The Impostor

Sophie McKenzie is the Richard & Judy selected author of psychological thriller *Close My Eyes* and *Sunday Times* bestseller *Trust In Me*. An author of over thirty titles, Sophie lives in London and has worked as a journalist, editor and creative writing tutor. Her many teen thrillers include the best-selling, multi-award-winning *Girl, Missing*.

Also by Sophie McKenzie

THE
IMPOSTOR

SOPHIE McKENZIE

canelo

First published in the United Kingdom in 2026 by

Canelo, an imprint of
Canelo Digital Publishing Limited,
20 Vauxhall Bridge Road,
London SW1V 2SA
United Kingdom

A Penguin Random House Company
The authorised representative in the EEA is Dorling Kindersley Verlag GmbH.
Arnulfstr. 124, 80636 Munich, Germany

A CIP catalogue record for this book is available from the British Library.

ISBN 9 781 83598 032 3

Cover design by The Brewster Project

Printed and bound in Great Britain by Clays Ltd, Elcograf S.p.A.

Look for more great books at
www.canelo.co | www.dk.com

For Ruth

ONE

It's Mum who proposes the toast.

'To Nathaniel,' she says, her voice trembling as she gazes around the table. 'May he rest in peace.'

'To Dad,' I murmur, the voices of everyone else echoing around me.

We're here, in the depths of an icy cold January, in the north London house where I grew up, to honour what would have been my father's seventy-ninth birthday.

He died six months ago, after a short series of increasingly devastating heart attacks. It's somehow fitting that Dad died in that way, his death as sudden and passionate as the man himself could be. He was a mass of contradictions. On the one hand, his reputation as the ruthless managing director of our family import business was well-earned and he always insisted that, despite the fortune he amassed, his children should fend for themselves with no hint of a trust fund or private allowance. No pocket money was given after the age of fourteen – we were all expected to find jobs if we wanted extra cash.

Despite all this – and his fierce temper when provoked – Dad was loving and gentle, especially towards me and my half-sister, Rae. It's funny. He made a great show of trying to treat all his children fairly – his own father caused huge upset in the family by leaving everything to Dad, and cutting Dad's younger brother, Uncle Edgar, out of his will. And yet Dad *did* treat us differently, being far tougher on the boys in all sorts of ways, small and large.

'Are you okay, Mum?' Tommy asks quietly.

Shaken from my musings, I look up. Mum is still holding out her glass over the empty pudding plates, a single tear trickling down her cheek. My heart seems to constrict as I take in the naked grief on her face. Mum was – is still – entirely devoted to the man she married at nineteen, when he was a business tycoon in his late thirties, with two failed marriages already behind him.

Tommy glances at me, then touches Mum's arm. She would never say it or show it overtly, but I've always been aware that my impulsive, charming, tousle-haired younger brother is Mum's favourite child, while my older half-sister – smart, beautiful, sharp-tongued Rae – was Dad's.

Mum looks down at Tommy, a startled expression on her face.

'Oh,' she says, looking around the table. 'Sorry, I... I...'

'It's fine, Mum,' Tommy says, squeezing her hand. 'It was a lovely toast.'

Mum smiles gratefully at him, then sinks back into her seat, wiping her face. She and Dad had a very traditional relationship, in which Mum always took a back seat, offering calm and kind support in the face of any turmoil thrown her way. Dad, in his turn, provided her with everything she wanted – not that Mum is in the slightest bit materialistic – and took care of everything outside the home. After decades together, I can't imagine how hard it must be for her to forge a life without him.

I catch her eye across the table. 'Are you all right?' I ask.

'Course she's all right,' snaps Zane, glaring at me. He turns to Mum. 'Aren't you, Donna?'

I bridle. My eldest half-brother, like Rae, the product of Dad's first marriage, has his mother's dark colouring but resembles Dad in all sorts of other ways, especially in the long slope of his nose and his tendency to short, explosive bursts of emotion. Zane has taken over from Dad as head of Carson Enterprises and, so far, the company seems to be thriving through the transition. Though both Zane and Rae are now in their forties, time has done nothing to moderate their passionate natures.

Mum looks down at the dining table, nodding, her cheeks now flushed. The meal is basically over. I've just helped her make coffee for everyone and most cups are half-drunk.

'I think I'll go up, actually,' Mum says, sounding a little injured.

I frown, feeling cross with Zane for upsetting her.

'I'm going to leave too,' Tommy says cheerfully, apparently oblivious to the tension in the room. 'I'm meeting some friends at Aces High. They've got a new DJ.'

Across the table, Zane bristles with disapproval. A shadow of concern passes over Mum's face. Tommy was the one aspect of their life together where she and Dad didn't see eye to eye or perhaps, if I'm honest, the one area where she stood up to Dad.

Tommy is thirty-one but still lives the same life he had as a teenager, playing video games in his room upstairs most of the day, then going to clubs in the evenings. Mum worries about him. I do too. But Tommy just sails through life without a care. Dad made him work at Carson Enterprises for a short period in his early twenties, but Tommy and a nine-to-five office job was a relationship that didn't end well and now Tommy basically lives rent-free at Mum's, food and home comforts provided, while making occasional spending money as a gaming influencer.

There's a flurry of activity, as Mum says goodbye to everyone and goes upstairs, while Tommy orders an Uber and disappears into the frosty London night.

I'm left alone at the table with Rae, Zane and Zane's girlfriend, Savannah. Sav, who is seven months pregnant and not drinking, sips at her apple juice then gets up and stretches her long, lean arms above her head. I stare enviously at the way her silk dress glides elegantly over her hips. She's thirty-two, the same age I was when Iris was born. Yet Savannah's bump is ridiculously, tidily round and she doesn't appear to have put on an ounce of extra weight. When *I* was seven months gone, I looked like a house and even now, four years later, I'm still a dress size bigger than I used to be. Rob, at home with Iris this evening, says it doesn't bother him, but I hate looking different from when we met.

'You okay, Sav?' asks Zane, eyebrows raised.

'I'm fine.' She smiles at him, her dark eyes gleaming in the candlelight. She pats her belly. 'Your son here just doesn't like sitting still.'

'Course he doesn't.' Zane chuckles.

I catch Rae's eye. We've privately bet each other on how long Zane's latest relationship will last. Rae reckons another twelve months, tops. I think Savannah will be so busy with her new baby that she won't have the energy to leave for at least two years. Neither of us think Zane and Savannah will stay together long term. Zane's previous long-term girlfriend finally decided she couldn't put up with his affairs anymore. Maybe I'm being cynical, but nothing about Zane makes me think he has really changed since then.

Zane clears his throat. 'Thank God Uncle Edgar didn't come. He's been a total pain in my arse this week, refusing to discuss the will or any of its details. It's like he wants to cut me out of the entire conversation.'

'You can hardly blame him for that, darling,' Rae says drily. 'Seeing as Dad cut him out of the entire inheritance.'

'Yes,' I add gently. 'Poor Edgar must have such conflicted emotions.'

'Oh, boo-hoo, Cassie.' Zane shoots me a withering glance. 'Don't be so wet.'

I purse my lips, feeling irritated. Zane would never have dared to speak like that to me when Dad was alive.

'I'm not being wet,' I insist. 'The will was a chance for Dad to make up for what *his* father did and he didn't do it.'

Silence falls around the table. Uncle Edgar has always deeply resented Dad inheriting our grandfather's entire fortune twenty years ago, a decision which Dad made no effort to rectify with his own succession planning. According to Dad's will, which is still going through probate, his entire estate, worth millions, will be divided between Zane, Rae, Tommy and myself. Mum now owns this house outright and has a monthly spending allowance, which is exactly what she herself wanted. But Uncle Edgar, who has worked in Carson Enterprises' finance department his entire adult life, inherits nothing.

'Edgar got their dad's fancy watch, didn't he?' Zane goes on with a wry chuckle. 'As for the rest, he only has himself to blame.'

'Oh, do shut up, darling,' Rae says with a sigh.

Zane hesitates for a moment. He and Rae are close, in a way that couldn't be more different from the bond I share with Tommy. I've seen them have furious rows, hurling huge insults at each other, then act immediately afterwards as if nothing happened.

'I just mean Dad didn't respect Edgar,' Zane says. 'He wouldn't have organised things like he did otherwise.'

Rae snorts. 'Dad might not have left Uncle Edgar anything, but he made him the executor of his will,' she points out. 'That's a mark of respect.'

'Actually, it just proves my point.' Zane snorts. 'Expecting someone who won't inherit from a will to do all the work involved in sorting it out is the *opposite* of respectful.'

'It *is* kind of weird.' Savannah wrinkles her nose.

'Anyway, the *content* of the will is beside the point,' grumbles Zane. 'Whatever the terms, Edgar's taking too long to organise everything. I'm sure we should be much closer to getting our money.'

I shudder at the meanness in his voice and Rae, who misses nothing, shoots me an enquiring look. I say nothing. There's no point. But I hate these kinds of arguments, bickering away over timing when we're all on the verge of inheriting a fortune. Dad's estate is made up of shares in the family business, which Zane now runs as managing director, plus houses in the States and Mallorca, two London flats and an array of investments. The plan is to sell everything except the business and divide up the proceeds.

'I'm grateful to Uncle Edgar for sorting it out,' I say.

'Yeah, you would be, Cassie,' Zane continues with a sneer. 'Come on, you have to admit that it would make more sense for *me* to have oversight of the estate sale. I'm the eldest child, head of the company *and* I've got the skills.'

Rae snorts. 'Adam had *better* skills,' she mutters, though not so loudly Zane can hear.

I shift awkwardly in my seat. Adam is the proverbial black sheep of the family. In birth order terms, he comes between Zane and Rae. Nobody in the family has heard from or spoken to him in over twenty years. I barely remember him.

'Let's not argue,' I suggest. 'We're all going to be so much better off soon.'

It's true. Rob and I have done a few calculations and it looks as if, when probate is finally granted, I'll come into several million pounds, after tax. We're planning to buy a house in London – a pipe dream until now – as soon as we get the money.

'You're right, Cassie.' Rae sighs, flicking her sleek dark hair over her shoulder.

The doorbell rings.

I frown. It's almost ten thirty.

'Who the hell is that?' barks Zane.

'I'll go and see,' I say, pushing my chair back.

I hurry out of the candlelit dining room into the soft glow of the hall. My feet tap loudly across the polished parquet floor. Tommy and I used to slide across here on tea towels when we were kids, until Tommy smashed into the wall and split his lip open.

I peer through the spyhole in the front door. A young woman is standing outside. She's dressed in a thin, shapeless coat, her arms folded across her chest. My first thought is that she must be the daughter of one of Mum's neighbours. Perhaps she's locked herself out or something. Despite the lateness of the hour, she doesn't look like any kind of threat.

Footsteps sound in the hall behind me. I glance over my shoulder as Zane, Sav and Rae appear in the hall.

'Who is it?' Rae demands.

'I don't know,' I say, opening the door.

The woman on the doorstep peers anxiously up at me. Now I can see her properly, I'm struck by how pretty she is: a pale, heart-shaped face surrounded by long, streaked blonde hair that tumbles over her shoulders. It's a similar length and colour to my own hair, though with twice the body and ten times the glamour.

She's like a grown-up Disney princess.

'Hello,' I say.

'Hi.' The woman looks from me to the others in a row behind me. Her eyes are huge and round and anxious. 'I'm so sorry to call round so late.' She hesitates, then says to me, 'You're Cassie, aren't you?'

My jaw drops. 'Do we know each other?'

'And you're Zane and… and Rae.' The woman looks over my shoulder at my half-siblings. 'I'm guessing none of you know who I am.'

I step back and she walks into the hall. The light shines off her golden hair. Her eyes are the palest of blue-green. There's something almost spellbinding about her.

'Brace yourselves,' she says with a smile, then her cold fingers touch my arm. 'I'm Mia. I'm your sister.'

TWO

I step back instinctively, shaking off Mia's hand.

'Sister?' I stare at her, wondering what on earth she means.

Zane strides forward so that he's standing next me. 'What the hell are you talking about?' he demands.

Mia blinks rapidly, her hand flying to her face as if he's slapped her. 'Nathaniel Carson,' she says quickly, looking round at us all. '*Your* father was also *my* father.'

Is she serious?

Mia is in her mid-twenties, I reckon, a few years younger than Tommy. Which means… I glance up the stairs, towards Mum's room. My stomach twists. If what Mia says is true, it means Dad must have had an affair.

He always seemed so devoted to Mum. Surely that can't be true, can it?

Rae grips Mia by the elbow. 'Come with me!' she orders.

The rest of us follow, as Rae steers Mia into the dining room. Before, it had glowed with a cosy, end-of-dinner warmth. Now half the candles have sputtered out and I'm aware of the congealed food on the plates and bowls stacked on the sideboard.

Mia hovers beside the table. I ignore the impulse to suggest she sits down or takes off her coat. That kind of welcome seems inappropriate under the circumstances.

Because she surely must be lying. But why? Is it some kind of prank? If so, on who? And for what purpose?

Rae pulls to the kitchen door, then stands opposite Mia next to me and Zane, while Savannah sits down at the table, now wreathed in shadow.

Mia folds her arms. A defensive gesture. She tilts her chin slightly upwards. For a fleeting second, I'm sure I see Dad in her expression. Then I shake myself.

'Explain yourself!' orders Zane, his voice fierce and loud.

Mia recoils, taking a step back. I feel a shot of sympathy for her. Rae puts a hand on Zane's arm.

'Ssh,' she cautions. 'We don't want to wake Donna.'

'I'm afraid it's a little late for that.'

I spin around. Mum is standing in the doorway, dressed in her cashmere robe. Her eyes are latched onto Mia, her expression one of complete and utter shock.

'Oh gosh, I'm so sorry, Mrs Carson.' Mia's face creases with worry. 'I know it's late and this is huge news. I guess I've had a while to get my head around it. Are you okay?'

'Stop!' Rae interrupts. 'We'll ask the questions.'

'When were you born?' Zane demands.

Mum walks over, her gaze still fixed on Mia. 'Who is your mother?' she asks softly.

'Just start at the beginning,' I urge.

Mia takes a deep breath. 'Okay, so, as far as I've been able to piece it all together, my mum and Nathaniel got together in the summer of 1997. I was born the following April.'

Mum gasps, her hand flying to her mouth. If this news is shocking to the rest of us, it must be devastating to her.

'So you're twenty-six now,' Zane says, narrowing his eyes.

Mia nods. I narrow my eyes. That means she was born when I was ten and Tommy just five.

'Go on,' Rae demands.

'I… I think my mother and Nathaniel met when he was in the Bahamas on business and Mum was doing an ad on the beach. She… she was a model. Apparently, Nathaniel was walking past and… and stopped to watch a bit of the filming.'

'I bet he did.' Zane gives a snort, earning a glare from his sister.

'Your mother was a model?' Mum asks, her voice faint.

Mia nods. 'Maryna Ishchenko. She was big for a bit in the nineties, then they moved away from that… from the heroin chic look and my mother found it hard to adapt.' She stops.

I glance at Mum. She looks dazed, as if she's struggling to take in what she's being told.

'Maryna Ishchenko,' Rae murmurs. 'That name sounds familiar.'

I nod, a memory shifting in my head. I'm fairly certain Ishchenko was a kind of second-tier supermodel for a while, but then faded into obscurity, succumbing to an accidental overdose a few years later.

'Wasn't she the one who snuffed it after a drugs binge?' Zane says with a nasty sneer.

I shoot him an angry glance. There's no need to be cruel.

A look of pain crosses Mia's face. She hugs her coat around her. The dark green wool is not just thin, as I first noticed, but also faded and threadbare at the elbows. 'That's right. I was only five at the time. My grandparents took me in. Raised me. Mum told them she didn't know who my dad was. He's not on the birth certificate and—'

11

'If your mother said nothing to anyone, how can you be so sure the, er, the relationship you describe took place?' Mum asks. She sounds formal, brittle, polite. But her fingers are fumbling anxiously with the cord of her robe.

'Yeah, I was working for the company back in '97,' Zane protests. 'I don't remember a trip to the Bahamas.'

'Like Dad would have taken you,' scoffs Rae.

Zane glares at her, then turns back to Mia. 'Even if your mother *did* meet our dad on some photo shoot,' he snaps, 'it doesn't mean they slept together.'

'I exist,' Mia says, evenly. 'I'd say that's pretty good proof.'

I glance uneasily at Mum again.

'Zane and Donna are right,' says Rae, glaring at Mia. 'It's easy enough to say an affair happened and that you're the result, but do you have any actual evidence?'

Mia slips a slender hand into the faux leather handbag hanging from her shoulder and draws out a rather crumpled greetings card. 'I found this a few weeks ago, when I was helping my grandparents clear out their flat. They've moved to sheltered housing.' She hesitates. 'There was a box of my mum's that neither of them knew about. Inside, I found an envelope of things that I think were from the affair; I'd never seen them before. Some pics of my mum from the photo shoot and a magazine article about Nathaniel. And this.' She holds out the card. It has a bunch of flowers on the front and the words *Happy Birthday* in silver foil. 'I think Nathaniel must have given it to my mum for her birthday.'

Mum gasps, the colour in her cheeks draining away. 'Flowers,' she says, flatly.

Rae and I exchange a glance. One of Dad's eccentricities was his dislike of cut flowers. He never bought them and refused to have them in the house but often signed cards with pictures of flowers on the front.

Mia hands Mum the card. Mum opens it up with trembling fingers. Inside is a brief message, printed in block capitals in faded black ink.

SWEETEST MARYNA. HAVE THE
BEST DAY. CAN'T WAIT TO SEE YOU
AND KISS YOU AND LICK YOU AND
***K YOU OVER AND OVER. N x

'Oh.' Mum's voice is strangled. She reaches for the chair behind her and sinks heavily into it.

Savannah, still sitting quietly at the table, leans forward and rubs at Mum's shoulder. It's a small, gentle gesture that is more than I'd have given her credit for, not that I really know her well. Perhaps Savannah relates. After all, she's had to cope with Zane for nearly two years.

'This card is bullshit!' Zane snatches it out of Mum's hand. He points to the message. 'This isn't even proper handwriting. There's no way to prove Dad either wrote it or signed it; it's just the initial "N" at the end.'

'Even if he *did* write it,' adds Rae, taking the card and examining it herself, 'and even if Dad and your mum had an affair, it doesn't make him your father.'

'Yeah, your whore of a mother was probably putting it about for everyone,' Zane snaps.

'Zane!' Mum, Savannah and I all cry together.

Mia's cheeks flush scarlet as she grips the edge of the sideboard behind her. If she's acting, she's brilliant at it. Then she looks up, defiant.

'The card is just the start of what I found,' she says evenly.

My heart skips a beat.

'Is that right, darling?' drawls Rae with heavy irony. 'Do go on.'

Mia straightens up. 'When I found the things Mum had saved, I worked through the timings,' she says. 'I couldn't get it out of my head that maybe Nathaniel *was* my dad. That Mum *had* known all along who he was. A friend of a friend is a paralegal, and she found out for me who was handling Nathaniel's will.' She pauses. 'Basically, I made a few calls and they put me in touch with the exec— the person in charge of the will.'

'The executor?' Rae demands.

'You've spoken to Uncle Edgar?' I gasp.

Mum stiffens in her chair.

'That's right,' Mia says. 'I told him everything and he said I should do a DNA test.'

Behind me, Mum lets out a groan. My stomach churns.

'Are you serious?' Rae demands.

'Why didn't Edgar say anything to us?' I ask.

'He insisted there was no point telling everyone until we knew the truth,' Mia explains. 'Apparently Nathaniel's DNA was already on file, so—'

'What?' Rae and I chorus.

Mia glances anxiously at Mum. 'Another paternity claim, I think. From about twenty years ago. Nathaniel had kept a copy of the report.'

I frown. I have never heard of such a claim and, from the look on Mum's face, she hasn't either.

'According to Edgar, that test proved Nathaniel *wasn't* the father on that occasion,' Mia explains. 'But his DNA data was still on the report, so Edgar sent that to the clinic.

14

Then I went along there in person and they took a sample of *my* DNA to… to do a comparison.' Her lip wobbles. 'I know this is difficult for all of you, but it was hard for me too. To know that I had a father all this time, and now it's too late to—'

'Spare us the sob story!' Zane barks. 'I assume you're going to tell us this DNA test confirms your theory?'

Mia nods. 'I got the results earlier today. I have an appointment to see Edgar about it tomorrow, but he'd told me you were all having this dinner tonight and… and I couldn't wait. I'd have been here sooner, but it was hard to get up the courage.' She reaches into her bag again and draws out a sheet of paper. She hands it to me, but Zane rips it out of my fingers before I have a chance to examine it.

'Wait a sec,' says Rae, suddenly sounding all lawyerly. 'You need a court order to use someone's DNA without their permission.'

'The exec— whatever, the person in charge of the will can give permission on the deceased's behalf,' Mia says softly. 'Edgar asked his lawyers about it. He said I needed to go to the clinic in person for it to be legally valid.'

I glance at Rae. She gives a curt nod.

'Why do the results of the test need to be "legally valid"?' Zane asks, his voice filling with suspicion.

'Because earlier this week I spoke to my *own* lawyer and…' Mia hesitates and a terrible sense of foreboding washes over me.

'And?' Rae demands.

'They said I'm entitled to the same share of Nathaniel's will as all his other children.'

THREE

The dining room erupts as Zane, Rae and Savannah all shout at once.

'Are you serious?' Savannah shrieks.

'You've got some nerve coming here on Dad's birthday,' Rae yells.

Predictably, Zane is loudest, booming out a long list of swearwords and ending with a furious roar. 'Get out!'

Mum sits like a statue at the table, her mouth gaping.

Mia's gaze rests on mine, a mix of resentment and resilience in those pale blue-green eyes. Zane repeats his order for her to leave, but Mia stands her ground.

'You can shout at me if you want,' she says quietly. 'And I am sorry to have interrupted your dinner, but I had no idea it was Nathaniel's birthday until Edgar told me.'

'You seem to have had quite the chat with our uncle,' Rae mutters.

'He's… he's been nice,' Mia says shakily. 'Kind.'

'I bet.' Rae rolls her eyes.

I frown. What is she suggesting? That prim, proper Uncle Edgar has had his head turned because Mia is young and pretty? Or simply that Edgar is a soft touch?

'I'd like to understand more about this… this DNA test,' Mum says, her voice low and troubled. 'You went in person to the clinic Edgar suggested?'

'Sounds like Uncle Edgar set the whole thing up to shaft us,' Zane says nastily.

'It was a legit clinic,' Mia persists. 'The same one that did Nathaniel's original DNA test twenty years ago. The name is on the report I gave you.'

Zane looks down at the paper in his hand. Rae moves closer, reading it over his shoulder.

'Does Uncle Edgar know you're here?' I ask.

Mia shakes her head. 'He didn't want a big showdown with everyone tonight, but—'

'Wait, are you saying he already knows these results?' Rae's jaw drops.

'That's right,' Mia says. 'The clinic sent them to both of us simultaneously. Like I told you, we got them earlier today.'

Rae lets out a low whistle.

Mum shakes her head. 'Why didn't Edgar say anything to us?' she asks.

'He wanted to talk to you all privately tomorrow, then organise a get-together a few days afterwards where you'd meet me. But I... I couldn't wait.' Mia makes an apologetic face. 'I hoped that if we talked in your home, Mrs Carson, everyone might be more sympathetic than if it was official and... and formal.' She pauses. 'I got the impression there's some bad blood between Edgar and, er, some of you.' She glances at Zane. 'I was trying to avoid a scene.'

'Right, well, I think we can say you've failed on that front, darling,' Rae snaps.

'Unbelievable nerve,' Zane growls. 'Coming here with this nonsense story.' Behind him, Savannah nods.

I glance at Mum again, still looking shell-shocked, then walk over to Mia. I touch her arm. She's shaking. I'm suddenly sure she's telling the truth. She looks at me, a hopeful spark in her eye. 'Edgar said we looked a bit alike, Cassie,' she says softly. 'I couldn't see it from the photos, but he's right, we do have similar colouring. Our hair… skin tone…'

I glance at our reflections in the mirror on the wall opposite. I guess we are both fair, but that's really where the resemblance ends. Her skin is fresh and unlined, while my dark blue eyes aren't anything like as striking as her sea-coloured ones. And she's not only a few centimetres taller than I am, but surely at least twenty pounds lighter. I catch her eye in the mirror and offer a small smile.

'I'm sorry we're behaving like this,' I say.

'Don't apologise for me, darling!' Rae's voice rises.

'We have nothing to bloody apologise for!' Zane bellows.

I hold up my hands, trying to calm them down. 'It's understandable that we're all shocked,' I say. 'But none of this is Mia's fault.'

'I'd say it's *all* Mia's fault,' Rae snaps.

I frown at her, then turn to Mia. 'You have to understand that none of us had any idea about you, which means this is… it's a *lot*.' I indicate Mum with a tiny tilt of my head. 'This is about much more than parentage. If what you say is true, there've been lies and a cover-up… and…' I trail off.

'Wait, though. Did… did Nathaniel know about you, Mia?' Mum's voice cracks as she speaks. Her fingers run tremulously along the collar of her robe.

'No,' Mia says. 'I honestly don't think my mum told anyone, not even him. I imagine that's why my DNA wasn't tested when I was a baby.' She indicates the report, still clenched in Zane's hand.

'This?' Zane snaps, crumpling the report in his fist. 'Let me tell you, this proves nothing. As far as I'm concerned, you're gold-digging pure and simple.'

'Okay, nobody should say anything else,' Rae commands, her eyes as sharp as her voice. 'Mia, you need to leave. It's totally inappropriate you ambushing us like this. If you want to take things forward, then you'll need to do it through your lawyer. And we'll respond through ours.'

Mia looks properly shaken. 'But… but I came here to avoid that.' Her lip trembles. 'I didn't think the money would be a big deal. You have so much. Honestly, what I really want is to get to know you all. I've never had brothers and sisters and—'

'You heard Rae!' Zane interrupts, his fists clenched. 'Get out! Now!'

I open my mouth, to try and calm everyone down, but before I can speak Mia is hurrying away, out of the kitchen. I scuttle after her, catching up as she reaches the front door.

I grab her arm and she turns. 'I'm so sorry,' she says. 'I really thought it would be… that I could…' A fat tear trickles down her cheek. 'I just wanted to meet you all.'

I squeeze her hand, feeling torn. 'Let everyone sleep on it,' I advise gently. 'Are you okay to get home?'

'I don't have a…' Mia presses her lips together, clearly trying not to cry again. 'I'll be fine.' And with that she rushes out of the house and along the front path, soon swallowed up in the shadow of the trees that line the gravel drive.

–

It's early the following morning and the family has gathered at Carson Enterprises to discuss how best we should respond to Mia. Mum has even managed to drag a grumbling Tommy out of bed, though he looks bleary-eyed after what was, I'm assuming, a late night at Aces High nightclub and, so far, has treated the whole idea of a secret sister appearing out of the blue as a joke. In contrast, Zane and Rae are still fuming and, as Mum, Tommy and I walk into my older brother's office, it's obvious the atmosphere between the two of them and Uncle Edgar is glacial.

I keep thinking how utterly distraught Mia looked in the face of Mum's horrified shock, Rae's scepticism and Zane's outright fury. Surely that couldn't have been an act or a lie?

Zane's office is a monument to minimalist glamour, with designer touches everywhere, from the Molteni&C coffee table to the leather-bound box files behind the desk. Glass walls on two sides reveal a grey-skied London morning outside.

Zane is standing behind his desk, with Uncle Edgar and Nina Owens, Carson's head of legal, at his side. Rae is sprawled elegantly across the armchair next to the coffee table. Mum, Tommy and I perch on the remaining chairs.

Uncle Edgar launches into a long-winded explanation of his original meeting with Mia and the steps he encouraged her to take. He then hands over to Nina Owens, who very solemnly confirms that the DNA test Mia took has been verified as legally admissible.

'I do apologise that Mia came to the house last night.' Uncle Edgar takes over the conversation again, speaking in typically clipped, formal tones. 'I had very much hoped and intended to be the one to tell you about her.'

'I do wish you had, Edgar,' Mum says miserably. 'I still can't take in what she said. Nathaniel... a love-child.' She looks down at her lap. 'I can't believe it.'

'Me neither, Donna.' Zane thumps his desk. 'Anyway, never mind the girl's ridiculous lies. How do we fight her outrageous claim?'

Nina glances anxiously at Uncle Edgar, who clears his throat. 'I'll take that one, Nina,' he says. 'I know you have a lot to be getting on with.'

Nina takes this as her cue to leave and scurries out of the room.

Uncle Edgar waits for the door to shut behind her then steeples his fingers, his expression very serious. My gaze drifts to the watch on his wrist. It's the gold Rolex that Dad left him, the one that used to belong to their father. It looks oddly brash on Edgar's slim wrist.

'I don't think there's any point fighting Mia's claim,' he says smoothly. 'The DNA test I organised proves her parentage without a shadow of doubt; legally her case to be recognised as Nathaniel's daughter is watertight. Her lawyer is currently applying to the courts to establish her right to inherit from his will. Once *that* is approved, Mia will be able to claim an equal share of Nathaniel's estate. Same as the rest of you.'

'No *way*,' spits Rae.

'Wow,' Tommy says, suddenly looking more awake. 'Are you serious?'

'I am,' says Uncle Edgar, solemnly. 'Nathaniel's wording is very specific. "*My biological children are, each and severally, to inherit...*" That's in line ten, and six lines after that, "*all my biological children are due an equal share except, solely, Adam Carson*".' He sighs. 'That "solely" rather nails it. I don't think there's any point spending money on a lost cause.'

'That's easy for you to say,' splutters Zane. 'It's our cash she'll be stealing, not yours.'

Uncle Edgar's face grows thunderous. 'I can assure you there is nothing easy for me about this.'

I chew on my lip. Rae once described our uncle as a kind of anti-Dad: softly spoken, when our father was loud and forceful; passive and reflective, in contrast to Dad's impulsive, man-of-action personality; and highly sensitive to criticism, unlike Dad, who always seemed energised by verbal attacks.

'Of course this isn't easy for you, Edgar,' Mum ventures quietly. 'It must have been terribly upsetting for you to hear Mia's story. A real shock.'

'I doubt that,' mutters Rae in my ear, too quietly for Mum to hear.

I wince, hating Rae's insinuation.

'I think we're getting ahead of ourselves,' I say. 'Surely the important thing here is that we have another sister. I realise that means Dad had an affair with her mother, but it was brief and it ended a long time ago.'

'That's *hardly* the point, darling,' Rae mutters.

'That's what I'm trying to say,' I go on. 'None of what happened in the past is Mia's fault. So we shouldn't take out our anger at Dad's... indiscretions on her.'

'You're right, of course, Cassie,' Mum says, sounding injured, as if I've reproached her. She stares down at her lap.

A throb of guilt pulses through me.

'I'm *not* angry at Dad,' Zane says with a scowl. 'Certainly not for screwing Mia's mother, *if* he did.' I frown at him. Zane pushes his chair back and strides away from his desk. 'What I'm angry about is that a nobody chancer slut is trying to con us out of our inheritance.'

'Jesus, Zane, language,' Rae protests. 'It's the 2020s. You can't call someone a slut just because you don't like them.'

'Oh, get off your woke high horse,' Zane snaps. 'She's not just a tart, she's the worst kind of one.'

'If everyone would please calm down, I'm sure we can find a way through the current maze,' Uncle Edgar says, casting Zane a disdainful look. 'I realise Mia's arrival is a shock and that it may, er, colour our recollections of Nathaniel.' He casts a sympathetic glance at Mum. 'But as I keep saying, the DNA test results are watertight.' He pauses. 'To be honest, I wasn't surprised. As soon as I met Mia, I saw a strong resemblance between her and Cassie.'

I look at Mum, who shrugs. 'I think she looks more like Tommy, myself.'

'Puh-leese,' Tommy mock-protests. 'My hair doesn't get as blond as Mia's unless I've spent the summer on the beach.'

'How nice,' says Rae drily. 'I'm sure it's fabulous over there at the Aryan end of the family, but just because Zane and I have our mother's colouring doesn't make us any less Carson. I don't see why being blonde and blue-eyed makes Mia *more* of one.'

'Actually, Mia has blue-*green* eyes,' I mutter.

'Do be reasonable, Rae.' Uncle Edgar clears his throat. 'All I'm trying to say is that I could see superficial similarities from the start and the DNA test Mia took has confirmed them.'

'How can you be sure the test wasn't tampered with?' Rae demands.

'I can assure you that it was undertaken in a highly respectable clinic,' Edgar says icily. 'The same clinic that Nathaniel used on, er, that previous occasion. I selected it myself on the basis of its longevity and reputation.'

'Well, fuck you very much for facilitating her lies!' Zane roars.

'Stop it, everyone!' I jump up, my heart thudding. 'If Mia really *is* our sister, then she's entitled to a share. And there's plenty to go around. Anyway, nothing's going to happen very quickly; probate won't be granted for a few more weeks at least, right?'

Uncle Edgar nods.

'Okay so, in the meantime, what have we got to lose by getting to know Mia a bit better?'

'I don't think that's a good idea,' Uncle Edgar says quickly.

'Uncle E.'s right about that, darling,' says Rae. 'Legally, it's better that we keep our distance.'

'I don't think I'd feel comfortable meeting her again,' says Mum.

'I definitely don't bloody want to,' snarls Zane.

I look at Tommy. He stares back at me with slightly unfocused eyes. Is he still high on whatever he took last night? A pang of worry for my brother flitters through everything else in my head, then I draw myself up. 'What about you, Tommo?' I ask.

Tommy grins, his gaze sharpening. 'Well, I already have two awesome sisters,' he says cheerfully. 'I can't see any reason to stay away from a third.'

'For God's sake!' Zane's voice drips with contempt.

Tommy winks at me. 'I'm in, Cas, whatever you want to do.'

'Right,' I say. 'Is there a contact number for Mia? An address?'

Uncle Edgar nods and hands me the file which contains his copy of the DNA test report along with the few bits of information he has gathered on Mia. There's not much here. Apart from her mobile number and current address, the file simply contains a copy of her birth certificate and a short paragraph outlining the main events of her life, all as Mia explained them to us yesterday. There are also pictures of her grandparents and her mother. I stare at the photo of Maryna. It must have been taken when she was about the same age as Mia is now. She's beautiful, with high cheekbones and the same colour eyes as her daughter.

I don't want Mum to catch sight of it, so I quickly take a snap of the contact info, then hand the file back to Uncle Edgar.

I'm still in shock at the idea I have a secret sister. It doesn't feel possible. And it certainly doesn't sit with the image I have of my parents' marriage. But if Mia really is who she says she is, and all the evidence suggests that she is, I owe it to her – and to myself – to find out as much about her as I can.

FOUR

I think about calling or texting Mia, then decide a surprise visit will give us the most information. After stopping to refuel Tommy with coffee and a muffin, the two of us head to her address in Wood Green.

'Is this it?' my brother asks uncertainly, as we stop halfway along a busy road outside a house that appears to have been converted into four flats. The stone in the front yard is cracked and icy, with a few hardy weeds poking through.

I let out my breath and it mists in the frozen air, then check the details on my phone again. 'Yup,' I say. 'Number 51, flat C. This is it.'

We approach the door as someone is leaving the building and slip inside after them, finding ourselves in a grubby entrance hall with doors on either side marked "A" and "B".

I follow Tommy up the stairs, where he knocks on flat C's front door. I hold my breath, suddenly nervous. How will Mia react when she sees us? Suppose she's not even home? Perhaps I should have rung first after all.

A moment later, the door swings open. Mia is standing there, dressed in grey joggers and a cropped, white jumper. Her hair is a little flatter than it was last night and she has no make-up on, but she's every bit as attractive. The boxy jumper sits high on her flat stomach, revealing a gold piercing through her navel.

Her eyes widen as she sees us both.

'Hello, Mia,' I say, letting an anxious smile play around my lips. 'I hope you don't mind us coming. I thought you'd like to meet—'

'*Tommy!*' Mia's eyes fill with joy. 'Oh, this is amazing! Come in, both of you.' She steps back to let us through to the narrow corridor. It's cluttered with piles of clothes and plastic bags. She shows us to the living room. It's tiny, just space for a couch and a huge flat-screen TV that takes up the whole of one wall. An Xbox and several game controllers are stacked in front of the television.

'How long have you had this place?' Tommy asks.

'Oh, it isn't mine,' Mia says. 'This is my friend Ellis's flat. I'm sleeping on the sofa.' She glances at the narrow couch, where a worn cushion has been placed over a neatly folded blanket. I frown. Is she really spending night after night on that thing? 'I… I don't have my own place.' She looks away.

Tommy and I glance at each other. I shuffle self-consciously from foot to foot. 'I… we wanted to come because.' I gulp. 'It was horrible last night, the way things ended.'

'It's my fault.' Mia glances up at me, her eyes glistening with tears. 'I shouldn't have turned up out of the blue. I've been kicking myself. But now… I'm… I'm just so happy you're here.' She reaches for Tommy's hand. 'I always wanted a brother.'

Tommy's chest visibly puffs out. 'It's lovely to meet you,' he says, squeezing her hand and giving her his biggest, most charming smile.

'We both want to get to know you,' I say. 'Everyone was at their worst, last night, and it's important to me that you have a chance to—'

The rest of my sentence is lost as Mia flings herself at me, her slight body pressing against mine as she squeezes me tight.

'Oh, thank you, Cassie,' she sobs. 'Thank you for believing me.'

I hold her, feeling awkward. Tommy puts his arms around us both and we stand for a moment, the only sound Mia's crying.

Do I believe her? Surely nobody could fake tears like this?

After a moment, Mia disentangles herself and steps back, wiping her face. 'Sorry,' she murmurs, 'I'm so sorry. It's just been such a difficult time. My grandparents going into sheltered housing and finding out about my real dad – *our* dad – and… and…' Her voice wobbles again.

I sigh. 'And getting excited about having a family who didn't exactly make you feel welcome last night?'

'That wasn't your fault or theirs,' Mia says quickly. 'It was me. I got it all wrong.'

Tommy is looking around the little living room, a look of horror on his face. I wonder if it's the cramped space or the clutter and mess within it that appals him most. His bedroom on the top floor of Mum's house is about four times the size and gets tidied by her cleaner twice a week. 'How long have you been staying here, Mia?' he asks gently.

Mia shrugs, lifting one slender shoulder. 'Almost two months now.' A hint of defensiveness creeps into her voice. 'I've got a flatshare lined up, but I can't move in until the weekend.'

'You shouldn't have to live like this,' Tommy says. He looks at me. 'Should she, Cas?'

I meet his gaze. Tommy is by far the most laidback of us siblings, but when he feels strongly about something he can be very insistent.

'Is there really nowhere else you can go until your flatshare comes through?' I ask.

Mia shakes her head. 'I've been here since my grandparents moved into their sheltered housing.' She pauses. 'It's not that bad. Ellis has been really kind letting me stay here. And it's super handy for work.'

'Work?' I ask.

'I have a part time job in a café in Islington.' A forced brightness creeps into her voice. 'I do a bit of modelling too, every now and then.'

'Like your mum,' I say.

She nods. 'What I really want is to be a photographer, but obviously *that* doesn't pay, so...' She looks down, her heart-shaped face reddening. 'I guess it must seem ridiculous to you having to scrape a living.'

Tommy blows out his breath. I can feel his eyes on my face.

'Of course it doesn't sound ridiculous,' I say. 'In fact, considering everything you've gone through, I think you're amazing.'

'You *so* are,' Tommy agrees. 'And you shouldn't have to live on people's sofas.' He runs his hand through his unbrushed curls. 'I'd invite you home with me, but I don't think Mum could cope with that just yet.'

Mia recoils. 'No, of course. I *couldn't*. She must hate me.'

'She doesn't hate you,' I reassure her. 'Honestly, Mum isn't like that. It's just for her, this is all about Dad being... you know...'

'Unfaithful and selfish,' Tommy says, sounding uncharacteristically terse. He hesitates, then his face lights up. 'Hey, Cas, why don't *you* have Mia to stay? Just for a few days till she moves into her flatshare. You've got a spare room. And it's still north London, so Mia could get to work, no problem.'

Mia gasps. 'Oh no, I couldn't do that.' Her words are insistent, but I can hear the yearning in her voice.

I stare at my brother, feeling exasperated. I'm totally up for helping Mia but having her come live with us is a huge leap, even if it is just for a few days. 'Er, by spare room do you mean our *junk* room?' I laugh. It sounds hollow to my ears.

'Whatever, we can clear it out, can't we?' Tommy beams with the generosity of a person who is giving away something that didn't belong to him in the first place. 'Come on, Cas, we can't leave Mia here.'

'I... I'm not sure,' I stammer. Inviting a complete stranger into my home, exposing her to my not-quite four-year-old daughter, feels like a step too far, even if she is my biological half-sister.

'Of course not, I totally get it,' Mia says, quickly. 'It means everything you just coming to see me here. It really does. I'd just like to get to know you.'

'Which will be far easier if you're both under one roof.' Tommy gives me an impatient look. 'Cas, I don't get what the problem is? You're always saying how hard it is for you and Rob to get out. Maybe you could persuade Mia to do a bit of babysitting for you while she's with you?'

'Oh, I'd love that,' Mia enthuses. 'You've got a little girl, haven't you?' I nod. 'I *adore* kids. I didn't mention it before, but up until recently I was working at a nursery. They had to make cutbacks and I was last in, so first out, but they gave me a great reference.'

'Really?' I say, my mind leaping at the new information. 'You've worked with young children?'

'Yeah, I'm DBS checked and everything.' Mia gazes at me with huge, hopeful eyes. 'I know I've no right to ask, but maybe I *could* come, just for a couple of nights until my flat's ready? It would mean the world.'

'Rob would agree to a couple of nights, wouldn't he?' Tommy asks.

'He would, I'm sure.' I nod slowly. My brother gives me an encouraging nod. His enthusiasm is infectious and hard to resist. At thirty-one, Tommy may have failed to launch, but his heart is definitely in the right place. And, after all, Mia is my sister. Why *shouldn't* I get to know her better? It's not like she'll be moving in permanently.

'Okay, then,' I say, smiling at her. 'Let's get you packed and over to ours.'

FIVE

It doesn't take long for Mia to put her belongings into three bin bags. Tommy and I help her carry them to my car. As I drive us home, I feel dazed by the sudden turn of events. It's only for two days, I tell myself. A chance to get to know a sister I didn't know existed twenty-four hours ago. Tommy, of course, is taking it all in his stride and he and Mia chat like old friends the whole way, with Tommy doing most of the talking.

'Sounds like you can turn your hand to anything,' he says. 'Waitress. Nursery assistant. Model. The modelling must be glamourous, no?'

'Not really,' says Mia. 'It's mostly waiting around. And I don't get jobs very often, to be honest.'

'What about the photography?' Tommy asks. 'Do you have a camera?'

'I had to sell it a while back,' Mia says, making a face. 'I'd love a Canon EOS. I go to all the free exhibitions. There was one in a gallery in Aldeburgh called *Male Gaze in the Twenty-first Century*. I really wanted to see it, but I couldn't to afford to get there.' She pauses. 'I can't drive. Not that I have a car anyway.'

'Well, Cassie and I both have one,' Tommy declares. 'So we can ferry you to the next gallery, yeah?'

I try to catch his eye in the rearview mirror. It's great that he's being so friendly to Mia, but I'd rather he didn't offer my services as an on-demand chauffeur, at least not without checking with me first.

'Cassie has Iris,' Mia points out, gently, picking up on my reluctance.

'And work,' I add. 'I'm a music therapist.'

'Er, what *is* that?' Mia asks. 'I mean it sounds amazing, but...'

'It's okay,' I say, smiling. 'Nobody ever knows. It's basically using music to help people with different kinds of needs: physical, emotional, social, cognitive. I work with a few private clients, but mostly I do referrals at a day centre.'

'How did you get into that?' Mia asks, wide-eyed. 'Are you a musician?'

'No, that is, I tried lots of instruments when I was a kid, but...' I sigh. 'I've always wanted to be a therapist and music therapy seemed like a really interesting way to do that. It's creative, sure, but mostly in terms of working out how music can help people.'

Mia nods, then asks a few further questions, with Tommy interjecting every now and then. He seems more animated than I've seen him in ages. I guess it must be fun for him to be the older sibling for once. At twenty-six, Mia is five years younger than he is, while I am five years his senior, but somehow, he and Mia seem much more alike in age – while I feel far older than both of them.

-

I park on our street at home then quickly message Rob to tell him about our new and temporary house guest. He texts back immediately with a thumbs up. Tommy is still talking as we get out of the car, now explaining to Mia about his love of climbing.

33

'It's my biggest hobby,' he says. 'Well, after gaming.'

I watch Mia as we walk into our three-bed terrace. Her eyes are wide, darting everywhere. The house is far smaller than my childhood home, where Mum and Tommy live and where Mia visited last night. Even so, Rob and I had to stretch our finances to buy it. Dad gave us a deposit – a generous gift which I'm well aware wasn't offered to any of my brothers. 'I know how much your mum wants you to live nearby,' he'd confided at the time. 'And if we leave you and your teacher husband to your own devices, you'll end up moving to the arse end of nowhere.'

'This is amazing,' Mia breathes, as she follows me into our open-plan kitchen diner. We had it remodelled when we moved in, just before Iris was born. Even now I shudder to remember those first six months, being so heavily pregnant and coping with what was basically a building site.

But now, as I gaze at Mia's awestruck face, I'm suddenly deeply aware of what a first-world problem dealing with house renovations is.

'Okay, I gotta bounce,' Tommy says cheerfully, 'but how's about the three of us meet up for brunch tomorrow?'

I nod.

'Thanks, Tommy,' Mia says.

A moment later, he's gone. I show Mia to the little spare room on the first floor. It's not as messy as I'd remembered. Despite the bags and boxes of old clothes stacked against one wall, the single bed is made up and there's hanging space in the slim wardrobe.

I remove a pile of old paperwork that needs to be sorted from the floor and retreat to the door. 'It's not much,' I say apologetically.

'It's perfect!' Mia clasps her hands together.

'There's no en suite, I'm afraid.' I point across the hall. 'You'll have to share the family bathroom with Iris.'

Mia nods, her gaze lighting on the room between her own and the bathroom. The door, featuring Iris's name in colourful wooden letters, is open, a scattering of toys and clothes in rainbow pastels visible on the carpet beyond.

'Iris.' Mia smiles. 'What a pretty name.'

I smile back. 'Would you like to come with me to pick her up from nursery?' I ask. 'After we've had a cup of tea?'

Mia nods eagerly.

I leave her to settle in, then go downstairs and put the kettle on. I guess I should let the rest of the family know that Mia is staying here for a few days, though I'm dreading their reactions: Uncle Edgar will disapprove; Zane and Rae will be furious. But it's Mum I'm mostly worried about. However generously she manages to acknowledge that her husband's infidelity isn't Mia's fault, Mia will always be a reminder of it.

Just as I'm considering how to break the news, I get a text from Rae. She doesn't hold back.

> Are you insane? Tommy has just messaged. What on earth are you thinking? It's legally, morally, emotionally a SERIOUSLY bad idea!!!!!

Great. If Tommy has told Rae about Mia staying here, then he'll definitely have told Mum. I let out a heavy sigh, then try ringing her. Mum will appreciate a call rather than a text.

The call goes to voicemail. Not a good sign.

I leave a message asking Mum to give me a ring as I have something to tell her, then re-boil the kettle. I realise, as I am putting bags in our teapot, that I have no idea how Mia takes her tea.

I hear her walk in and look up. She's changed out of her sweatpants and cropped, boxy jumper into a pair of high-waisted jeans that are tight on the hips and a T-shirt, equally close fitting. She's slim, yet impossibly curvy, like a Barbie doll. For the first time since I invited her to stay, I experience a pang of concern. Am I a complete idiot to be bringing someone so young and attractive into the house that I share with my husband?

I realise I'm staring and look away.

'Is this okay?' Mia says, uncertainly, looking down at her clothes. 'I thought if we were going to the nursery, I should be a bit smarter than sweatpants. And your house is much warmer than Ellis's flat.' She grimaces. 'I don't mean to be rude about him, but he *never* put on the heating.'

I nod. 'You look lovely,' I say, hoping that she can't hear anything other than reassurance in my voice. 'Now do you take milk? Sugar?'

'Actually, I'm vegan,' says Mia. 'Sorry, I should have mentioned it.'

'It's fine. We have some oat milk, if you'd like that?'

Mia nods and, armed with our mugs of tea and a plate of plain Hobnobs, which Mia selects as "definitely vegan" from the cupboard, we sit at the kitchen table.

Mia refuses sugar in her tea, but eats three biscuits one after the other, nibbling delicately but persistently at them. Heroically, I abstain, but my momentary feeling of self-congratulation vanishes as I put on my overcoat in front of the hall mirror. A tired face and slightly shapeless body are reflected back at me. Mia buttons up her thin, green coat. I wonder if I should offer her my puffer jacket, but I don't want to sound patronising.

–

Mia is smiley and charming with Bev, the long-standing head of the nursery staff. As Iris runs over, she immediately crouches down and asks about the drawing of a blue and red striped fish that Iris is clutching in her hand. I introduce her as Mia. We both agree not to confuse Iris with the term "aunt" at this point.

Iris herself is initially shy but opens up as we walk to the car and Mia asks what her favourite activity that day has been. Iris can't decide between tag in the playground, or a show and tell involving cupcakes. 'I had one with pink icing and rainbow sprinkles,' she lisps.

'Ooh, delicious,' enthuses Mia.

Iris reaches for Mia's hand and I nod to myself, relieved that my daughter seems so comfortable so quickly.

A similar pattern is followed when Rob arrives home that evening. He's tired after a long day at school – he was promoted to head of the science department at the start of the year. But despite the weariness evident on his face, he is his usual affectionate self, kissing me and letting Iris leap into his arms, before greeting Mia with a warm smile. After Iris is in bed, I cook dinner – a garlicky pasta using the oat milk in place of the dairy I'd normally put in the sauce – while Rob and Mia sit at the kitchen table across the room. Rob asks her a series of gentle questions, like where she went to school and if her mum had any other children. It turns out Mia's an only child, whose childhood was spent south of the river in Hither Green at a series of failing schools. I blush, thinking of the private

37

day establishments that I and my brothers and sister all attended, with their endless facilities and top academic records. Mia answers so freely and transparently and is so appreciative of the meal when it comes, insisting on clearing the dishes afterwards, that I decide I was silly to worry about her staying here. Mia is unpretentious, unselfish and without any edge. It might be hard for Mum to deal with her existence, but Mia deserves our time and our care.

As she sits back down at the kitchen table, she clears her throat. 'Er, would it be okay if I asked you something, Cassie? Well, two things actually.'

I nod.

'Did – this is awkward, but – do you know if Nathaniel had other affairs when he was with your mum? I know she was his third wife...'

I make a face, thinking how the same question has been running through my own head. 'I didn't think he had, but I guess maybe I was being naive.' I sigh. 'I know he left Zane and Rae's mum – that was his first wife – to marry an actress. So his second marriage definitely began as an affair. But that ended ages before he met Mum.'

'Your dad wasn't very complimentary about his second wife, was he?' Rob adds with a grin. 'I remember him calling her "that batshit crazy hippy bitch". Hey, and didn't she change her name from – what was it, Helen? To something woo-woo? Something about stars or—?'

'Harmony Moon,' I say. 'And just to be clear, Mia, Dad didn't normally talk about women as crazy bitches.' Mia nods, her eyes wide. 'I never heard him be rude to or about Mum.'

'That's because Donna is easy-going, calm and rational,' Rob points out. 'Not to mention beautiful, like her daughter.' He reaches for my hand and I bat him away, my cheeks pinking.

'Truth is, Mia,' I say, 'until you turned up with that DNA test, I honestly thought Dad had always been faithful to Mum. That's, er, that's partly why all this has been such a shock.'

'I see,' says Mia slowly.

'What's your other question?' I ask.

'I was reading about your – our – family,' Mia says. 'I know there's another brother, Adam, between Zane and Rachael – Rae. But I couldn't find anything out about him.'

I sigh again. 'Adam and Dad fell out years ago when I was a kid. Dad fired him from Carson, told Adam to get out of his sight, which Adam took so literally that nobody's seen or heard from him since.'

'Oh.' Mia frowns as she processes this new information. 'What happened?'

I shift uncomfortably in my chair. Dad caught Adam attempting to steal from company accounts. Dad didn't go to the police and the press never found out either so, despite the rumours that swirled around the business community for years, the attempted theft is not common knowledge. I understand why Mia's curious, but the last thing I want to do is reveal my family's biggest skeleton in front of her.

Sensing my awkwardness, Rob sits forward. 'Hey, Mia, tell us how you found out about Nathaniel being your dad. That must have been a moment, eh?'

Mia chats away, repeating the story once again. I sit back, smiling gratefully at my sensitive husband. He looks so handsome as he listens to her, a lock of his wavy hair falling over his forehead. And yet there are lines on that forehead that weren't there last year. And those dark shadows under his eyes are a reminder not just that he's tired but that the longer the three of us talk the later poor Rob will have to stay up. His promotion means that he often spends evenings on paperwork, though at least his new hours mean he's more likely to be able to drop Iris at nursery in the mornings. I'm about to suggest that Mia and I disappear to give him time to work, when Mia says something that jolts the thought right out of my head.

'Maybe it's wrong for me to ask for money.' She sighs.

I straighten in my seat. 'Why would you say that?' I ask.

Mia lifts one shoulder in an awkward, self-conscious half-shrug. 'Well, I… it's just that Zane and Rae – they were so *angry*. I mean, let's face it, I'm not really family like the rest of you are.'

'Nonsense.' Rob folds his arms, suddenly coming over all teacher-ish. 'You can't let them make you feel like that.' He leans forward conspiratorially. 'Don't get me wrong, I get it. The first time I met Zane and Rae, I was totally intimidated. They're both so…' He glances at me. 'Let's just say they're both very convinced of their own opinions. Entitled some might say.' He smiles. 'It's a private-school thing.'

I frown. Rob's right about my half-siblings, but I don't think it all comes down to education. After all, Tommy and I went to the same school as they did and we don't throw our weight around like Zane.

'Thank you for saying that,' Mia says softly. 'They are kind of intimidating.'

'They are,' I agree. 'And Rob's right to say you should stick to your guns. You've done a DNA test and it really doesn't matter what anyone else thinks.' I pat her arm. 'I'll tell you this much: I'm certain that if my – our – dad had known you existed, he'd have wanted to meet you and have a proper relationship with you. And he'd *definitely* want you to share our inheritance.'

'Do you really think so?' Mia suddenly sounds like a child. 'I so wish I'd known him. What was he like?'

'Terrifying,' Rob says with a chuckle.

I glance wryly sideways at him. 'He was strong,' I say. 'Passionate. But fiercely protective of the people he loved. Harder on men than women, I'd say.'

Mia nods.

'Definitely,' Rob adds. 'One more thing, Mia. You shouldn't worry about asking for a share of Nathaniel's inheritance.' He glances at me. 'There's plenty to go around, isn't there, Cas?'

'Absolutely,' I say, then wriggle uncomfortably in my seat, knowing that is hardly how Zane and Rae view the situation.

–

After we've eaten, I go upstairs to check on Iris. She's still awake, lying under the bed covers and staring up at the luminous stars on her ceiling.

'Hey, missy, you should be asleep.' I sit on the side of her little bed. 'Is everything okay?'

I'm expecting her to tell me about some playground dispute with one of her friends. But to my surprise, Iris turns to me with big eyes and says, 'Is Mia a fairy princess?'

I smile. 'No, she's a woman, just a bit younger than I am.'

Iris nods. 'She's very pretty.'

'She is,' I say. 'But you always have to remember that it's being pretty on the inside that counts. That means being kind and helpful but also able to say "no" if someone asks you to do something that makes you uncomfortable.'

'I know, Mummy.' Iris turns over and closes her eyes.

She's asleep a few moments later. As I leave her room, I get a text from Mum.

> Sorry for delayed reply. Hard for me with Mia, but I think you're being kind and generous to help her. Let's talk in a few days, once she's gone. Love you darling xx

What a relief. Feeling better than I have done all day, I head downstairs. Another message arrives as I reach the hall. It's from Tommy, confirming tomorrow's brunch. I walk back to the kitchen then stop in the doorway. Rob is standing at the sink, washing up the serving dish from dinner. At first, I can't see Mia, then I follow Rob's gaze through the window and spot her on the deck. She's on her phone, her golden hair shining under the security light as she paces up and down. She's frowning, clearly intent on her conversation. I look back at my husband. He hasn't taken his eyes off her.

'Pretty, isn't she?' I say archly, going over. 'Iris was just commenting on it.'

'Yeah?' Rob turns to me and kisses my cheek. There's no trace of awkwardness in his eyes. 'I hadn't noticed.'

I give him a playful thump on the arm. 'How long has she been out there?' I ask.

'Couple of minutes.'

I shake my head. 'She'll be frozen.'

'She's a grown woman, Cas.'

I sigh. 'Still.' I grab Mia's coat off the hall peg and go outside through the French doors. As I emerge into the icy air, I catch the end of Mia's sentence.

'Stop hassling me. I'm here, aren't I? It's fine.' Her voice is harsh and terse. A far cry from the wide-eyed innocence she's been displaying all day. She looks up and sees me and suddenly her voice changes again, back to sweetness and light. 'Ooh, listen, Grandma,' she trills. 'I've got to go. My lovely sister's here.'

She trips towards me, phone in one hand, hugging her arms as she shivers.

'I came to give you this.' I hold out the coat and Mia thanks me for being so thoughtful as we make our way back inside. 'Was everything okay, on the phone?' I ask. 'With your gran?'

Mia nods, rolling her eyes. 'She's just a bit protective,' she says. 'Always has been. I think she's scared I'll end up like my mum. She's worried about me being here for some reason, as if it isn't a million times better than Ellis's flat.'

'Right,' I say.

We take our seats at the table again and Rob pours us each another glass of wine. As I sip at the smooth, velvety Merlot, Mia explains about the various forms the lawyer needs her to fill in. She sounds overwhelmed and Rob is soon offering to help her with anything she needs. A small knot of anxiety twists in my stomach. I can't stop thinking how different Mia sounded when she didn't know she was being overheard. I tell myself that it's perfectly normal she should get annoyed with her grandmother on the phone. Normal too, that she might have a tougher edge to her than I've seen so far – or that she's wanted to put on display around me. She's had a hard start in life. It would be weird if she *didn't* have such an edge.

Even so, as Mia chatters on, full of her plans for her new flat, I find myself feeling relieved that she's moving out at the weekend.

Only two days, I think. Then we can get to know each other at a distance instead of this sudden and forced intimacy.

Just two more days.

SIX

The next morning Rob drops Iris at nursery and I start work on a lesson plan for a new music therapy client – a teenage girl recently disabled after a riding accident. I specialise in adults, rather than children, but I do sometimes see teenagers. They're often easier to work with than older people, being open to new ideas and generally very determined to make as much progress as possible – but you do have to work harder to win their trust at the start.

I sit at the kitchen table, reading the girl's profile and wondering how best to connect with her. Music therapy can get amazing results – provided you find the right way in. Everybody's different. Some people get a huge amount from just listening, others are eager to create the music themselves; it works on multiple levels. But for this girl, I'm guessing some activity that gives her a sense of control is going to be most helpful.

As I work, I hear Mia running the shower upstairs, then her footsteps padding across the landing. She appears downstairs later, just as I'm finishing a draft outline for the upcoming session. She's wearing jeans and another cropped jumper, tight over the swell of her breasts. Her belly piercing glints in the overhead light. Her hair is still damp, snaking over her shoulders and her face glows with health and life. She's only ten years younger than me, but it feels like a chasm. I experience a stab of envy. I seem to feel permanently tired these days and I know it shows on my face. It also makes it far too easy to gravitate towards sweet, carb-heavy snacks, which I know is the main reason behind my failure to lose those pregnancy pounds.

'Sleep well?' I ask, trying to hide the resentment I feel at Mia's appearance.

Mia nods, her huge eyes soft and full of gratitude. 'It was amazing to sleep in a proper bed and not be woken by people in the corridor outside Ellis's flat,' she says eagerly. 'I'm so grateful to you and Rob for letting me stay here.'

I smile, flooding with guilt at the meanness of my earlier thought. It's petty and unkind of me to resent Mia's natural beauty when she has had such a tough life. I indicate the cafetière, still half full of coffee, and invite Mia to take whatever food and drink she wants. She scoops some blueberries into a bowl, then slices an apple on top, carefully tidying up after herself as she goes.

'It must have been hard growing up not knowing anything about your dad,' I say as she joins me at the table.

Mia nods, nibbling at a slice of apple. 'I went through a phase in my teens where I asked my grandparents a lot of questions, but they only knew what Mum told them before she died – that she didn't know who my dad was. I hated Mum for that, for being so… so irresponsible and selfish.' She sighs. 'Of course, I feel guilty now. How awful that she *did* know but felt she couldn't tell anyone, not even her own parents.'

'Why d'you think that was?' I ask gently.

Mia shrugs. 'I've thought about it a lot. I know what you said yesterday, that if Nathaniel had been aware of me, he'd have wanted me in his life, but the most likely explanation I can see for Mum keeping quiet is that he just wasn't interested. I reckon she wanted to protect me from finding that out and probably thought that if she confided the ugly truth to anyone it might one day get back to me.' Her lips give a tiny wobble.

'Hey, hey… I don't believe that for a second. Isn't it more likely that your mum was embarrassed she'd got pregnant through an affair with a married man… ashamed even?'

Mia frowns.

'Not that she had anything to be ashamed about,' I add hurriedly.

'I suppose,' Mia says wistfully. Sadness fills her eyes. 'Maybe Mum didn't want to blow up his life.' She looks up, meeting my gaze. 'His family life, with you and your mum, I mean.'

I nod.

Mia pauses. 'But now here I am, blowing up all of yours.'

–

The next few hours pass quickly. Mia is a dream house guest. She not only washes up all the breakfast things without being asked but also tidies Iris's room, clearing toys into baskets, folding clothes and picking up the endless array of friendship bracelets that are scattered across the floor. We meet Tommy, as promised, for brunch. I notice every head turning as Mia crosses the cafe, while I trail invisibly after her. I push my resentment away. I've spent nearly twenty-four hours with the girl now and I'm more and more confident that she's exactly who she appears to be: a vulnerable, sweet-natured young woman who lost her mum at five and has grown up in relative poverty, but who retains a beauty that shines on the inside as well as the outside.

47

Tommy is his usual charming self, making Mia laugh as he describes his gaming influencer work, which she appears to be totally in awe of.

'But you're a model, Mia,' I protest. 'That's way more glamorous.'

She shakes her head. 'It's a snake-pit. Horrible. I'd so much rather be on the other side of the camera.'

'Well, when you get your share of Dad's money,' Tommy says, 'you'll be able to set yourself up as a photographer. I'll spread the word on all my socials; you'll be famous before you know it.'

Mia grins and blushes and I settle back in my chair, feeling more positive than I have done since she arrived. I'd be lying if I wasn't relieved that she'll be gone by the day after tomorrow. But I'm also sure that once Mum and Rae – and even Zane – get to spend a little time with her, they'll realise she's no threat to our family and is thoroughly deserving of her share in our inheritance.

I leave them at twelve in order to pick up Iris from nursery. Tommy is taking Mia to an exhibition, then they have plans for a movie.

I'm making a vegan pasta bake at home tonight for Mia's penultimate night in our house. Tomorrow will be Friday, her last night, and I'm thinking we'll celebrate with a takeaway. Maybe I'll even sound out Rae to see if she'd like to join us.

–

It's six p.m. and dark outside when the doorbell goes. I wipe my hands and go to the front door, Iris trailing at my heels.

Mia is standing outside, trying to sniff back the tears that stream down her face.

I stare at her, shocked. 'What's the matter?'

'It's... oh, I'm so sorry, I'm...' She stumbles inside and heads straight into the living room, pulling the door behind her.

Iris peers anxiously up at me. 'Is Mia okay?' she whispers.

'I'm sure she's fine,' I say. 'Go and finish your drawing. We'll come in to see you in a minute.'

Iris trots reluctantly away and I knock gently on the living room door, then peer inside. Mia is curled up on the sofa, her face in her hands. She's still sobbing, her shoulders heaving as she cries.

'Mia?'

She looks up. 'Oh, Cassie, I'm so sorry.'

'What on earth happened?' I ask, hurrying over. My head whirrs at one hundred miles an hour. Why is she upset and apologising? Is this something to do with Tommy?

Mia lets out a shuddering breath, then wipes her eyes. 'My flat's fallen through. I can't believe it. It's been planned for nearly a month and now I'm back to square one and I'm going to have to go back to Ellis's sofa and—' She dissolves into tears again.

'Hey, hey.' I draw her into a hug, the damp of her tears seeping through my sweatshirt and onto my shoulder. 'Why has it fallen through?'

'Landlord changed his mind, apparently.' She sniffs, drawing back. 'The worst thing is that he offered the people I'm supposed to be sharing with a smaller place. They had to agree then and there, and there's no room for me.' Her voice cracks. 'I've not just lost where I'm going to live, but the people I was going to live *with*. Sometimes it feels like I'm just never, ever going to catch a break.'

Another tear leaks out and trickles down her cheek. She wipes it away. 'I'm so sorry to get so upset. It's just the shock.'

'Of course.' I pat her arm. 'There's no need to apologise. And don't even think about going back to that sofa. You can stay here as long as you need.'

As soon as the words are out of my mouth, I wish I'd phrased the offer a little less generously, maybe setting a time limit for her visit or explaining that I need to check in with Rob before committing us to a longer stay. But Mia flings her arms around me.

'Oh, thank you, Cassie, I can't tell you how much it means to me to have a sister like you.'

'No worries,' I say gruffly, now feeling mean. 'I'm sure you'll be fixed up with a new place in no time.'

–

Another week passes. Mia makes herself invaluable at home, taking over almost all the laundry and cooking several dinners, even when she's spent the day at her waitressing job. She is careful to take herself off in the evenings, so Rob and I get time to ourselves, and I have to admit she massively eases the strain of juggling everything. I invite Rae over for supper midweek and, though she is still suspicious of Mia, she at least acknowledges the girl is highly likeable. Mum is fine too, though says she needs a bit more time before meeting Mia again, while Uncle Edgar calls me to explain that Mia's claim to be legally recognised as Dad's daughter should soon be approved. 'I still can't see a point in anyone challenging it,' he says, 'but I'm afraid Zane is still committed to doing so.'

I frown. Zane is still not answering my calls. It's typical of him to be high-handed about this. He could at least speak to me, even if just to say he disagrees with me taking her in.

—

Two weeks after she moved in, Mia gets a last-minute, one-day modelling job in a studio in south London. She leaves the house before anyone is up on Tuesday morning. A while later, I'm home from dropping Iris at nursery, and tidying up the breakfast things. I'm just thinking how used I've already got to Mia clearing up after us all, when the doorbell goes.

Zane stands outside in the cold air, a very serious expression on his face.

'Hi,' I say, bracing for the attack over Mia which I'm sure is about to issue from his lips.

'Hi, little sis.' To my surprise Zane smiles and leans over to kiss my cheek as if this is a planned and highly pleasurable social visit. 'How are you?'

'I'm, er, I'm fine. I wasn't expecting you.'

'I know, but I thought best to turn up without making a big deal of it, so we could chat. And when Mia's not here.' He strides past me into the house. I shut the front door, feeling the warmth of the hall radiator under the blast of icy air from outside.

'How did you know Mia was out?'

'Tommy told me she's off on some slutty modelling job.' Zane raises his eyebrows. 'Like mother, like daughter, eh?'

I stiffen, feeling awkward. 'Zane, if you've just come here to be mean about Mia then I really don't have the energy. If you'd give her a chance, you'd see she's actually a nice person who's had a horrible life in lots of ways and—'

'Hey!' Zane interrupts. 'I'm not here to give you a hard time, okay?' He smiles and I think for the millionth time how he doesn't have any of Dad's charisma or Tommy's charm.

Still, at least when he's smiling, he seems less intimidating.

'Just give me one minute!' He turns and pounds up the stairs, taking the steps two at a time.

I hurry after him. 'Um, Zane, if you're after a bathroom there's one down—'

'Is Mia staying in here?' Zane opens the door to the little spare room and peers inside. The room is neat and tidy. The scant possessions that Mia has brought with her are out of sight, presumably either in the little wardrobe at the end of the single bed or in the small set of drawers that form the bedside table.

'What are you doing?' I demand.

For answer, Zane strides over to the wardrobe and opens the door. He peers inside, then gives a disdainful sniff and turns to the drawers by the bed. Over his shoulder I catch a glimpse of a bra and some socks.

My discomfort morphs into anger. 'Stop it, Zane, you can't just go through Mia's things.'

He glances around at me, making a face. 'She won't leave proof lying about here, of course.'

'Proof?'

'That her story is fake.'

I roll my eyes. 'Come on, Zane.'

'Okay.' He holds his hands up in surrender, then stalks back out onto the landing.

I follow him down the stairs again, feeling cross and confused.

As we reach the hall, Zane turns to face me. 'I'm sorry for barging in,' he says, sounding more like a man trying to express regret than one feeling it. 'But please hear me out.'

It's the last thing I want to do but perhaps once he's said whatever is on his mind he will leave. 'Go on.'

'Mia's claim to our inheritance rests on her being Dad's daughter,' Zane says. 'And the proof of that rests on two things – firstly, that her mum and our dad had a fling nine months before she was born.'

'So?'

'I checked the exact dates when Dad was in the Bahamas back in '97 – the company has a record of the flights he took and they do fit with when Mia says her mum was there, though it's impossible to get any info on her photo shoot as the credited photographer is dead and I can't find the names of anyone else involved.'

I frown. 'Okay, but the fact that Dad was there kind of supports Mia's claim, doesn't it?'

Zane nods. 'It's circumstantial, but yes. So then there's the second proof – Mia's DNA test results.'

'I know all this, Zane,' I say. 'She showed them to us that first night. Uncle Edgar said it was a perfectly reputable clinic that did the test.'

'That might be what Edgar thinks, but it doesn't make it true,' Zane says. 'Who's to say the clinic wasn't in league with Mia, helping to falsify her DNA?'

'Do you really think that—?'

'In an ideal world, I'd take Mia's DNA myself and get another test done, but that's illegal without her permission, so the next best thing is to go to the clinic and speak to whoever took Mia's DNA. Find out what *really* happened.'

I shake my head. 'Isn't that overkill?'

'No.' Zane hesitates. 'I've been thinking about it and you have to admit there are plenty of people who'd love to get their hands on Dad's money. Who knows what lengths they'd go to.'

'That may be so,' I concede, 'though you're talking about serious crime. But there's no way that one of those people is Mia. She doesn't have the resources or... or the personality to carry out such a massive fraud.'

'Okay, but what if there's someone *behind* Mia, using her as... as a "front", as it were?'

'A front?'

'Yeah, I think that somebody worked out that our dad and her mum were in the Bahamas at the same time, nine months before Mia was born, and decided to invent a fictitious daughter in order to get their hands on our money. Mia's the face of the operation, but she's not the brains.'

'Oh, right,' I say drily. 'So who is?'

'I don't know,' says Zane. 'But Valentino Rossi would be first on my list.'

I purse my lips. Val Rossi and Dad were once great friends but fell out when Dad accused Rossi of cheating him in a business deal about twenty years ago. Rossi, for his part, has always protested Dad was the cheat and that a significant chunk of Carson Enterprises rightfully belongs to him.

'So you're saying that after two decades, Val Rossi decides to scam us to get his hands on some of Dad's money? What does Mia get out of that?'

'Probably a cash payment for playing her part, though I'm sure Rossi will take most of it for himself.'

'Stop!' I say, my head spinning. 'Zane, this is crazy. It sounds like something out of a bad movie. Way too far-fetched to be believable.'

'It is if *I* say it.' Zane leans against the wall behind him. 'That's why I want you to come with me.'

'Come with you?' I stammer. 'Where?'

'To the DNA clinic, of course,' he cries. 'We need to go and investigate together. Nobody will believe *me* if we find something suspicious, but they'll believe *you*.'

I stare at him. 'Are you serious?'

Zane nods. 'Come on,' he says, his voice firing with energy. 'We've got an appointment with the clinic manager at ten thirty.'

SEVEN

The Silver Tree DNA testing clinic is on the first floor of one of the big private health centres on Harley Street.

Zane strides in with his usual swagger. I scuttle after him, feeling self-conscious. I'm certain this is a wild goose chase. Uncle Edgar already checked out the clinic before sending Mia here. I've only agreed to come with Zane because I can see he isn't going to shut up until somebody proves to him that she really is our father's daughter.

Also, if I'm here, Zane won't later be able to twist whatever the clinic tells him to suit his own agenda.

The reception area is busy for a private facility, with almost half the leather couches occupied. A small boy about the same age as Iris is rolling a toy car over the glass coffee table in the centre of the room. A screen on the wall shows the news. It's flanked by a pair of bland, pastel paintings.

Zane raps his knuckles on the countertop, impatient for the receptionist to finish talking to the woman ahead of us. His intense presence fills the waiting room.

I touch his arm. 'Calm down,' I whisper.

He grunts something under his breath. I can't make it out.

'May I help you?' The young, heavily made-up receptionist is free at last.

'I have an appointment with the clinic director at ten thirty,' Zane barks, his voice deep and fierce.

The receptionist blinks at the force of his words. She glances at her screen.

'You're Mr Carson?' she asks.

'That's right,' Zane says.

The woman's gaze drifts to me, her eyebrows raised. She is young, barely out of her teens, yet her face is caked in foundation and her eyes lined in jet-black kohl. *You're more attractive than you think*, I want to tell her.

Instead, of course, I simply say. 'I'm here for the same meeting.'

'This is my half-sister, Cassandra,' Zane announces.

'Right, okay, Ms Carson, Mr Carson,' the receptionist says. 'Mr Edwards will just be a minute. Please take a seat.'

Zane and I sit down on either side of the coffee table. The little boy with the car looks up. I smile at him. Zane scowls.

After a couple of minutes Mr Edwards appears: a balding, bespectacled man in an elegantly cut suit. He ushers us into his office, and we sit in front of his leather-topped desk in wing-backed armchairs.

'I'm so pleased we were able to make time for this meeting,' he says smoothly.

'Let's cut the crap.' Zane leans forward. 'Do you have the reports?'

I stare at him. Which reports is he referring to? I thought we were just here to ask a few questions.

Mr Edwards nods. I get the impression he has dealt with many emotional people over the course of his career and totally has the measure of Zane. He certainly doesn't seem fazed by his abrupt manner.

'As I explained on the phone,' Mr Edwards says, his voice silky smooth, 'the rules around the release of DNA test information are very carefully drawn and tightly enforced, for reasons which I'm sure you can appreciate.'

'I know that,' Zane grunts ungraciously. 'But this is a contested result.'

'If I might clarify.' Mr Edwards holds up a perfectly manicured hand. 'The result of the DNA tests themselves are *not* contested. They are *legal* DNA tests, done to the highest specifications. To be clear, it's the *inheritance* claim with which you're involved that is contested. There is absolutely no possibility that the two test reports you asked to discuss today have ever been tampered with.'

I stare at him, feeling bewildered. I had no idea Zane had asked for anything in advance.

Zane turns to Mr Edwards. 'The tests were both done here. I need you to confirm that *all* protocols were followed on *both* occasions,' he barks.

'I can assure you they were,' says Mr Edwards soothingly. 'The clinic has always had strict chain of custody rules. Now, as I was explaining, when an inheritance claim is contested, it's possible for the executor of a will to receive information that would otherwise be privileged. Your uncle, Mr Edgar Carson, has given me permission to discuss the findings of both tests with you. Here they are.' He draws two sheets of paper out of the folder on his desk and places them in front of us.

I peer closer, eager to understand.

Both sheets contain summaries of DNA parentage results and feature three columns full of mysterious letters and numbers, headed respectively "case number", "child's name" and "alleged father".

The first sheet is dated twenty years ago and shows the initials "D. D." under "child's name" and "N. C." under "alleged father".

I stare at the "N. C." initials. This must be the paternity test which Mia said Dad underwent two decades ago.

Mr Edwards taps his finger against the paper. 'As you already know, this historic paternity test is the reason Nathaniel Carson's DNA was originally tested.' His finger slides down the page to the bottom where the line "*Probability of paternity 0%*" is written in bold.

I nod. It's weird seeing the test result here and thinking how Dad took it without Mum or us knowing. Does his doing the test mean he thought he *was* the father? Or that he was convinced he couldn't be? I shake myself. Right now, it hardly matters.

Mr Edwards' hand moves to the second sheet of paper. This one shows the initials "M. I.", presumably for Mia Ishchenko, under "child's name" and, again, "N. C." under "alleged father". This time the probability of paternity is given as 99.9998%.

It looks identical to the page Mia showed us the other day.

I glance at Zane. His lips are pressed tightly together as he studies both sheets of paper.

'As you can see the alleged father, "N. C.", is the same in both the recent test results and the one done twenty years ago,' Mr Edwards explains. 'There is no doubt this data represents the DNA of Nathaniel Carson.'

Zane nods. 'Yes, I accept that. I've already seen the DNA test from the previous claim.'

I glance at him in surprise. 'You have?'

'Edgar showed me that first night. I went round and demanded the facts,' Zane says. 'However, our acceptance of Dad's DNA here is irrelevant. What matters is whether or not Mia's DNA is genuine.'

For the first time, Mr Edwards bridles. 'As I've already explained, all protocols were followed in the undertaking of her test and the chain of custody of the samples was strictly observed. I've also shown your uncle Ms Ishchenko's signed form, and I believe the young lady in question has provided video proof to your uncle of her attendance here too.'

I glance at Zane. 'It does sound conclusive, don't you think?'

'No,' Zane barks. 'All of that just proves she was here at the time the test was supposedly done. It *doesn't* prove the test is accurate.'

I meet Mr Edwards' gaze. He looks as baffled as I feel.

'What are you suggesting?' I ask. 'How could Mia have faked a DNA test?'

Zane sits upright, his face contorted with a frown. 'I'm suggesting that whoever is behind this whole… farrago… bribed whoever did Mia's test to provide fake results.'

I gasp. Behind the desk, Mr Edwards blinks rapidly. 'I can assure you that all our staff are thoroughly vetted, there's no way—'

'I want to talk to whoever did Mia's test,' Zane demands. He snatches up the results sheet and points to the initials of the clinician. '*There!* "B. H." – who is that?'

Mr Edwards frowns. 'It isn't possible for you to speak to them, I'm afraid. Apart from anything else, I have to protect the privacy of my staff and—'

'Privacy, my *arse*.' Zane's voice rises to a shout. He jumps to his feet. 'Do you realise what's at stake here?'

'Zane.' I tug at his arm, standing up too. 'Calm down.'

He shakes me off. 'Who was it?' he yells at the director. 'Give me their name or I'll have this clinic closed down for fraud.'

His words echo around the office. Mr Edwards stands and stares at Zane in stony silence, letting a few seconds pass before speaking again.

'Well,' he says, 'I think we've covered everything I can help with, Mr Carson.' He turns to me. 'Ms Carson, thank you so much for your time.'

For a moment, Zane stands, clearly still fuming. I blow out my breath. How stupid I was to think coming here would resolve things for him. He's like a conspiracy theorist, where a fact given as a solution to a problem is heard, instead, as part of that same problem.

'Zane, let's go,' I say softly.

Zane heaves an angry sigh, then stomps out of the office and through to reception, leaving me to shake hands with Mr Edwards and offer an apology for my half-brother's behaviour.

I brace myself as I return to the waiting area. But there's no sign of Zane here.

'He left,' the receptionist says quietly.

I hesitate. No doubt Zane is waiting for me outside. I really don't want to have to deal with his rants all the way home. I blow out a shaky breath.

'Are you all right?' the young receptionist asks.

I turn and smile at her. I intend to give her an empty platitude. But what actually comes out of my mouth is: 'It's just such a mess.'

'I know.' The young woman smiles back. 'It often is when things are... contested. Your... your brother is obviously very upset.'

I nod. 'I just wish there was a way to prove to him the results are genuine, but he won't believe it.' I press my lips together. What am I doing, sharing our family fallout with this complete stranger?

'He wants to speak to the clinician who did the recent DNA test, doesn't he?' she whispers. 'I heard him shouting. He said her initials, "B. H.".'

I roll my eyes. 'Sorry,' I say, 'I imagine half the waiting room heard.'

'It's just...' She hesitates. 'Normally I wouldn't say anything, but it *is* a bit odd.' She looks around. 'Mr Edwards won't like me telling you, but the person your brother wants to speak to... the nurse who did that test...'

A sense of foreboding washes over me. 'What about her?' I ask.

The receptionist looks up at me. 'It happened the day afterwards. She was on her way home from work and... and she was killed in a hit-and-run car accident.'

EIGHT

I stumble out of the DNA test clinic in a daze. Zane is pacing along the pavement, oblivious to the drizzle that clings to his head and shoulders. I raise the hood of my jacket and hurry over to him.

'Bloody waste of time!' Zane roars. 'But I'm not letting it lie. I'm going to find out the name of the—'

'She's dead.'

He stares at me. 'What?'

'The nurse who took Mia's DNA died in a car accident the very next day. The receptionist just told me.'

Zane's jaw drops, then he turns on his heel. 'Right,' he snarls. 'I'm going to go back in and get that Edwards man to come clean and—'

'No.' I grab his arm, digging my fingers in forcefully. A drop of rain trickles down my face and I wipe it away.

Zane glares at me. 'What?'

'You're not going back in there and you're not haranguing the director or the staff either.'

'Oh, aren't I now?' Zane sneers. 'Why is that?'

'Because it'll be counterproductive, just like everything you did inside the clinic.' I let go of his arm and put my hands on my hips. I have never spoken to Zane like this; we've never been close enough. Growing up, the thirteen-year age gap and lack of time spent together meant he was always a distant figure, and since then we've met purely at family gatherings and a few social functions. He's never invited a bigger connection and, to be honest, has always seemed entirely uninterested in both me and Tommy. Up until now I've thought of him as an insensitive and ruthless man, but as I look into his eyes right now, I glimpse the vulnerability that lurks deep under the surface. I soften my voice. 'Look, I get why you wanted to press that Edwards guy for information, but if you'd been a little more appreciative or open—'

'You mean if I'd been a soft-boiled pushover,' he mutters.

'Sometimes soft-boiled pushovers win the race.' I grin. 'Which one of us got the useful information here?'

Zane makes a face. 'Okay,' he grunts. 'Point taken. But if we don't try and talk to the clinic again, how will we find out what happened to the nurse? Or if it was connected to the Mia fraud?'

'Firstly, there's no proof at all that there *is* any "Mia fraud",' I say. 'I grant you it's a weird coincidence that the nurse who did her test died the day afterwards, but it doesn't *prove* anything.'

Zane shrugs, clearly not convinced.

'Secondly,' I continue, 'we can find out what happened to the nurse ourselves. We have her occupation, her initials from the test form – B. H. – and we know she was killed in a hit-and-run on her way home from work a few weeks ago, the day after Mia did her test. That gives us a date and a rough idea of place.'

Zane is already searching on his phone. The rain eases as I take mine out too.

It doesn't take long to find details online.

They make for chilling reading.

In what may be a racially motivated attack, Blossom Harrington, a 34-year-old registered nurse, was struck down by a vehicle as she crossed a road close to her house. Forensic investigators claim that, far from stopping, the vehicle sped away after the assault.

'The driver of the car displayed a callous disregard for life by driving off instead of calling the emergency services,' says DI Pickard, who is heading up the murder investigation.

I glance at Zane, as he looks up from his phone.

'Brutal,' he mutters.

'But they're saying it was probably a racially motivated attack,' I say. 'Nothing to do with the nurse doing Mia's DNA test the day before.'

'That's just their theory,' says Zane bitterly. 'It's obvious to me that the nurse was involved in the DNA fraud and that whoever killed her wanted her out of the way.'

'Whoa.' I stare at him. 'That's a massive assumption.'

'Come on, Cassie,' Zane protests. 'Surely you can see this situation is dodgy as all hell.'

'No, I don't see that,' I say firmly. 'In fact, the only thing I *am* certain of is that even if there's a distant possibility that Mia somehow faked that DNA test – and I still don't see how she could have done that – there's no way she could have killed this nurse, Blossom Harrington. She can't even drive.'

'So she says,' Zane growls.

'Seriously, Zane, she grew up in the heart of south-east London with public transport and no money. Who d'you think would've paid for driving lessons?'

Zane gives a sullen shrug. 'So what if she doesn't drive? I already told you I'm sure she's working with somebody else. *They* could have carried out the hit-and-run.' Zane clenches his jaw. 'I'm going to start digging into Val Rossi; he's definitely the most likely candidate.' He lowers his voice. 'He'd do anything to get revenge on Dad and is certainly capable of funding a DNA test and guiding Mia through a long con. Plus, he was very rude to me and Savannah at the Braeburn Charity Gala a couple of months ago.'

I shake my head. Rudeness hardly implies guilt.

'How is Sav?' I ask, wondering how Zane's dark mood might be affecting his girlfriend. When I was heavily pregnant, I felt weepy and uncomfortable almost all the time. After the birth, I suffered from post-natal depression for about six months and without Rob's solid, steady presence at my side, I don't know how I would have coped.

'Sav's fine,' says Zane curtly, with a dismissive wave of his hand.

I shake my head. Could he be any more self-absorbed? As we walk to his car, the sun comes out and the damp pavement around us gleams wetly.

'Are you going to tell Rae about this?' I ask. 'Or Uncle Edgar? It's just Mum's upset enough about Mia as it is and you stirring things up isn't going to help.'

'I won't say anything for the time being,' Zane says as we reach his car. 'But once I've investigated, we'll definitely have to call another family meeting.'

I heave a sigh and get into the car.

As Zane drops me at home, he murmurs a warning: 'Be careful.' His low, concerned whisper sends a shiver down my spine. I give myself a shake. I'm ninety-nine per cent sure he's wrong about Mia, while his theory about Val Rossi masterminding some sort of elaborate inheritance con is beyond outlandish.

Inside, the house is silent and I take advantage of the peace and quiet to do some ironing, while mulling over this morning's discoveries. Iris is on a playdate, and by the time I've picked her up and got home again, it's almost six thirty. I'm hoping Rob will have sorted dinner and, indeed, as we walk in the delicious smell of roasting vegetables fills the air. Iris runs upstairs to her room to fetch the tablet she's allowed to play on for half an hour every evening. I take off my coat and, smiling at the prospect of greeting my husband in the kitchen, wander down the hall and open the kitchen door.

But it's not Rob standing by the hob; it's Mia.

She's humming a tune under her breath and stirring a thick, creamy sauce. Her back is to the door, so she doesn't see me. I stand, staring at the pale green cardigan she is wearing. It looks very familiar. I move a little closer. The sleeves are hitched up to her elbows, revealing the barbed wire tattoo that rings the skin of her lower arm. I peer at the collar of the cardigan. There's a tiny nick in the fabric and the top button is missing.

It's *my* cardigan.

I fill with sudden rage. How dare Mia wear my clothes? Where did she even get that cardigan? What else has she been snooping through?

I clench my fists. Part of me wants to demand an explanation, but Iris could reappear at any second. I don't want to risk flying off the handle in front of her.

Instead, I back out of the room and, checking Rob isn't in the living room, hurry upstairs to find him.

He's sitting on our bed, reading something on his phone. My gaze lingers on the handsome slope of his nose in profile. His shirt is undone to the waist, revealing the taut muscles of his chest and abs.

'Hey.' He looks up as I hurry in. He's unshaven, his chin covered in stubble. 'Good day?'

I can tell, immediately, he's in the mood to get physical. It's the flicker of interest in his gaze, the subtle shift of his body weight on the bed.

We often make love in the early evening, with Iris absorbed in her tablet, before the day catches up with us and we crawl into bed too tired to think about anything except sleep.

It's the last thing I want right now.

'Did you notice what Mia is wearing?' I hiss.

Rob frowns. 'Eh?'

'She's rooted around in my drawers... my *clothes* and she's wearing one of my cardigans. I don't like it. In fact, I think it's creepy.' I suddenly wonder if perhaps Zane's suspicions are more based in reality than I've let myself think. 'You'll never guess what—'

'That cardigan came from a bin bag at the back of our wardrobe that you told me weeks ago you were going to take to the charity shop.' The sexual interest vanishes from Rob's gaze. 'I told Mia she could have whatever she wanted from it.'

'Oh.' I stare at him, the memory of my pre-Christmas clear-out suddenly flooding back.

'Mia said something earlier about her jumpers being too warm in this house, when the heating is on and needing something lighter, so I remembered the bag was in there and gave it to her.' He scowls. 'Are you telling me you have a problem with that?'

'No,' I say, now feeling guilty. 'Of course not.'

'Honestly,' Rob goes on. 'If you'd seen the poor girl, she kept saying she didn't want to take it without asking you first. I had to practically force it on her.' He sighs and stomps away, into our en suite.

I blow out my breath. I feel stupid for having jumped to conclusions. But also a little resentful. Of course I don't mind Mia wearing things I was going to throw out anyway, but I'd still rather have been asked in advance. More than that – if she wasn't living with us, it wouldn't have happened. I wander into Iris's room, but she's not there, so I go back downstairs, to find that she is now sitting with Mia at the kitchen table. A tray of roasted vegetables drizzled with thick, pale sauce rests, steaming, on the countertop, while a pan of rice bubbles on the hob.

'Mummy, look!' Iris calls me over. 'Mia's found a new game for me. It's for dressing up dolls.'

Mia looks around at me and smiles. 'Hey, I hope you don't mind,' she says. 'The kids where I used to work *loved* it.'

I nod, as Mia stands up, leaving Iris bent over the tablet. My eyes can't help but linger on that cardigan. Mia wears it far better than I do. Not to mention the tight white T-shirt underneath.

'Casual elegance,' I say, forcing myself to smile at her. 'It's a hard look to pull off.'

She glances down at the cardigan, her cheeks pinking. 'Oh, gosh, I'm so sorry. I knew I should have spoken to you first. I mean, Rob said it was okay, but—'

'It's fine,' I say. 'Honestly, you should keep it, it looks great on you.'

As soon as I've said the words, I regret them. They are all about the guilt and resentment I feel, not any desire to give Mia my clothes.

'Oh, no, that's okay,' Mia says. 'It's a bit big on me actually, so—' She stops, her hand flying to her mouth. 'Oh, I'm so sorry, that must have sounded really rude.'

'You're fine,' I say, though inside I feel ridiculously churned up. I'm well aware that Mia is slimmer and more attractive than I am. It's stupid to be upset about it. And it's certainly not Mia's fault. I change the subject. 'Hey, what's in that sauce?' I point to the tray of veggies on the countertop. 'It looks delicious.'

'Just something my mum used to make,' Mia says. 'My gran kept all her recipes.'

A look of sadness crosses her face. I'm about to ask her more about her mum, but just then Rob comes in with some information he's unearthed about inheritance claims from illegitimate children. He and Mia sit side by side at the table, Mia leaning slightly towards him as she peers at his mobile.

After a few minutes, Iris's tablet times her out of her play session. She's tired and whiny, demanding to play a little longer and I brace myself for a showdown. But before she can get too grouchy, Mia scoops her up as if she's known her all her life and jiggles her on one knee, while still nodding and listening to Rob.

A tendril of envy winds around my heart. Mia is so lovely – sweet-natured, great with Iris and stunningly beautiful. Sitting there between my husband and daughter, she looks entirely at home.

While I, standing across the room, suddenly feel like the outsider.

I shake myself. I'm being ridiculous to think like this. I pour a jug of water and take it over to the table. Rob looks up and meets my gaze. I smile at him and see in his eyes an understanding that I'm trying to make up for my earlier insecurity and irritation. He smiles back as I pass him a glass of water.

Against the odds, it turns into a lovely evening. And it's followed by several more. Mia has a seemingly effortless ability to fit in with our household. Iris adores her, yet Mia always knows when to help out and when to slip away and let us be a family together. She's funny too, making Rob and I laugh with tales of the rather pompous photographer on her recent modelling shoot. She also mentions that she's seen several potential flats already and is going to view another soon. She sounds genuinely positive that something will come of one of these and she'll soon be moving on. And yet I can't shake my sense of doubt about her. However brightly her smile lights a room, I'm always aware of a shadow lurking in the corner.

—

It's the Monday morning of the following week and I'm up, but still not properly awake, when Mia appears in the kitchen with tears in her eyes, to tell me that none of last week's possible new flats have worked out. I reassure her, as I did before, that she can carry on staying with us, though this time I'm careful not to add "for as long as you need". I can't help but wonder if Mia is really looking for a new home as hard as she says. But as soon as I've had the thought, I feel guilty – I know how difficult it is to find a decent, affordable rental in London.

That afternoon Mia says she's going to view yet another place but is home within the hour, explaining as she sobs that the flat had gone before she got there. It occurs to me that the two company-owned London apartments might be free. Perhaps Mia could move into one of those for a few months? I email Edgar straightaway, to ask.

He replies that evening, explaining that unfortunately there are long lets in both flats. I also get a text from Zane – his first communication since our trip to the DNA clinic last week. He asks me to meet him tomorrow, adding:

I have important news

I frown, wondering why he feels the need to be so mysterious, but I'm soon distracted by Iris falling and scraping her knee on the hall floor, and Rob announcing he's popping out for a quick drink with his brother.

By the time Rob returns, Iris has long since fallen asleep, while Mia has already disappeared upstairs to her room, so Rob and I chill on the sofa. Rob tells me about his day and how he dealt with a year nine student kicking off in the science lab. Then he moves closer, his eyes gleaming, and suggests we go to bed.

We make love with smothered giggles, not wanting to make a noise that Mia, just across the landing, might hear. I'm just drifting off to sleep afterwards, when my phone, plugged in to charge across the room, rings.

'Leave it,' mumbles Rob, more than half asleep already.

But I'm already stumbling over to pick the thing up. Sav is calling and my first thought is that there's something wrong with her pregnancy. Adrenalin shoots through me and as I say 'Hello,' I'm wide awake.

Shuddering breaths are all I can hear down the line.

'Sav?' My voice cracks. 'Is that you? Are you okay? Is it the baby?'

'It's… It's Zane,' she sobs. 'He's been in an accident.'

'What kind of accident?'

'Car. Hit-and-run.' Sav dissolves into tears.

I freeze, as the thought shoots through me: a hit-and-run was how Blossom Harrington, the DNA clinic nurse, died.

'Is Zane all right?' I ask. 'Where is he? Did he say anything about what happened?' There's no reply, just more muffled weeping. '*Sav?*'

'Oh, Cassie,' she sobs. 'He's dead. Zane is dead.'

NINE

It's hard to focus. The idea that a ferocious, larger-than-life spirit like Zane's can just have been snuffed out is impossible to process.

I call Tommy as soon as I put the phone down on Sav. It's gone eleven, but I doubt he'll be in bed yet and I know he'll feel as shocked as I do. Indeed, he expresses exactly the same sense of stunned horror that is running in circles around my head. He also insists that he'll come right now and pick me up to go over to Zane and Sav's house.

'We should sit with her until her mother arrives, Cas,' he urges. 'She likes us a lot more than Rae.'

I get dressed, then go down to the kitchen to wait. Rob pours me a whiskey and places an extra cardigan over my shoulders. I lean against him, feeling the heat and strength of his body. As we sit in silence, the pad of Mia's footsteps echoes on the stairs. I glance up at Rob, alarmed and, reading my mind, he slips out to tell Mia what has happened.

A few moments later he creeps back in.

'I explained to Mia you needed a bit of space,' he says, rubbing my arm. 'She actually offered to babysit Iris so that I can come with you to Sav's house. What do you think?'

I gaze at him. Tempting though it would be to have him at my side, we haven't ever left Mia alone with Iris

74

overnight and I'd hate our daughter to wake up and find neither of her parents here without any warning. Plus, Rob has a full day at school tomorrow.

'It's fine,' I whisper, kissing him softly. 'I'll have Tommy with me. Once he's here, you get back to sleep. I'll tell you how everyone is in the morning.'

—

Tommy and I say very little as we drive. Zane and Sav's house is in Putney, which would normally take ages from north London but at this time on a Monday night we sail through the streets. By the time we arrive, both Rae and Uncle Edgar are already there. I give Rae a hug, trying to imagine how I would feel if I lost Tommy. In typical Rae style, she is dry-eyed and stiff-limbed, but there's no mistaking the pain of her grief.

How awful for her, I think, to not have anyone to really share the full force of it with. Uncle Edgar had the same kind of awkward, troubled relationship with Zane as the rest of us. It was only Rae whom Zane seemed truly to love — and be loved by.

I offer my sympathies, but Rae brushes them aside, briskly explaining that it's too late for Savannah's mother to drive all the way from her home in Leeds right now, but that she's coming first thing in the morning.

Sav appears and collapses into my arms.

'Thank goodness you're here, Cassie, I just can't believe it,' she keeps weeping.

One of her friends arrives at this point and quickly takes charge. She steers Sav upstairs, insisting they should do a guided meditation together. It is clear this isn't something either of them really want me involved in, so I leave them to it and head to the living room, where Uncle Edgar, Tommy and Rae are deep in conversation.

They look up as I walk in.

'Rae's been on with the police,' Tommy explains. 'It looks like Zane was killed on his way home after dinner with clients.'

'What happened exactly?' I ask.

Rae shakes her head.

'Nobody knows,' Uncle Edgar says solemnly. 'There were no witnesses and no CCTV on the road where he was run over.'

'So, what... a drunk driver or something?' I hold up my hands in a gesture of despair. 'Don't they have any leads?'

Uncle Edgar shakes his head. 'I'm afraid there's not much for them to go on. They say they'll investigate cars on surrounding roads, but there's a lot of traffic.' He sighs. 'I don't hold out much hope that they'll find the culprit. It's such a shock, isn't it? I, er, I was just getting ready for bed when Rae called.'

I glance over at my half-sister. 'Did Savannah call you?'

'No,' Rae says, pursing her lips as if angry at the question. 'Actually, *I* called her. I was still down on Zane's phone as his emergency contact.'

I nod. Tommy catches my eye. 'How's Sav doing?' he asks.

I shake my head. 'Just lost, I think. Like we all are.'

'Such a terrible, terrible accident,' murmurs Uncle Edgar. 'One moment of careless driving and... a life snuffed out.'

'How do you know it was an accident?' Rae demands.

Uncle Edgar frowns. 'Well, what else, Rae dear?'

'The driver didn't stop,' Tommy points out.

'Well, there could be lots of reasons for that,' Uncle Edgar says. 'Cowardice. Fear of arrest, of losing their licence at the very least.'

'Apparently the paramedics are certain he died immediately,' Tommy adds quietly. 'Even if the driver had called an ambulance straightaway, it wouldn't have saved him.'

'They don't know that for sure,' Rae snaps.

'No, of course,' Uncle Edgar says soothingly. 'We're all so sorry. When a senseless accident like this hap—'

'Stop calling it an accident.' Rae's voice rises.

I look at her, wondering what Zane told her about his ongoing investigation into Mia's DNA test. I suddenly remember the mysterious text message he sent me earlier.

I have important news

My throat tightens. Whatever that news was, I'm certain it had something to do with Mia. What else would Zane be contacting me about?

'You think that... that it was deliberate?' I ask, my voice catching in my throat.

Rae shrugs, her lips trembling.

It's a bright winter morning, three days after Zane's death. Edgar has called an emergency family meeting at Carson Enterprises. Everyone I pass on the way up to the tenth-floor boardroom glances in my direction, an expression of shock and sympathy on their face. It seems surreal to me that the entire staff are working away, despite the circumstances but, as Tommy grunts when I meet him and Mum outside the elevator, consumer electronics don't import themselves.

As the initial shock subsides, it's obvious that we are all reacting in different ways. Rae, alone, is distraught. Uncle

Edgar is focused on the practicalities, while Mum – who never had an easy relationship with Zane – remains quietly phlegmatic.

For myself, it's not grief that I feel. At least, not like when Dad died. We knew the end was coming then but even so the shock of his passing felt like the world shifting underneath me. Right now, the shock is like a thunderbolt, more surreal than painful. It's not as if I was close to Zane. I can count on the fingers of one hand the times we spent on our own together – and even our last, recent, trip together to the DNA clinic was mostly about me trying to rein him in.

Uncle Edgar is keen to fill us in on the police investigation, explaining that the detectives on the case don't seem to have a single clue about the car that ran Zane down. Apparently, they've checked all the cameras in the area and tracked down every car in the time frame with visible numberplates – but come up with no new leads.

It's clear from the way he speaks that Uncle Edgar has logged Zane's death as a tragic, random accident. I keep thinking of the message Zane sent me and wondering if I should tell someone – but it's hardly proof of foul play, so I don't. Or, at least, I haven't so far. Instead, I edge closer to Rae, placing my hand on her arm. She gives me a brief shake of the head to indicate that she's not after sympathy right now.

I sit back and sigh, as Uncle Edgar keeps talking about how the company is intending to handle the loss of their managing director. I can't quite believe Zane isn't about to stride in, rude and sweary as usual. At home, Rob has been wonderful, full of concern and support, while Mia – to her credit – has kept in the background, stepping up unobtrusively to help out with small things around the house, including playing endlessly with Iris.

I glance at Rae again, as Uncle Edgar launches into a fresh speech about how the Carson family will always pull together in times of trouble. It strikes me that the family Rae grew up with has now completely gone. She lost her mother to cancer ten years ago, then Dad last summer, while like the rest of us, she hasn't seen her other brother, Adam, for over twenty years.

I think there have been several attempts over the years to track him down, but none of them successful. He wasn't even at Dad's funeral.

Uncle Edgar suggests a short break so we can refill our coffee cups. As everyone else heads for the insulated cafetières on the drinks table at the end of the boardroom, I lean over to Rae and whisper: 'Do you have any idea about Adam... where he might be?'

'None,' Rae says, her face rigid with pain. 'I've left messages with all the people he used to know, but he... it's been so long.' Her voice cracks. 'It's so hard now though, without Zane.'

'I'm so sorry, Rae.' I squeeze her hand. My thoughts scoot back to a Christmas visit from her, Adam and Zane when I was little. Rae often came to stay with us and I was used to her being bossy and impatient in our games, but Adam and Zane, being in their mid to late teens at the time, were far rarer visitors. Zane, as ever, was aloof and uninterested, but Adam played with me for hours. When I picture them both, it's Zane's sneer I imagine — and Adam's gentle smile.

Uncle Edgar clears his throat. I look up to see that he's resumed his position at the head of the big boardroom table.

'I am now going to ask Nina Owens to outline the procedures and protocols the company will follow in the wake of this… our terrible bereavement,' he says. 'I felt it was more appropriate for this information to come from legal than myself. Rest assured that what Nina is about to say represents the view of our other directors. We felt it made more sense to discuss everything internally in advance of this meeting, to spare yourselves the strain of admin and logistics at this difficult time.'

Rae frowns, looking up for the first time.

Nina rises to her feet. She expresses her own sorrow for our loss then adds crisply: 'As from today, the running of day-to-day affairs will be undertaken by a committee comprising all department heads.'

'And I'll be at the helm,' Uncle Edgar adds, 'focused on key strategies and providing an overview on policy and direction.'

I gaze around the room. Tommy is a couple of chairs down on my right. He has a faraway look on his face, as if uninterested in the detail of how the company will continue after Zane's death. Sav sits opposite him, her face wreathed in misery and as unengaged in the conversation as Tommy. Being here must be unbearable for her. I think back to the later stages of my own pregnancy. I was physically so helpless by then – unable to run or even pick something up off the floor – but even more vulnerable psychologically – full of fears and anxieties about the impending birth. My baby was really just an idea to me at that point. All my focus was on the act of labour and how terrifying it seemed. It was Rob who got me through those last few weeks: absorbing my fears and insisting he wouldn't let anything bad happen either to me or to our baby.

I don't know what Sav's relationship with Zane was like, but surely she must have leaned on him a little too? And now all that support has been wrenched out from under her, just when she needs it most.

Mum sits next to Sav, one hand on Sav's arm, the other idly in her lap. She might not have got on with Zane, but I'm certain Mum can relate to the loss his partner is feeling now. As Nina moves on to the company's strategic plan for the quarter, I can see Mum frowning. I'm guessing she thinks this is inappropriately insensitive, considering the naked grief being displayed by both Zane's sister and his pregnant girlfriend.

Mia is at the other end of the table, staying as far away from Mum as possible. She's listening eagerly. To be honest, I'm surprised Rae didn't object when Uncle Edgar said Mia would be here, but perhaps she's just too consumed with her grief over Zane to focus on Mia right now.

'We just need to vote to rubber stamp these interim measures.' Nina clears her throat. 'Now, assuming there are no objections to our proposal, I'd—'

'I object.' Rae looks up, her eyes sparking with sudden energy. 'I don't think it's appropriate for Nina and Edgar and some random committee to take charge.'

Nina looks at Uncle Edgar, who frowns. 'It's not a random committee, Rae, it's the Carson Enterprises board of directors. Surely you can see that we're best placed to run things?'

'I only see that you're best placed to run this company into the ground,' Rae says icily.

I stare at her. She's not normally quite this rude. Direct, yes, but with wit and verve and plenty of our father's charm. Right now, she sounds more like Zane. An unexpected arrow of loss pierces through me. Even if Zane was often difficult to the point of boorishness, it's hard to accept that he isn't in the world any longer.

'I don't think—' Uncle Edgar splutters.

'I don't care what you think,' Rae spits. 'I want to take charge. And, bearing in mind that this is a family firm which now belongs to me, Cassie and Tommy, I can't see why I shouldn't, unless one of them objects?'

Everyone looks at me.

My jaw drops. 'I… I'm not sure,' I stammer.

Rae rolls her eyes, then turns to Tommy and fixes him with a fierce look. 'I'm guessing you're not the slightest bit interested in who runs the place, Tommy,' she says haughtily, 'but I'm sure even you can see I'd do a better job than Uncle Edgar.'

The atmosphere grows even more tense as Edgar glares at Rae, while Tommy looks down at the table. I wriggle uneasily in my seat.

And then Tommy looks up. I'm expecting him to shrug and perhaps yawn, then tell Rae he's happy to go with whatever she wants.

Instead, there's a mischievous grin on his face.

'Tommy?' Rae suddenly sounds uncertain.

'I think we should sell the company,' my brother says.

Nina gasps. Uncle Edgar frowns. '*What* did you say?'

Tommy's grin deepens.

Rae frowns. 'Is this a joke?'

'No.' Tommy sits up. 'We should sell. Make as much money as possible.' He glances around the room, clearly enjoying the look of consternation on Rae and Uncle Edgar's faces. 'We sell, divide the money between us, and each spend our share on something we feel passionate about.'

'What about Dad's legacy?' Rae protests.

'Indeed,' Uncle Edgar says, with feeling. 'Anyway, you... you can't just dictate a sale. What about all the staff who work here?'

'*That*'s not the issue.' Rae sniffs. 'I'd be making half of them redundant anyway.'

Uncle Edgar's eyes widen. He grips the edge of the table.

'Er, excuse me, but isn't it a majority vote?' Mum asks timidly. 'If Tommy wants to sell and Rae wants to take charge, then doesn't Cassie have the casting vote?'

Everyone stares at me. I shake my head, feeling totally overwhelmed.

'What about me?' Sav demands. 'Surely I decide what happens to Zane's share?'

'Actually, you don't,' Rae says. 'I've gone over the terms of Dad's will and it's very straightforward. If you and Zane had been married, you'd potentially have a case. But you weren't, so you don't.'

The atmosphere in the room grows more tense. Sav stares at Rae like she's stabbed her. 'But we were going to get *engaged* this year,' she splutters.

'Precisely,' Rae snaps. 'That's not being married, is it, darling?'

Mum lets out a nervous cough.

'Are you sure about this, Rae?' I ask. 'What about Zane and Sav's baby?'

Rae shakes her head. 'There's no proof it even *is* Zane's baby.'

Sav gasps.

'Rae!' I stare at her, shocked she can be so cruel.

'You're all missing the point.' Rae rolls her eyes. 'Dad's will isn't through probate yet, so Zane didn't actually have his share of the inheritance when he died. Under the terms of the will, if one of the siblings dies *before* probate is granted, their share is divided among the surviving brothers and sisters.' She pauses. 'Like I said before, a spouse *might* be able to make a legal case, but not random girlfriends. The will very clearly prohibits that.' She pauses. 'I think it was Dad's way of protecting us from gold-diggers.' She smirks, looking pointedly at Savannah. 'We seem to have seen a lot of those recently.'

My cheeks burn at Rae's rudeness.

'How dare you!' Savannah pushes herself up from the boardroom table, tears springing to her eyes. 'I've got nothing. I'm not even on the title deeds of Zane's house. Where am I supposed to live?'

'Didn't Zane leave you something in his own will?' Mum asks, looking confused.

'He hadn't made one,' Sav says. 'He said we'd do it once the baby was born.' She glares at Rae.

'I'm sure no one will object if you stay on in Zane's house until you can make other arrangements,' Rae says crisply.

'This isn't fair!' Sav's voice rises to a shriek. 'You *know* Zane would have wanted his child to have a proper inheritance.' She turns to me and Tommy. 'You two can't let her do this.'

I stare helplessly at Sav, then turn to Tommy. He's staring down at the table. I look over at Rae.

'Sav's right,' I stammer. 'Surely there must be—'

'I didn't make the rules of Dad's will,' Rae retorts. 'And it's not my fault if Zane didn't do a will himself.'

'This is *such* bullshit.' Savannah grabs her coat and storms out of the boardroom.

TEN

A tense silence fills the boardroom.

'Well, I guess that just about wraps things up,' Rae says drily.

'Excuse me,' Mia pipes up from the far end of the table. She'd been sitting so quietly I'd almost forgotten she was there.

Everyone looks at her.

'You said the estate including the company divides between the surviving siblings. Well, I'm one of them, aren't I? And there's definitely proof that I'm Nathaniel's biological child.' Across the table, Mum stiffens. 'Don't I get a share?'

Rae glares directly at Mia – such a fierce angry look I'm astonished Mia has the confidence to hold it and stare stubbornly back. The room falls silent.

Tommy leans across and nudges me. I look at him. He's gazing at Mia with a look of sneaking admiration.

Uncle Edgar clears his throat. 'Actually, Mia makes a good point,' he says slowly. 'Once her application to be recognised as a beneficiary of Nathaniel's will is approved by the courts, she'll have an equal say in terms of the estate. We should delay a vote on whether or not to sell the company until then. Nothing can be done until probate is granted anyway.'

'I see,' Rae snaps. 'Go on then, Mia. You've obviously thought about this. Which way do you vote? Tommy wants to sell, because he's an idiot. I want to run the company and think I'd make a great job of it. Cassie as usual is trying to see all sides and hasn't declared yet.' Rae shoots me an irritated glance, then fixes her gaze on Mia again. 'What about *you*?'

My eyes rest on Mia, expecting again that she'll look entirely out of her depth. In fact she looks at Rae with calm, confident eyes, her mouth set in a determined line.

'I'll need to think about it.' She looks at me. 'Just like Cassie. But right now I can't see why I *wouldn't* want to sell. I'm not… that is… I wouldn't have the first idea about running the company but I could definitely do with the money it would raise.'

'*Yes!*' Tommy hisses triumphantly.

Rae clenches her jaw.

'Well, I think there's nothing more to be gained by talking further at this point,' Uncle Edgar says, tersely. 'I suggest we pick up discussions again once Mia's position vis-à-vis the inheritance has been established. That will give Rae time to flesh out her proposal for taking over the company, and Mia and Cassie time to think over their response. Hopefully I should have a date for probate by then too.'

The meeting breaks up. Rae swoops out first, then Uncle Edgar and Mum leave together. Tommy has made a beeline for Mia and they are now deep in conversation.

I suddenly feel disgusted with my entire family. How can we have let ourselves get caught up in a row about money and power, when Zane has only been dead a few days? I grab my coat and head out without a word to anyone.

I take the lift to the ground floor and stand on the windy concourse outside Carson Enterprises, with my back to the brick wall, letting the air cool my cheeks.

'Cas?'

I turn around. Savannah is in front of me, her eyes red-rimmed and the tip of her nose, peeking over her scarf, pink from the cold.

'That was so awful in the boardroom,' she says, her voice trembling.

'I know.' I squeeze her arm. 'I'm so sorry for how Rae spoke to you.'

'I couldn't give a toss *how* she speaks,' Sav says bitterly. 'I just don't want her getting away with this plan to cut me and my baby out of the family inheritance.'

I stare at her. 'I honestly don't think that is Rae's *plan*, as such,' I say slowly. 'I think it's how she sees the terms of Dad's will. And as Uncle Edgar didn't put up a fight over it, I'm guessing he thinks she's seeing it correctly. Legally at least.'

Sav looks mutinous, then puts her hand on her belly and winces.

'Are you okay?' I ask.

'Yeah, it's just… I'm sure it's just the baby kicking.'

I nod.

'Look, Cas, I was thinking…' Sav looks beseechingly up at me. 'Would you talk to Rae for me? She likes you. You could tell her I'd be happy to provide the baby's DNA for a paternity test. Prove he's Zane's.'

I wrinkle my nose. 'Oh, Sav, I don't think Rae is really in any doubt about that; she was just… being provocative.' I sigh. 'Anyway, even with proof, it won't change the terms of Dad's will.'

87

'No, but maybe Rae would listen if *you* point out that Zane's baby is still entitled to *something*, whatever the will says.' She hesitates. 'It's not just about the money; it's about making sure Zane's wishes are followed.'

I nod, slowly. 'I don't mind talking to Rae and, for what it's worth, I agree with everything you're saying. But she's likely to say that the way the will has been set up reflects *Dad's* wishes and that she wants to follow those.'

'Don't you think that's strange?' Sav asks, frowning. 'Why would Nathaniel have organised it like that? I can't believe he'd have wanted to cut Zane's baby out.'

I shrug. 'It's hard to foresee every possible scenario and I expect Dad assumed Zane would die a long time after him and have plenty of time to make sure his own family was looked after. To be honest, I think it's probably like Rae suggested, that Dad wanted to protect the family. Not from *you*,' I add hurriedly. 'But he wouldn't have imagined Zane dying just at this point, before the will came into force *and* before you two got married. And he didn't know you were pregnant, did he?'

'No, I only found out myself after he died, but—'

'You have to remember how much bad blood there was between Dad and Uncle Edgar back when *their* father left everything to Dad. I expect Dad thought keeping his own will simple would make sure everything was fair.'

Sav winces again, her hand on her stomach.

'Let me put you in a taxi home,' I suggest. 'All this stress can't be good for you or the baby.'

Sav shakes her head. 'I'm fine. Though, there is one thing…'

I raise my eyebrows.

'I keep wondering if Zane's death wasn't…' She bites her lip. 'I just wonder if it was really an accident.'

My blood chills. So far, I haven't told anyone about the text Zane sent me just before he died and whether the "important news" he wanted to share is something connected to his death.

'Why, er, would you say that? The police are saying it's a random accident.'

'It's just weird that this so-called random accident happened on a road with no CCTV, when Zane often said how London has the most cameras per square kilometre in the western world.' She hesitates and I'm certain there's something else she's thinking.

'What?' I frown. 'Did Zane say something that indicated he'd been threatened? To make you think he was being deliberately targeted?'

'No. Nothing like that. It's just... Zane was so convinced Mia was a fraud. I keep wondering if... maybe it's stupid, but could Mia have killed him?'

I shake my head. 'Mia was with us that night, at our house all evening. I'd have known if she'd gone out.'

'Okay.' Sav hesitates. 'But even so... I know Zane talked to you about his suspicions and that the two of you went to the DNA clinic together last week.' She looks at me. 'What exactly did you find out there?'

'Nothing about the test itself, but we did discover something about the nurse who saw Mia and collected her DNA.' I pause. 'She was killed the following evening... in a hit-and-run.'

'But that's how Zane—' Sav gasps. 'That *can't* be a coincidence.'

I make a face. 'I don't know.'

'Come on, Cassie, it *can't* be.' Sav grabs my arm. 'The day Zane died, he told me he'd found something that would prove Mia isn't who she says.' She hesitates. 'Or...

or at least something that *might* prove it – a lead to the truth, if not the truth itself. I asked him to show me whatever it was, but he said there was nothing to show yet and he needed to speak to you before he did anything. Did he say anything like that to you?'

'No, well…' I fidget from foot to foot, feeling uncomfortable. 'He sent a message that evening. It just said he had "important news". But that was it.' The wind whips a strand of hair across my face. I smooth it back.

'I'm sure Zane was killed because of what he found out,' Sav says. 'I've told the police, but the family liaison officer insists there's nothing relevant to Mia on his phone or his PC and without something more concrete to go on…' She trails off and I notice that her face is too pale and there are dark rings under her eyes.

'Are you sleeping okay?' I ask.

'I'm fine.' Savannah waves her hand impatiently, dismissing my concern. 'I've gone through Zane's online schedule – it's linked with mine so I can add our obstetrician appointments. It's all regular meetings and a couple of business lunches that have been in the diary for months. But there is one thing that stands out.' She hesitates.

'What's that?' I ask.

'Zane made an arrangement to see Valentino Rossi this morning,' she says. 'He's head of Carson's biggest rival, isn't he? Do you know why Zane wanted to talk to him?'

'As a matter of fact, I do.' I take a deep breath. 'Zane thought Rossi might be behind Mia. Organising for her DNA test to be faked. Stage-managing everything. All as revenge for being cheated by Dad – as Rossi sees it – all those years ago.'

Sav clutches my arm. 'Suppose the text Zane sent you was something to do with Rossi? Some sort of proof that Rossi was involved?'

'I guess it's possible.' A sense of foreboding creeps over me. 'You know, when Zane and I first went to the DNA clinic I thought his suspicions were ridiculous.'

'And now?'

I shrug. 'I just don't know. To be honest, I've kind of been trying not to think about it.'

As I say the words, the full weight of just how confused I feel hits me for the first time. On the one hand, Mia appears preternaturally kind and sweet, and the idea that anyone would carry out an inheritance fraud on my family seems ludicrous. And yet the past ten days have revealed two suspicious hit-and-run deaths, both of which are at least partly linked to Mia's claim to be Dad's daughter. There's also my nagging suspicion that there's more to my new half-sister than meets the eye. I'm well aware that I might just be envious of her youth and beauty, but I can't get the doubt out of my head:

What if Mia is manipulating all of us?

A shiver wriggles its way down my spine. If Mia's involved in deception and murder, what am I doing letting her sleep under my roof? Right next door to my three-year-old daughter?

'Okay, then.' Sav's eyes widen. 'I'm going to keep Zane's appointment with Val Rossi. It's only ten minutes round the corner. Finish what Zane started and find out if Rossi is in league with Mia.' She looks pleadingly up at me, as a gust of wind whips her hair across her face. She smooths it away. 'Will you come with me? I'd go on my own, but the man was super rude to me and Zane at this gala we went to a while back.' She pauses. 'He's kind of scary.'

I sigh, remembering Zane mentioning the same interaction. I can understand why Sav doesn't want to visit Val Rossi by herself, but surely it's crazy to think that such an established and successful businessman could be involved in a dramatic inheritance con? On the other hand, if all the stories are true, Rossi has more of a motive than most to get his hands on Dad's money.

'Please, Cassie?' Sav asks, her eyes wide and fearful.

'Sure,' I say heavily, looking at the pregnant swell of her belly. Val Rossi has a reputation for being fierce. I can hardly let her go on her own.

ELEVEN

Unlike Carson Enterprises, Rossi Import Holdings is no longer a family firm. Nevertheless, a huge oil-painted portrait of Valentino Rossi still hangs behind the reception desk, an intense glare emanating from his face. I've only met the man once before, when I was out with Mum and we bumped into him. He was as brusque and unsmiling as in his picture.

Feeling trepidatious at the prospect of blundering into his office today, I take the glass elevator to the fourteenth floor, Sav at my side.

The waiting area up here has a breathtaking view over the east end of London, which is, famously, where Val Rossi grew up as the eldest child of a large, poor, single-parent family and, along with his mum, regularly went without meals so that the younger kids could eat.

As Sav peers out of the window, she touches her belly and winces again. Is that really just the baby kicking? I can't imagine the stress she must be under; she seems to have subsumed all her feelings about losing Zane into fury over the inheritance.

'Are you okay?' I ask quietly.

'It's not the money,' she says, ignoring my question. 'It's the rejection. One minute I have a partner with the capacity to support me and our new baby, the next his family are kicking me into the wilderness.'

'That's not how *I* feel,' I protest. 'And it's not how most of the family feel. There's no way Mum or Tommy or I will see you or Zane's baby suffer.'

'I know.' Sav falls silent. 'Thanks, Cassie.'

I gaze out over the cloudy skies and grey stretch of Thames water below us. There's no reason why, even if the terms of the will do deny Sav any money, those of us who *are* inheriting shouldn't offer her a portion of our own share. But I resist saying any of this for now. There's the situation with Mia and her claim to sort out first. If her appeal for a quarter of the inheritance is accepted, I'll need to talk to her and my other siblings – not to mention Rob – before making Sav any offers.

Val Rossi's PA appears after a few minutes. She frowns when I explain we are here on behalf of the late Zane Carson, hoping to meet Mr Rossi in his stead. She clearly expects Rossi to refuse to see us and is openly surprised when he orders us to be shown straight into his office.

He's waiting across the room, a sympathetic smile on his face.

'Cassandra. Savannah.' He extends his arm and pumps first my hand, then Sav's. 'I'm so sorry for your loss.'

'Thank you.' Emotion bubbles to the surface of Sav's voice.

I press my own lips together and give Rossi an appreciative nod. He ushers us to the chairs in front of his huge desk, the sympathetic smile still fixed on his face.

We all sit down, Sav easing herself gingerly into her seat.

Val Rossi must be in his seventies now, but he's still a handsome man. His mane of dark hair is streaked with silver and swept off his face, which is tanned and remarkably unlined. He smells of something elegantly herbal and his fingernails are perfectly manicured. There's a neatness to him, in contrast to Dad's chaotic charisma, but he has his own charm and a very easy smile.

'What a terrible loss for you both,' he is saying. 'I saw the meeting Zane scheduled to see me and I confess I was curious, though I didn't imagine anyone would keep the appointment.' He gazes at me, expectantly. 'What can I do for you?'

Sav looks at me, clearly indicating I should take the lead. I clear my throat, wondering how to begin. 'I don't know if you've heard,' I say slowly, 'but a young woman recently came forward, a Mia Ishchenko.' I pause. 'She says she's my... that Nathaniel is – was – her father.'

Rossi presses his fingertips together, steepling his hands. He doesn't take his eyes from mine; his gaze is more than a little intimidating.

'Mia has done a legal, fully verified DNA test that backs up her claim,' I explain, 'but Zane was suspicious.'

'He thought Mia was a gold-digging con artist,' Sav interjects.

A faint smile crosses Rossi's face. 'That sounds like Zane. His father's voice, eh?'

For the first time I hear just a hint of venom in his tone. I waver. Perhaps it is stupid for me and Sav to be here, telling this man our family secrets. I decide to be more circumspect.

'Sav noticed Zane was planning to meet you and... and we wondered if perhaps you knew anything about Mia yourself?' I ask gently. 'We're not accusing you of anything, just wondering what you've heard?'

Rossi purses his lips. 'Mmn. Of course, I *had* heard about the paternity claim and assumed, naturally, that a share of Nathaniel's inheritance was the target.'

I wince. Mia has always been so insistent that, first and foremost, she wants to get to know her family. That the money is secondary.

'I think it's more complicated than that,' I say.

'I don't.' Sav's pent-up words burst out of her. 'I think Zane was right that Mia's a fraud and I think you know something about it.' She points a finger at Rossi, the other hand resting protectively on her rounded belly.

Rossi recoils. 'Me?' He looks genuinely startled. 'What possible reason would I have for knowing anything about your family's dirty laundry?'

'You could be behind Mia. Manipulating her. Telling her what to do and say, how to act.' Sav's voice trembles with emotion.

Rossi's eyes widen angrily. '*Excuse* me?' he demands.

'Sav!' I put a hand on her arm hoping she'll pick up the hint to restrain herself. I turn to Rossi. 'Please understand this is hugely upsetting for my... for Savannah here. She's just lost her partner and is weeks away from giving birth.'

'It's not that,' Sav says, wrenching her arm away. 'It's just that something about Mia's claim – the timing, quite apart from anything else – well, it stinks and Zane was the only person who saw that.' She hesitates. 'I really don't mean to be rude, but Zane thought you might be involved and his hunches were usually right.'

Rossi's eyes rest on her. There's a sharp intelligence in his gaze. 'You're wrong about that,' he says crisply. 'Zane was hot-headed and impulsive and this often led him to act on hunches that backfired, sometimes spectacularly. His father was definitely aware of that.'

'That's an outrageous—' Sav hisses.

'I don't know when you last discussed my brother with my father,' I interrupt quickly, 'but I imagine it was a while ago. And though you're right of course that Zane was definitely, er, irascible, he had calmed down a lot in recent years.' I pause, forcing myself to hold Rossi's penetrating gaze. 'It's also the case that Zane wasn't the only person suspicious of Mia and her claim.'

'I see.' Rossi taps his fingers together again.

Savannah presses her lips together and stares down at the carpet.

'Look.' Rossi leans forward. 'Full disclosure. I'm not involved with Ms Ishchenko or in on her… con trick, if it is one. Firstly, I have no interest in Nathaniel's inheritance. I neither need nor want his money and, if I did, this seems a very underhand not to say high-risk approach to getting it. Nathaniel and I had our differences when it came to business trading, but we are – were – both straight shooters.'

'But you accused him of cheating you years ago,' I splutter.

'I never said "cheat". That was the press.' Rossi clears his throat. 'Nathaniel and I were both going for the same highly lucrative piece of business. It was a once in a life-time opportunity and your father bulldozed over me to acquire it. He was ruthless, prepared to go to any lengths to get what he wanted. I decided after that episode there was no place in my life for him, so I cut all ties. My wife was livid. She was great friends with Helen at the time, though the two of them soon lost touch once she became Harmony Moon.'

'Who's Helen, er, Harmony Moon?' Sav asks, looking up.

'Dad's second wife,' I explain. 'The one he left Zane and Rae's mum for. She changed her name when she left Dad and joined a commune.'

Sav stares at me. 'Are you serious? Zane never mentioned her.'

'Poor woman,' Rossi adds with a sniff. 'The way Nathaniel treated her was horrific. I heard him once telling her she'd be a terrible mother, calling her a "useless slutty bitch".' He shakes his head.

I blow out my breath. There's nothing about Rossi's demeanour that suggests he's lying. Though I guess a good liar would be more than capable of appearing honest.

Was Dad really so horrible to his second wife?

I suddenly don't want to hear any more. I stand up. Sav makes a pained face as she follows suit, pushing herself slowly off her chair.

'Thank you for your time, Mr Rossi,' I say.

'Wait, Cassandra.' Rossi stands up on the other side of his desk.

I turn to face him.

'If you really think this... Mia person is a fraud, why don't you go to the police?'

'We have no concrete proof, nothing to go on other than Zane's insistence and some circumstantial, er, events.' I shudder, remembering the car accidents that killed the clinic nurse last month, then Zane just a few days ago. Were those hit-and-runs carried out by the same person? Were Blossom Harrington and my half-brother deliberately targeted? 'I'm not sure enough about any of this to do anything,' I tail off, lamely.

'And yet you must have your suspicions, like Zane did, or you wouldn't be here?' Rossi raises his eyebrows.

I press my lips together, unwilling to be drawn.

Sav is already walking to the door, one hand pressed against her side. As she walks out into the carpeted corridor, Rossi says quietly to me: 'If someone *is* pulling Mia's strings, then my best guess is that it'd be your uncle.'

I stare at him. 'Uncle Edgar?'

Rossi nods. 'He wasn't left anything in Nathaniel's will, was he? At least that's the line that's going around?' He looks at me expectantly.

I give a curt nod. 'I don't see—'

'It's history repeating itself, isn't it?' he goes on. 'Firstly, Nathaniel inherits everything from their father and Edgar is forced to play second fiddle with a job in accounts. And now Nathaniel passes the whole estate to his kids, cutting out Edgar entirely.'

'What are you saying?'

'On its own, a bit of historic resentment might not be enough,' Rossi continues smoothly, 'but being cut out of a second massive inheritance might have pushed him over the edge. It's certainly grievance enough for a motive.' He pauses. 'I'd definitely look into your uncle if I were you.'

Is he serious? I open my mouth to ask if he really thinks Uncle Edgar would be capable of fraud and murder, but Rossi is already buzzing for his PA. She appears instantly in the doorway.

'Let me see you out, Ms Carson,' she says firmly.

Rossi offers his hand and gives mine a brisk shake, then picks up his phone and turns away.

Feeling summarily dismissed, I make my way outside to join Savannah by the PA's desk, my head spinning.

'Oh, what's wrong?' The urgency of the PA's voice cuts across my thoughts.

She's standing beside Savannah, who has gone a ghostly white and is clutching her side again, face screwed up in pain.

Sav looks up at me, panic in her eyes. 'It's the baby,' she gasps. 'Something's not right.'

TWELVE

Three hours have passed since our visit to Val Rossi. I've spent all of them in the obstetrics department of the private hospital where, thanks to the healthcare insurance Zane organised for them both, Savannah has now been admitted with abdominal pain and bleeding. Sav is with the doctor now, while Tommy and I sit outside in the waiting area. I've used Sav's mobile to try and contact her mother, but my calls go straight to voicemail and so far I've had no response to my texts. Thankfully, Rob was able to pick up Iris earlier, explaining to his headteacher that there was a family emergency, so I don't need to leave the hospital just yet.

'It's too much,' mutters Tommy beside me. 'I can't lose someone else.'

I glance at him. 'Easy,' I say. 'I don't think Sav's life is in danger.'

'The baby's might be,' Tommy says with a sigh. 'I don't think I could cope with Zane *and* his unborn child both going in the space of a few days, not so soon after Dad.' He sits back, wringing his hands. 'Do you think we should call Mia?'

I shake my head. 'She barely knows Savannah.'

'It's just she's family, our half-sister,' Tommy says. 'Zane and Sav's baby is as much hers as it is ours.'

'That's not what Zane thought,' I murmur.

Tommy grunts dismissively, then frowns as he catches sight of my face.

'What is it?' he asks.

I take a deep breath and tell him about the suspicious death of the DNA clinic nurse who did Mia's test and how Zane was convinced that Mia's claim to be part of our family was an elaborate fraud backed and funded by Dad's business rival, Val Rossi. 'Sav and I went to see Rossi earlier. He insisted he wasn't involved, but…' I trail off, remembering Rossi pointing the finger at Uncle Edgar.

'Come off it, Cas,' Tommy says crossly. 'There's nothing to be involved *with*.'

'I didn't think so at first either, but… but you have to admit it's a weird coincidence that Blossom Harrington *and* Zane were both the victims of hit-and-runs.' I hesitate. 'And maybe Mia's sometimes a bit too good to be true.'

My brother frowns. 'What are you talking about?'

'Well, she's always so thoughtful and nice about everything. But I overheard her speaking to her gran on her first night with us, and she sounded really mean. Like a completely different person.'

'So what?' Tommy protests. 'After all, Mia's gran brought her up. She's basically her mother, and who *doesn't* sometimes get irritated with their mum?'

'I guess.' I sit back. 'But what about the timing? Don't you think that's a bit of a coincidence? Mia happens to find out about her parentage only after Dad dies and leaves a massive fortune to his children?'

'She explained how she found out. The only coincidence is that her grandparents happened to be leaving their flat within a few months of Dad dying. Which isn't really *much* of a coincidence, when you think about it.' He pauses. 'Come on, as a plot to cheat a family out of a load of money, there have to be less risky and convoluted methods, don't you think?'

I sit back. Perhaps Tommy's right. Even so, Val Rossi's parting words keep echoing in my head.

I'd look into your uncle if I were you.

–

The afternoon wears on. Rae is in a long client meeting at work but sends several texts to see how Sav is doing, while Mum and Uncle Edgar drop in for a visit on their way to some charity tea in central London.

Sav explains that, after some worrying bleeding, her pregnancy has now stabilised and the baby is fine. 'Though the doctor says I need to avoid stress until the birth.' She makes a face.

We spend the next hour or so in Sav's room. Tommy makes everyone laugh with a story about a recent climbing accident in which he lost a pair of thermal gloves. He makes a mundane incident sound far funnier than it can possibly have been at the time. After another few minutes, the nurse chivvies us out, insisting we should head home and let Sav rest before her mum – who has finally picked up her messages – arrives in the next hour or so.

'I'm so relieved everything's okay with the baby,' Mum says, linking arms with me as we return to the waiting room.

'Indeed,' says Uncle Edgar, who is strolling just behind us. 'After losing Zane so violently, I can't imagine the stress for that poor girl if she had to go through another trauma.' He shakes his head.

The four of us pause in the waiting room to say our goodbyes. Mum draws Tommy aside for a quick word, leaving Uncle Edgar and I momentarily alone.

As my uncle checks his mobile, I rest my gaze on his lined, pinched face. He looks nothing like Dad did. Rae once put it well when she said that, as they got older, Dad seemed to "spread and melt" into a bigger, bolder version of himself, while Edgar "hardened and set" into somebody slighter and more uptight.

My thoughts drift to Val Rossi's accusation again.

'Uncle Edgar, where were you when you heard about Zane... I mean when you got the call that night?' The question blurts out of me too forcefully and I blush.

Uncle Edgar looks up at me, bemused. 'At home, Cassie. I told you before, I was getting ready for bed. Why do you ask?'

I hesitate, trying to soften my tone. 'Were you *with* anyone?'

Uncle Edgar frowns. 'What do you mean?' he asks, an edge to his voice.

'Nothing,' I say. 'I just wondered if you were alone when Rae called?'

'What a question!' The tips of his ears turn bright red. I stare into his eyes, my heart thudding. There's not just guilt in his expression; there's shame too. As if I've totally caught him out. 'I don't think who I spend my time with, or where I am when I spend it, is really any of your business.' Uncle Edgar presses his lips together in prim disdain, an expression that Zane used to say made his face look like a cat's arse. 'Is that all, Cassie?'

I nod, my mind reeling.

As Uncle Edgar stalks angrily away, I lean back against the wall. Why would he act like I was being offensively curious unless he had something to hide? He clearly doesn't want to be pinned down on where he was or what he was doing the night Zane died. Was that because he was driving the car that ran Zane over?

My chest tightens.

'We're going now, my love,' Mum says gently, materialising in front of me.

I nod, unable to speak.

'Are you all right?'

I nod again, forcing a smile onto my face. As Mum and Edgar leave for the car park, Tommy and I make our way out to the main entrance. Tommy is chattering away about an upcoming climbing trip. I'm barely listening.

'What is it, Cas?' he asks at last. 'You look like you did after you ate those dodgy oysters on Mum's last birthday.'

We emerge into the cool air and fading light of the February afternoon.

'It's Uncle Edgar,' I breathe, as we walk to Tommy's car. 'Something doesn't add up.'

'What do you mean?'

I hesitantly set out my fears. 'Do... do you think it's possible that Uncle Edgar came up with this entire situation?' I ask. 'Inventing Mia, getting her to pursue a claim so that he can get a share of Dad's money after all, then killing Zane when he got too close to finding out?'

'You're kidding!' Tommy laughs. Then stops, as he sees from my expression that I am, in fact, deadly serious. 'Come on, does *any* of that sound like boring Uncle E.?'

I shrug.

'He's... he's too small scale,' Tommy says, wrinkling his nose. 'I mean, I agree that he's a bit of a cold fish and definitely bloody calculating enough on the money side of things. But I can't see him coming up with a masterplan involving a fake sister – and I definitely can't imagine him behind the wheel of the car that killed Zane. Or that DNA nurse from the clinic a few weeks before.'

'Okay, but he had the means, the motive *and* the opportunity,' I point out. 'He might even have known Mia's mum – or at least that she and Dad were in the same place at the same time. Suppose Dad *did* flirt with her – maybe even have a fling with her? Of all of us, Edgar's most likely to have known about it. Then perhaps he learned about Mia later and realised that the date of her birth more or less fitted with the date of her mum and our dad meeting up. It's not a huge leap from there to getting her to pretend she's actually Dad's daughter.'

'What about the DNA test?' Tommy protests.

'Again, Uncle Edgar was in the perfect position to manipulate it. As executor of Dad's will he's responsible for dealing with any challenge that comes up. He knew about Mia and her claim ages before us. He could have organised a fake test – maybe not easily, but he could have done it.'

'How?'

'I don't know. Perhaps he bribed that nurse, Blossom Harrington, to fake Mia's DNA somehow, like Zane thought. Then when Blossom came back for more money, he realised he'd never be free of her and decided to kill her.'

'Right.' Tommy looks doubtful. 'But why start something so risky and complicated in the first place?'

'That's easy,' I say, bitterly. 'Uncle Edgar was cut out of his own father's inheritance. You know he's always resented that. And then last year the brother who got the lot dies and doesn't leave him a bean. Surely that's a motive?'

'I guess when you put it like that,' Tommy says hesitantly. 'Do you think we should talk to Edgar? Confront him?'

'I don't think there's much point doing that,' I say slowly. 'I just asked if he was alone when he found out about Zane and he got furious with me. I can't imagine how angry he'd be if we let on we think he might have committed fraud and murder. There's no way he'd come clean. *And* he'd know we suspected him.'

Tommy makes a face. 'Then *what*?'

'So...' I hesitate, an idea circling around my brain. 'Rob has Iris, which means I have time right now.'

'Time for what?' Tommy checks his phone. 'It's just gone four.'

I stop walking. 'I want to look at Uncle Edgar's schedule and his recent messages and see if I can find out what he was doing on Tuesday night. Maybe also look for any evidence that he's in league with Mia – or the DNA clinic nurse.'

Tommy's jaw drops. 'Are you serious?'

I nod. 'I know it sounds mad, but at least if we find nothing, it'll make it more likely he *isn't* involved.' I sigh. 'Not that I have any idea how to get into his phone or his computer.'

'Actually,' says Tommy, with a grin, 'I might be able to help with that.'

THIRTEEN

'How could you possibly get into Uncle Edgar's computer files?' I ask, as we get into Tommy's car.

Tommy grins. 'Remember when I worked at Carson Enterprises?'

My mind flashes back to the brief, rather tempestuous period when Dad insisted that Tommy, who had been drifting since leaving school two years previously, joined the company as a management trainee. At the time, Tommy was highly resistant. He was used to spending his time gaming and on climbing trips with his buddies. But Dad forced him to enter the management programme and his first three months – as a marketing executive assistant – didn't go too badly. Unfortunately, Tommy's next rotation was in the finance department, of which Uncle Edgar was head. It was a disaster. Tommy lasted less than two weeks, then stormed out, refusing to spend another minute in the building. I think at that point Dad wanted to lay down the law: Tommy either knuckled under at Carson or found paid work somewhere else. But Mum interceded, suggesting he be allowed to train as a climbing instructor instead.

Tommy did that training and passed with flying colours but never took it any further. In fact, since leaving Carson he's never had a proper job.

'Cassie?' Tommy urges, starting the engine of his car.

His voice brings me back to the dull afternoon and the hospital car park outside the car.

'Okay, Tommy,' I say. 'How does you working for Uncle Edgar years ago help us now?'

Tommy taps the side of his nose to indicate he's going to keep this particular detail secret for a while longer. 'You'll see,' he says. 'We just need to get into his office and tonight after work is the perfect opportunity.'

Another hour passes. It's dark as well as cold outside now, but Tommy and I sit snugly in a café overlooking the entrance to Carson Enterprises and wait until people start heading home and the office building begins closing down for the night. I text Rob to say I'm with Tommy, which I'm aware implies that we're still at the hospital. I don't want Rob to know what we're doing. Not yet anyway.

I know I should feel guilty about this, but I'm too full of other emotions to give the guilt much attention. The idea that Mia might not actually be Dad's daughter makes me feel physically sick. That my own uncle might be behind the fraud — and possibly even Zane's death — makes me even sicker. It all seems too cruel and too complex to possibly be true. And yet I can't shake off my suspicions.

'Uncle Edgar's PA just left,' Tommy whispers.

I follow his gaze through the steamed-up windows and peer across the concourse. I can just make out Miranda, my uncle's long-time assistant, strolling slowly along the pavement in the direction of the Tube.

Tommy gulps down the remains of the coffee in his cup. 'Ready?' he asks. 'We need to time it before reception hands over to security at six thirty.'

I nod, getting up and putting on my coat. 'Let's go.'

It's freezing as we cross the concourse. I tug my coat tightly around me until we reach the heated lobby of Carson Enterprises. The tasteful pale grey walls are decorated with a mix of abstract art and framed business excellence award certificates. The reception staff here know us both, of course, and when Tommy calls out that we're here to pick up a scarf I left in the boardroom during this morning's meeting, they nod and wave us through.

As we walk to the lift my palms grow cold and clammy. Sneaking into Uncle Edgar's office to search through his files goes against every value I hold. It's not just deceitful, it's illegal.

Inside the elevator, Tommy presses the button for the tenth floor and leans back against the stainless steel, examining his hair in the mirror. Unlike me, he appears to be taking our adventure completely in his stride.

'Just another day at the office, eh, Tommo?' I murmur under my breath.

Tommy glances at my reflection in the mirror. 'Don't sweat it, sis. We need to know what Edgar's done. That's it. We're not going to steal anything or hurt anyone.'

I nod, but my guts knot with anxiety as we walk along the soft carpet of the tenth-floor corridor, past the boardroom and the managing director's office, which was Dad's for so many years and then, for a short while recently, Zane's.

Uncle Edgar's office is tucked around the corner. It's smaller than the MD's office, with only a tiny window onto the lights of the London evening. Miranda has a desk directly outside, squashed next to a large filing cabinet.

I hesitate, my eyes on the cabinet's drawers.

'He's not going to have left anything about Mia with his PA or in any file she can directly access,' Tommy points out, striding through the door into Uncle Edgar's office. 'And he doesn't use messaging apps. It'll all be in emails. Edgar's old school.'

'Okay, so how do we get into his emails?' I ask, following Tommy inside.

The office is neat as a pin. The desk, set with a big computer, takes up nearly a third of the room. Two chairs are set in front of it and there's a shelving unit and cupboards in the same polished wood opposite. The shelves are lined with carefully labelled box files.

'It's so tidy,' I murmur. 'So stark.'

'Course it is.' Tommy gives a snort as he walks over to the desk and leans over the computer. 'Uncle Edgar's a total control freak.' He looks up. 'You know, Dad was difficult and had a temper, but people *liked* him. *Nobody* in this place likes Uncle Edgar. Why d'you think I only lasted ten days working for him?'

'Cos you're lazy and don't like being told what to do?' I counter.

Tommy glances over and makes a face at me.

'No,' he says, and for the first time I hear a hint of peevishness in his voice. 'Uncle Edgar's tricky. He was a horrible boss.'

'Maybe you just think that because he set high standards?' I suggest, unwilling to let my little brother entirely off the hook. Even Mum, who adores him, acknowledges that Tommy has issues with authority and, despite his wide circle of friends and charming persona, is drifting through adulthood without passion or purpose.

'Oh, give it a rest.' Tommy rolls his eyes, then places his hand over the mouse. He's wearing Dad's signet ring,

I notice, the initials *NC* engraved in the gold. 'Edgar likes to micromanage his staff. It really pisses everyone off. It certainly drove me nuts. *There.*' He points to the screen. The login is asking for a username and password. I frown as Tommy enters *edgar_carson*, the standard Carson Enterprises username style, then glances sideways at me, a triumphant expression on his face.

'Er, Tommy,' I start. 'I don't want to rain on your parade, but a username isn't—'

'I know the password too,' Tommy interrupts, bending over the computer.

'How?' I demand as he taps at the screen. 'From when you worked here? Jesus, Tommy, even Uncle Edgar will have altered his password after ten years.'

'Of course,' Tommy says, still tapping away. 'But when he changes it, he just switches out the number at the end. Look.'

He shifts sideways a little, so I can see him typing:
Cain&Abel18

He presses enter and the screen judders to indicate the password is wrong.

'Not surprising,' Tommy says. 'He was already on "17" when I worked here, but I thought it was worth a shot.' He carries on trying numbers. I shake my head, unconvinced this will work. But, sure enough, *Cain&Abel29* opens up the entire screen.

I stare at the desktop, anxiety fluttering now in my chest. So far, we've just talked about snooping. Now, here we are actually doing it. Tommy clicks on the email icon. There are two options: the official Carson Enterprises email and Edgar's private Gmail.

Tommy hovers over the Gmail account, which immediately asks for another password.

'Now what?' I ask.

For answer, Tommy crosses the room and removes the first box file on the left of the top shelf opposite. A small black book sits behind it. Tommy takes it out and grins at me. 'See? Old school. Uncle Edgar writes all his personal passwords in here, like the old man he is.'

Still grinning, he flicks through the book, then calls out the Gmail password.

I'm into Edgar's personal email account in seconds. As I scan the inbox, a door slams nearby. I jump, then meet Tommy's gaze.

'There must be someone in the corridor,' I whisper. 'Why don't you keep watch while I check what's here.'

My heart races as I scan the email subjects. There are only three messages dated the day Zane died: a reminder of a dental appointment, a newsletter sent out by my uncle's antiques dealer and a short message from Gigoletta Services, confirming a mysterious sounding "personal delivery" for 9.30 p.m. that night.

That's more or less when Zane was killed. I glance over at Tommy, still peering up and down the corridor.

'I think I found something,' I whisper. 'Uncle Edgar was expecting a delivery around the time Zane died. D'you think it's a cover? Seems odd that he'd have—'

'Where was the delivery from?' Tommy asks.

'Gigoletta Services.'

Tommy lets out a low whistle. 'You're kidding? Well, I guess it isn't that surprising.' He smirks. 'No wonder Uncle Edgar didn't want to tell you what he was doing.'

'What d'you mean?' As look at the name "Gigoletta Services" again I realise what Tommy is saying. My cheeks burn as I put the name into the search engine, and sure enough.

'It's an escort agency,' I say flatly.

'So who did Edgar have delivered?' Tommy glances around again with a grin. 'Blonde, brunette or redhead?'

I sink into the chair behind the desk. '*That's* why he looked so embarrassed when I asked if he was alone that evening. Ugh. I can't believe he pays for… for…'

Tommy shrugs. 'I'm not surprised at all. I mean, I can't exactly imagine Edgar chatting up some woman in a bar.'

'But he's in his seventies,' I protest. 'He can't… I mean, how would… Does it work when you're that age?'

Tommy frowns. 'Now you're being naïve, Cas.' He pauses. 'Still, I guess it counts Uncle Edgar out of running Zane over. He can't have been in his car doing that *and* at home getting laid by a hooker – or whatever Boomers call them.'

I shake my head. 'Uncle Edgar could have paid someone else to do the hit-and-run.'

Tommy raises his eyebrows. 'I guess if he's prepared to pay for sex, then why not death?'

I scowl at him. 'Don't be so flippant; this is serious.'

'Sorry.' Tommy makes a face. 'It's just… don't you think it's all just a bit far-fetched?'

'Just keep a look out.' I turn back to Uncle Edgar's emails and scan through them, looking for anything out of the ordinary that might indicate a liaison with a hitman.

Of course there isn't anything. I sigh. Nobody would leave an email trail over something like that.

'Cassie, let's go,' Tommy hisses from the door.

'Just one more minute,' I say, a fresh idea sparking. 'I'm going further back, to see if there's anything in the emails connecting Edgar to Mia or the DNA clinic.'

'Okay, but hurry!'

My hands are clammy as I tap quickly at the keyboard. I input a time frame going back six months, plus all the search terms I can think of, from "*DNA*", "*test*" and "*clinic*" to both Mia's name and the name of the nurse, Blossom Harrington, as well as random related words such as "*daughter*", "*secret*" and "*plan*".

After a couple of minutes I've found nothing except the recent threads of emails from Mia's lawyer and Mr Edwards at the DNA clinic, which simply confirm what Uncle Edgar has already told us. I blow out my breath, feeling frustrated.

Tommy looks up from the door. 'We're pushing our luck now, Cas. We need to go. Have you found anything?'

I shake my head. 'If there ever was anything, Uncle Edgar's deleted it.'

'Right,' Tommy says, giving me a rueful smile. 'I guess that's it, then.'

I stare at the computer screen. The little bin icon in the bottom left of the email menu catches my eye. 'Hey, I wonder if Uncle Edgar knows you have to empty the trash to properly get rid of it?'

'Probably not.' Tommy frowns. 'But we've already been up here longer than—'

'It'll just take a sec.' My fingers fly over the keys, trying my search terms again. I get nothing from either Mia's or Blossom's names, nor from the words "*DNA*" or "*clinic*".

'Cassie,' Tommy hisses from the door. 'Come *on*!'

'Just one more minute.' I type in the word "*lie*".

An email flashes up, dated a few weeks after Dad died. I peer more closely and read.

From: harmonymoon@lissaycommunity.org

To: edgar_carson@carsonenterprises.com

Edgar. Nathaniel might be dead, but he still owes us,
not the other way around. The lie is justified.

'Tommy!' He looks round and I beckon him over.
'Look at this! It's from Harmony Moon. You know, Dad's
second wife.'

I stand aside, so Tommy can read the email. His eyes
widen. 'What the hell?' he gasps. 'What do you think "*the
lie is justified*" refers to?'

'It must mean Mia.' My heart thuds as the reality of
what I'm saying hits home. Surely, this is the only explanation that makes sense of everything.

Mia is a snake – and I've let her into my home.

'Why must it mean Mia?' Tommy wrinkles his nose.

'We know there was no love lost between Harmony
Moon and Dad *or* Edgar and Dad. It's clear from this
Harmony reckons they've been hard done by, that Dad
should have left them something in his will and that
they've created the "lie" of Mia to get their hands on that
inheritance.'

'It still seems a stretch.'

I peer again at the email. 'Not if you look at the date.'
I point to the timing of the email. 'This was sent to Uncle
Edgar four or five weeks after Dad died. That's exactly the
timing you'd expect if the two of them were cooking up
Mia as a con on the rest of us.'

'Are you seriously suggesting Uncle Edgar has
committed *fraud*?'

'Committed *what*?' Uncle Edgar's voice booms around
the office.

My head flies up. Our uncle is staring at us from the doorway, wide-eyed with shock. I gasp, as he glares at us. 'What the *hell* are you two doing in here?'

FOURTEEN

My head spins. Beside me, Tommy's mouth gapes open. We back away from the computer.

'I asked you to explain what you're doing in here?' Uncle Edgar strides into his office and turns the computer towards himself.

'We, I...' I stammer.

'It's not what it looks like,' Tommy squeaks, sounding suddenly about ten years old. My mind flashes back to a visit to Uncle Edgar's house when we were kids. Tommy was caught stealing a gold florin from our uncle's antique coin collection, hoping he'd be able to use it to buy sweets. Edgar completely lost it, shouting and swearing so violently that, for a moment, I thought he was going to hit Tommy. Perhaps, looking back, he might have done, but just then Mum came into the room and Uncle Edgar was forced to resume his usual mask of coldness and calm.

Uncle Edgar's eyebrows shoot up. 'Oh? And what does it *look* like, Tommy? Because to me, it looks like you two are ferreting about my private emails and accusing me of fraud.'

I glance at my brother. His face has drained of colour. He says nothing.

I take a deep breath. Maybe we should just tell the truth.

'A few things have made us suspicious of Mia,' I say, keeping my voice even. 'We were looking for clues in your emails to... to her being a fake.'

'For heaven's sake! The idea that poor girl is making her story up is just ridiculous.' Uncle Edgar narrows his eyes. 'And why would you think *I'd* have anything to do with it?'

'We're sorry,' Tommy blurts out, 'but you have to admit you have a motive. Your own father left everything to Dad, then Dad cut you out of his will too.'

I wince. It's too blunt. Uncle Edgar looks taken aback. 'You seriously think I've connived in some outlandish plot to conjure up a fake daughter and fraudulent DNA, just in order to get my hands on Nathaniel's money?' He draws himself up, his cheeks pinking with fury. 'You disgust me. Get out!'

Tommy takes a step towards the door, but I hold my ground.

'Please, Uncle Edgar, surely you have to admit it's possible that Mia's whole story is made-up? Zane was suspicious of her and now he's... gone.'

Uncle Edgar glares at me. 'I do hope, Cassandra, that you're not suggesting I had anything to do with Zane's passing?'

'Of course not,' I lie. An image of the Gigoletta website flashes before my mind's eye. 'But we're trying to keep open minds and the truth is that even if you were, er, with someone at your house, there are still... ways...' I hesitate, feeling supremely awkward. 'If you have money, you can pay people to... to do things.'

Uncle Edgar's face flames with colour. 'What exactly are you accusing me of?' he hisses.

'Nothing!' Tommy says quickly. 'It's not that.'

'We just want you to explain this.' I step over to the computer and point to the email from Harmony Moon, still open on the screen. 'What is this justified "lie" she's referring to? Is it Mia? Did Harmony Moon come up with the… the idea of a fake daughter?'

Uncle Edgar pulls the keyboard more closely towards him. 'That email has nothing to do with Mia,' he says briskly. He prods at the keyboard and a second later, the message – and every other item in the trash – has been fully and finally deleted.

I stare at the blank screen. The words from the email are still burned in my head, but all proof of them is gone. Surely Uncle Edgar's desire to get rid of it so urgently implies he has *something* to hide?

I meet his gaze. There's no guilt in his expression, just angry defiance.

'You have to tell us what that email was about,' I insist.

'Yes,' Tommy urges. 'If the justified "lie" isn't about Mia, what *does* it refer to?'

Uncle Edgar glares at us, his mouth set in a grim line. 'I can't tell you, but I swear on my life it has nothing to do with Mia.'

He looks away.

'At least tell us why Harmony thinks Dad owed you both?' Tommy demands. 'Is she talking about money?'

'Enough, Tommy.' Uncle Edgar shudders.

'But—'

Uncle Edgar holds up his hands and Tommy falls silent. Uncle Edgar clears his throat. 'All I will say – and this is my final word on the subject – is that Harmony had to put up with a *lot* from Nathaniel.'

I frown. Is that true? It chimes with what Val Rossi suggested. And yet Dad was generally respectful of women. I never heard him be rude either to or about Mum and he was always loving and caring with me and Rae. Even if he didn't treat Harmony Moon as well, it's hard to believe that he left her so aggrieved that she'd chuck a hand grenade like Mia into our family, especially decades after they broke up. No, there must be another motive.

'Please listen to me.' Uncle Edgar's voice is suddenly gentle. 'Both of you.'

I look into his sorrowful eyes. The misery there is real, but I'm still sure he's hiding something. 'What?' I ask.

'Mia is an innocent victim in all this,' he says softly. 'I know you don't want to hear it, but she's proof of your father's… shall we say… frequent and arrogant disregard for personal responsibility.'

'That's not fair,' I protest.

'Isn't it?' Uncle Edgar purses his lips. 'Well, here's something else you may consider "not fair". I'm afraid to say I think you and Tommy are acting in the same peremptory, unkind way that Nathaniel regularly demonstrated.'

I stare at him, shocked to my core.

'Tell us what you really think, Uncle E.,' Tommy drawls sarcastically.

Uncle Edgar indicates his office door. 'You need to leave now, or I'm going to call down to security and get you both thrown out.'

I want to fight back, to tell him that he's wrong about Dad and that I'm certain that no matter *what* he says, the email from Harmony Moon *was* about Mia. But it's clear that our uncle isn't going to say any more and, anyway, Tommy is already striding angrily into the corridor.

I have no choice but to slink after him.

We make our way downstairs in silence. As we step out into the cold air, Tommy blows out his breath.

'Well, that was horrible.'

I glance at my brother. He hates confrontation. Always has.

'I know,' I say soothingly, stroking his arm.

'Maybe we should leave all this alone now,' Tommy ventures uncertainly.

'Maybe.' I hesitate. 'Do you think Uncle Edgar was telling the truth?'

'About comparing us to Dad in the least flattering terms possible?' Tommy rolls his eyes. 'Yes, definitely.'

'No, about the email from Harmony Moon not being about Mia?'

'I don't know, Cas, but you have to wonder why on earth Harmony Moon would be involved. I know that revenge is a dish best served cold and all that, but even still...' He frowns. 'It just seems so random, for her to suddenly conjure up a fake daughter to attack him with, when he's not even alive anymore.'

I press my lips together. 'Perhaps his death was the catalyst,' I suggest, thinking it through. 'That tracks, especially if Harmony Moon's motive was financial. Maybe she's always resented not getting more money off him and after he died, she saw an opportunity. Sending Mia to get a chunk of the inheritance she feels cheated out of – it might have felt like her last chance to get even.'

'Come on.' Tommy makes a face. 'Surely, she's moved on by now? She lives in a hippy commune in the middle of nowhere, for goodness' sake. That hardly says: "I'm a materialistic bitch and I want your money", does it?'

I shrug. 'Who knows what she thinks. She's clearly been exchanging emails with Uncle Edgar. I think it's totally possible she came up with the entire scam.' I look at him. 'You said yourself that Uncle Edgar is a micro-manager, good at details. Well, maybe Harmony Moon is the one who came up with the big picture... the overall plan?'

'I guess,' Tommy says, frowning. 'But how on earth are we going to find out?'

FIFTEEN

Tommy and I part company at the Underground station and I make my way home, lost in thought. The more questions I ask the fewer answers I get. In fact, every step I take seems to lead to more uncertainty. More confusion. As I open the gate and turn onto our front path, my heart fills with dread. How am I going to face Mia feeling as I do? The thought of her lying to our faces revolts me. But there's no point confronting her without more evidence. Apart from anything else, if I'm right that she's a fraud, then she is almost certainly dangerous too. I don't want to put myself or my family at risk and the thought of spending another night under the same roof fills me with horror.

The house smells of something sweet and buttery as I walk in. Iris rushes out to hug me before I've even taken off my coat.

'Mummy! Come and see what me and Mia have done.'

I let my daughter drag me through to the kitchen. Mia and Rob are sitting at opposite ends of the kitchen table. They both look up as I walk in. Rob gives me a weary smile, his eyes drifting straight back to his laptop. Mia beckons me over, almost as excited as Iris to show me whatever they've been doing. A tea towel is spread over a tray, set on the table in front of Mia.

'Look, Mummy!' Iris whisks the tea towel away.

I peer down at the tray. It's full of cookies, each decorated with a photograph printed on edible paper. I peer more closely. The photos are all of my family and Rob's. Iris is on the cookie in the middle of the tray. She's surrounded by cookies of her grandparents and Uncle Edgar, plus Zane, Rae, Tommy and Rob's sister and her family. Rob and I are positioned at the top of the tray, while Mia's picture is in pride of place, right next to Iris's.

'I ordered the rice paper transfers using pictures off Rob's phone,' Mia explains.

I experience a flash of concern that my husband has handed over his phone like that, then push it away. I'll talk to Rob about Mia later.

'It's us!' Iris jumps up and down with excitement then points to the cookie picture of herself. 'I'm right next to Mia.'

My stomach tightens. 'They look amazing, Iris,' I say, forcing myself to smile. 'Did you make the cookies?'

She nods. 'But Mia got the pictures and helped me put them on with icing.'

'Amazing.' I say the word again, but clearly with insufficient energy.

Iris's face falls. 'But it's *us*, Mummy. All our family. Including Mia.'

Her words send a jolt through me. What makes Iris think that? I look straight at Mia. '*Family*?' I ask, trying to keep my tone light.

She stares anxiously back at me. 'Er, I know what we agreed about not saying too much, too soon,' she murmurs, 'but Iris asked if I was her cousin because... because you and I look a bit alike, and... and I couldn't lie to her.'

'Oh.' My head spins. Iris is watching me, her little fore-head knotted in confusion. Across the room, Rob raises his head. 'What exactly did you say to Iris?' I demand. Even as I'm speaking, I know I sound too accusatory, especially in front of my daughter. But it's too late. The words are out and Rob, Mia and Iris are all staring at me, clearly baffled by my vehemence.

'Er, I... I explained I was your long-lost sister,' Mia stammers.

'Just like a princess in a story, Mummy.' Iris clasps her hands together.

I clench my jaw. 'I see,' I say, trying and failing to sound light-hearted.

'I told Mia it was fine.' Rob's voice is stern too now. It sounds a warning note.

I glance across and see the question in his eyes: *What on earth is wrong with you?*

'Of course it's fine,' I say. 'It's great.' I back away. 'Just need the bathroom. Be right back.'

'Okay, I'll put on the kettle,' Mia calls after me. 'By the way, I have another modelling job; I'll be away for the start of next week and...'

The rest of her sentence is lost as I hurry out through the hallway, up the stairs and into our bedroom. I sink onto the bed, my head in my hands.

I should never have let Mia into this house. Not until I was totally sure she is who she says.

I need her to leave as soon as humanly possible.

'Cassie?'

I look up. Rob is walking over, concern on his face. He sits down beside me and takes my hand, running his finger over my wedding band. 'What's the matter? You were acting really weird just now.'

I jump up and shut the bedroom door, then tell him in hushed whispers that I'm terrified Mia may be part of an elaborate con trick.

'The more I find out the more worried I get,' I explain, then proceed to tell Rob how Zane's suspicions led me to Val Rossi, who, in turn, led me to Uncle Edgar. I repeat the line in the email Harmony sent to him.

Nathaniel might be dead, but he still owes us, not the other way around. The lie is justified.

'I think Harmony Moon and Uncle Edgar may be behind Mia's claim to be Dad's daughter, pulling the strings so to speak, in order to get their hands on money they both think they are owed. Harmony probably came up with the idea, then Edgar recruited Mia, gave her all the background info she needed and organised a fake DNA test.'

'Seriously?' Rob frowns, a look of consternation on his face. 'That's a huge accusation.'

'That's not all,' I say. 'Zane was getting too close to the truth, so I think Uncle Edgar might have paid someone to… to kill him.'

'*Murder?*' Rob's frown deepens. 'You can't really think Edgar would—? Come on, Cassie, this is ludicrous.'

'Look at the facts,' I persist. 'Zane died in a hit-and-run, which is the same way the DNA clinic nurse who did Mia's test was killed.'

'So what?' Rob rolls his eyes. 'Are you saying Edgar killed the nurse too?'

'Why not?' I persist. 'Uncle Edgar has a huge motive. His salary as head of accounts at the firm is good, obviously, but it's nowhere near what the rest of us are looking at through the inheritance. And remember he's now been cut out of that inheritance not once but *twice*. And you should have heard him talking about Dad; he sounded so bitter. I'm willing to bet Harmony Moon feels much the same.'

'You have to be kidding me, Cas.' The hint of revulsion underneath my husband's bewildered tone hurts like a knife. 'Sounding bitter is *not* a motive.'

'Rob, listen—'

'No, *you* listen.' He shakes his head. 'I know Zane died suddenly and that must be really hard for you, but it's crazy to read some kind of sinister coincidence into two London hit-and-runs over the space of several weeks. And as for snooping through Edgar's emails… I'm shocked you and Tommy even considered doing it.'

'We had to know the truth,' I protest.

'You're seeing a conspiracy where there isn't one.' Rob pauses. 'I think if you'd had as hard a life as Mia has, then this wouldn't be happening.'

'*What?*' I recoil. 'What does that mean?'

'Did you know that when Mia was a kid, her mother got involved with a man who beat her. Which Mia *witnessed*. She remembers being terrified on several occasions when she was the same age as Iris is now. Imagine that? And look at what happened soon afterwards. Maryna couldn't cope, hence the drugs and the overdose, leaving Mia without a mum *or* a dad.'

'We don't know any of that about her mum's boyfriend is true,' I point out. 'She could be making the whole thing up.'

'I was watching Mia while she was telling me and I'd bet this house she wasn't lying,' Rob says, his voice rising in frustration. 'I'm from a tough background too, remember? I get where Mia's coming from.'

'Please,' I say, stung. 'Having divorced parents isn't the same as an entirely absent dad and a dead mother. And, as I keep saying, she could be lying.' I cross my arms, feeling indignant. 'Your problem is that you just can't see past those big kitten eyes of hers.'

'That's not fair,' Rob snaps. 'And if you won't trust my instincts, then what about all the stuff that we know is historically accurate? Nathaniel *was* in the Bahamas at the same time as Maryna's photo shoot. Mia *was* born nine months later. Why won't you accept *those* facts?'

'I'm not saying they couldn't have met. Maybe there was even a one-night stand in the heat of the moment,' I say. 'I accept that Dad wasn't perfect. But that doesn't make Mia his daughter.'

Rob shakes his head. We sit in silence for a moment, then he looks up. 'What's really going on here, Cas?' he asks, softly. 'Are you, maybe, jealous over Mia? Angry that Iris and I both like her?'

'No, of course not,' I insist, my cheeks burning.

'Really? Because I don't know how else to make sense of you acting like this.' Rob rises to his feet. 'You've had every advantage compared to that girl. She's had a really awful upbringing and deserves compassion from you, not this paranoia that's almost verging on... on cruelty.' And with a final disappointed look, Rob walks out of the room.

I listen to his steps on the stairs as he goes back down to the kitchen and Iris and Mia. After a while I hear the chink of crockery, but nobody calls up for me to come to dinner.

I don't have any appetite anyway.

SIXTEEN

The next morning I drop Iris and go to the Sound Heals clinic in Gospel Oak. It's Friday, my busiest morning of the week, with back-to-back music therapy sessions: the first with a Parkinson's group where I have to work hard to encourage most of the participants to join the singing, drum beating and recorder playing; the second with a selection of dementia sufferers at various stages of decline.

As soon as I'm done, I call Rae and insist we meet urgently.

An hour later we're taking a lunchtime walk in Regent's Park, near Rae's law firm. I repeat, once again, everything I've found that suggests Mia may not be genuine.

My half-sister's reaction couldn't be more different from Rob's.

'None of this surprises me, darling,' she says. 'I've actually been searching for Mia on social media,' she says. 'There's *nothing*. And it's not like Mia Ishchenko is a common name.'

'I guess there could be a good reason for that,' I venture.

'A good reason for a twenty-six-year-old part-time model to have literally no presence online?' Rae snorts. 'I'd like to hear it.'

I swallow. 'So what do you think we should do about Harmony Moon's email? I'm convinced the justifiable "lie" she's talking about is Mia, but Uncle Edgar was adamant it wasn't and—'

'We need to track down Harmony and demand an explanation,' Rae interrupts bossily. 'Where is this Lissay Community, anyway? It sounds Scottish.' She's already looking on her phone. 'Ah, it's in north Devon. Set up by James Lissay, who *was* from Scotland, in the 1980s.' She looks excitedly up at me, her dark eyes sparkling with anticipation. 'When shall we go?'

I chew on my lip. It's Friday today. Mia told us last night she'll be leaving on Sunday for a two-day modelling job. That will be the perfect time for me to be away from home, when I don't have to worry about her being around Rob and Iris.

'How about we set off this Sunday?' I suggest. 'We can stay overnight somewhere, come back on Monday?'

'*Perfect*, darling,' coos Rae. 'I've actually got a client in Bath due a face-to-face meeting. Maybe I can combine our trip with seeing them on our way home.'

I call Tommy and let him know our plan. My younger brother still isn't quite so convinced of Mia's guilt as Rae and me, but he agrees to come with us. Later, I tell Rob I'm just piggybacking on a work trip of Rae's in order to spend a day and a night in the countryside. I know it's another lie, but I can't bear the confusion – and possibly the contempt – I'd see in his eyes if I were to explain what I'm actually doing, and why.

Luckily, I only have three regular clients on Monday, one of whom is away on holiday anyway. I call the other two and postpone their sessions to Tuesday.

I think about taking Iris on our trip, but she has nursery on Monday morning and, anyway, having a small child in tow will make our journey harder. I comfort myself with the thought that at least Mia won't be around while I'm away.

-

Early on Sunday morning Rae picks up first Tommy, then me, in her smart, sleek Audi and we set off for north Devon. The journey takes just over four hours, including two rest stops, and it's almost two p.m. by the time the three of us make our way down a direct track and finally arrive at Lissay. The community is bounded by a high wooden fence stretching as far as the eye can see in both directions. A banner strung over a huge wooden gate marks the entrance: *Lissay Community, est. 1984. Wild and free* ☺

Rae, who has driven the entire way after refusing my offer to share the burden, leans over the steering wheel as she reverses into a patch of dry earth to the right of the gate.

'Why are we parking here and not going inside?' Tommy asks from the back seat.

I point to the sign nailed to the gate post: *No cars beyond this point.*

'Great,' grumbles Tommy. 'I bet it's all dirt tracks and knit your own crystals.'

'At least you're not wearing Louboutin ankle boots, darling,' Rae says with a sigh, stepping gingerly out of the car. 'I forgot to pack my Hunters.'

'Do you two have any idea how overheard-in-Waitrose you sound?' I say with a chuckle, opening the passenger door. After the stuffy journey, the wintry breeze is pleasantly cool on my face. I take a deep breath. Despite the distant whiff of manure, the air is fresh and clear. I zip up my jacket and stomp over to the gate, glad that *I'm* wearing walking boots. Someone has given the wood a coat of sand-coloured paint fairly recently, but plenty of chips and dents are visible. I look for a doorbell but can't see one.

As Rae and Tommy join me, footsteps sound on the other side of the gate. Does whoever is there already know that we're here? We haven't rung ahead – none of us wanted to use the Lissay Community registered landline number. As Tommy pointed out, we'll get more out of Harmony Moon if we catch her unprepared for our visit.

I knock on the gate. Two loud raps.

Rae adjusts the collar of her Prada trench coat. 'It just occurred to me,' she whispers. 'Might this place be a cult?'

'Yeah.' Tommy's eyes widen. 'With one of those charismatic leaders who sleeps with all the young women, then makes everyone commit mass suicide?'

'For goodness' sake, it's just a commune.' I roll my eyes. 'Come on, both of you! Brace yourselves for mud and… and try not to flaunt your wealth too conspicuously.'

'What wealth?' grunts Tommy. 'I don't even get an allowance. As you well know.'

'I'm a working woman, darling,' adds Rae indignantly.

I shake my head. 'Just because—' I stop, as the large wooden gate swings open.

A man whose greying hair is fashioned into a series of long, thin braids walks towards us. His weatherbeaten face makes it hard to guess his age; he could be anything from forty-five to sixty.

'Good afternoon,' he says with a pleasant smile. 'We do *so* appreciate your interest, but I'm afraid if you're here to look around I have to inform you that Lissay isn't open to tourists at this time of year.'

'We're not tourists,' Rae says abruptly.

The man raises his eyebrows. 'I see.'

'We're looking for someone,' I say. 'Our… er, our stepmother.'

'Her name is Harmony Moon—' Tommy turns to me. 'Does she use Carson as a surname? Or did she go back to her maiden name?'

The man is staring at him. 'You're Harmony Moon's stepson?' He sounds shocked.

'One of them,' says Tommy. 'She was married to my dad before he got together with my mum.'

'But after he was married to *mine*,' Rae adds.

'Sorry, it must sound very confusing,' I add.

'Not at all.' The man extends his arm. His hands are surprisingly delicate, with long, slender fingers, though there are rough calluses on all the knuckles. 'I'm Cloud. Harmony's a friend.' He glances at Rae, real curiosity on his face. 'You're Rae, aren't you? Harmony Moon talks very fondly of her time with you, when you were a little girl.'

A look of bewilderment flashes across Rae's face. I'm guessing she doesn't have much memory of the period Cloud is referring to. At forty-four, Rae is eight years older than I am and would have been about five or six during Dad's brief marriage to his second wife.

It has never occurred to me before, but it makes total sense that Harmony Moon might have felt close to Rae during the short period she and Dad were together.

Cloud ushers us through the gate. It opens onto a large field, most of which is laid out in long rows of turned-over earth, several featuring straggly plants. A cluster of people in overalls are working next to the greenhouse in the top corner.

'This is where we grow our food,' Cloud says proudly. 'We're a community of seventy-two, including twenty children. Everyone plays a part. Of course this is far from our busiest time of year outdoors, but there's plenty to do, even in February. Right now we're sowing cabbage and cauliflower in the greenhouse. Oh, and chitting potatoes too.'

Tommy glances sideways at me. *Chitting?* he mouths, with a wink.

I frown at him.

'What are they doing?' Rae points to the group next to the greenhouse.

'Harvesting late sprouts,' Cloud says. 'Hopefully a few leeks, too.'

We walk towards the gate at the end of the field. High hedges shield whatever is on the other side from view on either side, but through the gate I can make out another field, peppered with wooden shacks.

'Do you have animals here?' asks Tommy, sounding a little nervous.

'Just a few goats and some hens,' says Cloud. 'Eggs and milk are good sources of protein for the children, but most of the adults here eat an entirely plant-based diet.'

He opens the gate and we walk through onto a mud track, as the sun comes out, bathing the community spread out beyond us in glowing light.

A large hut stands in the centre of another field. Its roof is a mass of solar panels and purple batik curtains hang at the windows. Smaller cabins are dotted all around it, each with their own small patch of ground in front.

'Everyone together, but with their own space to retire to,' says Cloud proudly. 'That is the heart of Lissay.'

'What's the big hut for?' I ask.

'That's where we eat our evening meal,' says Cloud. 'There's a roster for cooking. We also do various crafts. Ken who joined us a few years ago is a jeweller, so we've got a growing business in reclaimed metalwork earrings.'

'How lovely,' says Rae politely.

'Which one of these cabins is Harmony Moon's?' I ask.

'I'll take you over,' says Cloud, pointing to one at the far end of the field.

It's larger than most of the other cabins, with planters along both window ledges. I'm sure in the spring these will burst into bloom, but right now they look rather sad.

Cloud loosens his boots at the door. 'Shoes off, please,' he says, walking inside.

The three of us obediently leave our footwear by the door. Somehow, Rae has managed to avoid getting any mud spatters on her fancy ankle boots. They stand polished and upright between my battered walking boots and Tommy's trendy trainers like a governess gazing reproachfully at a pair of recalcitrant students. Then the three of us follow Cloud into a large living area where the heat from a small wood burner creates an almost suffocating warmth, after the chill outside. I'm expecting the scent of patchouli and a load of hippy décor but, to my surprise, the walls are plain panelled wood, and the sofa and armchairs are covered with smart red and purple throws. A stainless-steel stand mixer sits on a plain granite countertop in the kitchen area at the end of the room. The only hint of anything New Age-y is the row of crystals along the window ledge.

'Here she is,' Cloud says.

I turn as a tall, slim woman sashays through the far door.

SEVENTEEN

Harmony Moon must be in her late sixties. Her face is as lined as her friend Cloud's but there's an almost youthful beauty in her high cheekbones and almond-shaped eyes. Her long, grey-streaked hair is pinned back at the sides with butterfly clips and she's dressed in an elegant jumpsuit and thick wool socks. Her jaw drops as she catches sight of us.

'Visitors for you,' says Cloud, grinning. 'I'll leave them to explain, need to get back to the gate.' He disappears.

Harmony Moon glides towards us. 'Hello?' she says, uncertainly.

I quickly introduce us and her eyes widen, first in shock then in recognition as she peers closely at Rae.

'It's been so long,' she says, with a hint of reproach in her voice. 'I don't think I've seen you since you were six years old, Rachael.'

'Rae, please.' Rae clears her throat. 'Er, it's nice to see you.'

Harmony Moon stares at her. 'Children?'

Rae shakes her head. 'You?'

'No.' Harmony Moon makes a face. 'Your father saw to that.'

My ears prick up. What does *that* comment mean? Val Rossi's claim that Dad called Harmony Moon a "useless, slutty bitch" drifts into my head again.

Just as I'm wondering how to get Harmony Moon to say more, Tommy jumps in.

'Gosh, that sounds awful,' he says, warmly. 'What did Dad do? To stop you having kids, that is?'

I tense, wondering how Harmony Moon will react to such a direct question.

Beside me, Rae looks equally alarmed.

'It would just be so good to get your side of the, er, relationship,' Tommy says, smiling. 'Especially after all these years.'

I hold my breath, as Harmony Moon lets her fingers flutter over the row of crystals on the window ledge. She gazes mournfully through the glass at the cloudy sky outside.

'I had some early success as an actress,' she says at last. 'But during and after our break-up Nathaniel made me sound so crazy that nobody would hire me.'

I catch Tommy's eye. Surely that can't be true?

'Social invitations dried up,' Harmony goes on. 'Before long all I could do was run away here and lick my wounds. It was entirely Nathaniel's fault.'

I shuffle awkwardly from foot to foot. Clearly, it's not going to be a problem to get Harmony Moon to open up. We haven't even taken off our coats and she's already trash-talking Dad.

'Would you like some tea?' she says, switching to polite host as if sensing my discomfort.

'Thank you,' I say.

'That would be nice,' echoes Rae.

As Harmony Moon fusses over a pan of water on the hob, she keeps up a non-stop commentary on the commune.

'There's no gas here, but we do generate our own electricity. Enough to power lights and a hob each, anyway. We try not to waste anything. It took a lot of getting used to when I arrived and I'm still not a great one for the farming side of things but Cloud does my share of that and I make my contribution baking bread.' She indicates the stand mixer as she places four steaming mugs of tea on a tray and brings it over to the table next to the sofa.

Rae, Tommy and I perch on that, while Harmony takes her mug and sits on the armchair opposite. She tucks her feet underneath her and sips carefully at her tea.

'I heard about Nathaniel,' she says. 'I'm... well.' She pauses. 'I'm sorry for your loss.'

'Thank you.' I pick up a blue mug and cradle it in my hands. 'You must be wondering why we're here.'

'Dad left a will,' Rae starts.

'I heard.' A smile creeps across Harmony Moon's face. 'Everything to his children equally, except Adam of course.' She pauses. 'Edgar told me.'

My heart thuds at this acknowledgement that the two of them have been in touch.

'Is that right?' Rae says waspishly.

Harmony Moon lets her fingers flutter over the crystals on the window ledge again. She points to a smooth, greenish-yellow gemstone. 'Peridot,' she says. 'My signature crystal. It stands for harmony, growth and renewal.' Despite the slender elegance of her silky jumpsuit and sleek, pinned-back hair, I notice that the paint on her nails is cracked and peeling. 'What does Nathaniel's will have to do with me?' she asks, her voice suddenly tight and terse. 'Our divorce was finalised decades ago.'

'It's Mia,' Rae says, flatly.

'Who?' I watch Harmony closely as Rae explains how Mia turned up out of the blue on what would have been Dad's birthday. Her expression is one of mild confusion, as if she genuinely has no idea who Mia is.

'So Nat cheated on Drippy Donna.' A look of grim delight appears on Harmony's face.

I stiffen, glancing at Tommy, who is frowning.

Harmony catches our expressions and raises her hand in an airy wave. 'Sorry,' she says, not sounding sorry at all. 'I know Donna's your mother but honestly, I always wondered what Nathaniel saw in her. Anyway, back to this Mia girl.' She sniffs, picking up the yellow-green crystal she pointed to earlier. 'I suppose she wants a share of the inheritance?'

'That's right, and...' I falter. Now we're here it sounds melodramatic to say we suspect Mia may be a fraud. Ludicrous even.

'Mia's whole story is a lie.' Rae's voice is bitter. 'Zane knew it and she killed him.'

Harmony's slightly sardonic manner evaporates in an instant. 'Zane is *dead*?' Her hands fly to her mouth.

I bite my lip, feeling awkward that we have waited so long to reveal this shocking news.

Rae nods, her eyes glistening in the light from the window, then goes on to explain about the hit-and-run.

'Which is exactly how the nurse who did the DNA test on Mia died,' I add.

'A DNA test that Uncle Edgar organised and most probably had faked,' Rae adds.

'Wait. You think Mia and Edgar killed them? This nurse and... and Zane?' Harmony looks appalled.

'Yes,' says Rae.

'Maybe,' I say.

'Oh, come *on*, darling,' Rae chides me. 'It's the only logical explanation.'

Harmony Moon raises her eyebrows.

'It's a very complicated situation,' I explain, shooting a look at Rae. 'I don't know about the nurse, but Mia and Uncle Edgar both have alibis for Zane.'

'That doesn't mean they didn't hire someone to murder him,' Rae points out. 'Mia is clearly working with somebody who has deep pockets and the resources you'd need to carry off a major con. We think Edgar is involved, but he isn't necessarily the only one.'

'I'm not sure I'm following.' Harmony Moon's fingers tighten around the peridot crystal. 'I hope you're not suggesting that *I* might be part of—?'

'We're not suggesting anything,' I interrupt. 'It's just… we found an email you sent Uncle Edgar a few weeks after Dad died. We wondered… well, this is what you wrote.' Harmony frowns as I recite the message. '*Edgar. Nathaniel might be dead, but he still owes us, not the other way around. The lie is justified.*'

Harmony Moon's face is a mask, but she's gripping that crystal so hard her knuckles are white.

'We really need to know, and Uncle Edgar refuses to tell us.' Tommy sits forward. 'What's the "lie" you're referring to?'

Harmony Moon stares at him.

'It's Mia, isn't it?' Rae blurts out. '*She's* the "lie" that will enable the two of you to get what you believe you're owed from Dad… his money.'

'How *dare* you!' Harmony Moon rises to her feet.

'Rae didn't mean to sound so accusatory,' I say quickly. 'Like I said before, we're just trying to understand.'

Rae looks down at her lap.

Harmony Moon shakes her head. 'I never *heard* of Mia before today. She has nothing to do with that email you're talking about.'

My stomach gives an uneasy twist. She sounds as completely sincere as Uncle Edgar when he said the same thing.

'But you do remember the email?' Tommy asks slowly. 'What's it about, if it's not about Mia?'

Harmony Moon sits down again. 'Sorry but no, I can't give you any details,' she says. 'It wouldn't be fair.'

Fair on whom? I frown, intrigued. Rae is open-mouthed, clearly eager to push Harmony to explain. I touch her arm lightly to indicate she should hold fire for now.

'I know this is hard for you, Harmony,' I say gently, 'but you sound angry in the email. Can you at least tell us why you thought Dad "owed" you?'

'Yeah,' adds Tommy. 'What did Dad do that upset you so much? Is it something to do with that thing you said before, about him somehow stopping you from having children?'

There's a long pause. Harmony looks like she's debating with herself what she should and shouldn't tell us. My guess is that part of her is longing to dish the dirt on Dad and my heart quickens in anticipation.

'Terrible parenting,' she says at last. '*That's* what upset me about Nathaniel.' She pauses. 'I'd go so far as to say, *evil* parenting.'

'*What?*' Rae asks sharply.

'I don't understand,' I say. 'Are you talking about Mia? Because if Mia *is* a lie… and not Dad's daughter at all, then how could he have been an evil parent to her?'

'I didn't say Nathaniel was evil to Mia. How could I?' Harmony Moon snaps. 'I didn't know she existed until five minutes ago.'

'So what did you mean, then?' I ask. 'Which one of us was Dad the evil parent to?'

'Not me, darling, that's for sure.' Rae folds her arms, looking askance.

I look at Tommy. I can see the same confusion on his face that I feel myself. Our father wasn't perfect. He was regularly absent because of work, often prone to bursts of bad temper and – it seems undeniable now – wasn't entirely faithful to Mum, but he provided for us and was fun to be around – and though he certainly gave us every academic and extra-curricular opportunity growing up, he also insisted we worked for our pocket money and refused to set up trust funds or indulgent allowances. Most of all, he was always loving and invested in our lives. Flawed, certainly. But never "evil".

'Evil's a strong word,' I start. 'Could you explain what—'

'I'm sorry but I can't say any more,' Harmony Moon interrupts. 'I shouldn't have said what I said…'

'About Dad as a parent?'

'Yeah, how was he "evil"?' Tommy shakes his head in confusion.

'He wasn't.' Harmony Moon's cheeks pink. 'I was just lashing out.' She takes a deep breath. 'Let's just say your father wasn't exactly trustworthy when it came to other women. I'm sorry, but… but that's the truth.'

The three of us fall silent. Even if Mia isn't really Dad's daughter, and even if he didn't have an affair with her mother, that DNA test he submitted to twenty years ago suggests he was unfaithful to Mum at least once. And if he could betray the trust of a woman I'm certain he loved, how much more likely that he slept around when he was married to Harmony Moon?

'So you're saying the justifiable "lie" in your email has something to do with Dad and other women?' I ask.

'No.' Harmony Moon sighs. 'I'm just saying that my time with your father was a very unhappy one. He didn't like men paying me attention and made it clear he thought I was "easy".' She shakes her head and I think again of Val Rossi's "slutty bitch" comment. Harmony Moon purses her lips together, deepening the fine lines around her mouth. 'When I mentioned earlier that Nathaniel stopped me from having children, what I meant was... that he pressured me into a hysterectomy.'

I stare at her.

'Why would he do that?' Rae splutters.

'What do you mean "pressured"?' Tommy asks.

Harmony Moon shrugs, looking uncomfortable. 'I had some... some gynaecological issues. Nothing life threatening. There were various treatment options, but Nathaniel insisted the hysterectomy was the best course of action. That it made the most sense, medically.' She pauses. 'He could be very forceful and I was very vulnerable. I regretted the operation as soon as I'd had it done.'

'But if it made sense medically?' I ask, feeling confused.

'That wasn't Nathaniel's real reason. He made that perfectly clear through all his jibes and sneers.' Harmony Moon's voice rises. 'He basically implied that I was a slut and needed to be neutered like an animal.'

Jesus. I exchange a look with Rae. She shrugs as if to say, *We're getting nowhere.*

'I'm really sorry you felt so... er, that Dad treated you so badly, Harmony Moon,' I say carefully.

Rae nods slowly. 'We're grateful for your time.'

'Okay, then.' Harmony Moon's eyes linger on Rae's face, her voice suddenly gentle again. 'I really am very sorry to hear about Zane,' she says softly. 'That must be a terrible blow for you, especially with Adam not being around.'

Rae looks up, her expression hardening. 'Oh, I'm used to Adam not being here,' she says, then her voice cracks. 'But, yes, it is hard… without Zane.'

Tommy shuffles uncomfortably on his chair.

I look down at my lap.

Harmony Moon clears her throat. 'When is the funeral?'

'There's no date yet,' I explain. 'The police are still performing a postmortem.'

'I spoke to them yesterday,' Rae says, her voice wobbling a little. 'They said they should be able to release Zane's body later this week. We'll probably hold the funeral in a fortnight or so.'

'Well, please send me the details,' Harmony Moon says. 'In fact, perhaps you could leave your number?' She's looking at Rae expectantly, but Rae is dabbing her eyes and doesn't notice, so I quickly scribble both our mobile numbers on a scrap of paper from my bag and hand it to Harmony Moon.

'Thank you.' She stands up. 'And now, perhaps it's time for you all to leave.'

EIGHTEEN

Rae, Tommy and I spend Sunday night in a hotel in Exeter. I call Rob from my room before going down to eat. He asks what we've been doing and I find myself skittering over the events of the afternoon and avoiding any mention of our visit to Harmony Moon. I hate myself for this lie of omission; I've never been remotely dishonest with him before. Even though I know telling the truth would probably lead to a row, which is the last thing I want, it feels horrible to be keeping something so significant from him. At least Rob confirms Mia has left for her modelling trip. The thought that she isn't at home with him and Iris brings me a huge sense of relief.

Over dinner, Rae, Tommy and I discuss our meeting with Harmony Moon.

'I'm certain she was lying about knowing Mia,' Rae insists. 'The more I think about it, the more likely it seems that Mia, Harmony Moon and Uncle Edgar are in league with each other. It makes total sense. Harmony and Edgar set Mia up to claim a share of Dad's inheritance, and they split whatever she gets three ways.'

'I guess that does make sense,' I say. 'But Harmony's reaction when we talked about Mia seemed totally genuine. She acted like she'd never heard of her.'

'Of course she did, darling. "Acted" being the operative word,' Rae says crisply.

I nod, slowly.

'I'm not so sure,' Tommy says with a sigh. 'Leaving aside whether either of them are capable of murder, I'm not sure if either she or Uncle Edgar have the temperament for such a... a massive plan as inventing a character and all the flourishes you'd need to go with that.' He wrinkles his nose. 'Harmony's theatrical enough, but I don't see her following through. While Edgar's life is too small, too focused on details. He might know how to fiddle the books but I can't see him organising a fake DNA test. Or coaching Mia in how to con the rest of us.'

Rae shrugs. 'I'd say that makes him and Harmony Moon a good team, don't you think?'

'What about that "evil parent" comment then?' Tommy insists. 'How does that fit in?'

'Tommy's right.' I sigh. 'It doesn't make any sense.'

'For goodness' sake, darlings!' Rae removes her perfectly manicured hand from her wine glass and waves it dismissively in our direction. 'You heard Harmony. She was just lashing out, trying to hurt us when she said that. She thought Dad was evil to *her*, not *us* – all that stuff about ruining her career and pressuring her into a hysterectomy she didn't want.'

I fall silent, Harmony Moon's words echoing in my head: *That's what upset me about Nathaniel... evil parenting... I didn't say Nathaniel was evil to Mia. How could I? I didn't know she existed until five minutes ago.*

So if not Mia, whom did she mean? Was she really just lashing out, like Rae says? Or does she think Nathaniel was "evil" to one of us? It can't be Rae – Rae herself was adamant about that. And definitely not Zane, who was Dad's heir-apparent all his life.

What about Adam? It's true that Dad fired him. But he had tried to steal a fortune from the company, and Dad never called the police, which he would have been entitled to do. Besides, even though, in the heat of the moment, Dad told Adam to "get out of my sight", nobody seriously believes he intended him to stay away forever.

However hard I look, I can't see anything he did to any of his children as "evil".

'I don't think Harmony Moon was simply lashing out,' I say slowly. 'But I don't think she meant everything she said about Dad either.'

Rae raises her eyebrows. 'Go on.'

'I reckon it was calculated,' I say. 'She slagged off Dad in a way that she knew we'd find hurtful in order to focus our attention on *him* and away from *her*. I think that "evil parent" remark was intended as a diversion. Part of her attempt to cover her tracks.'

'That's it!' Rae claps her hands together. 'That's *exactly* it!'

'I suppose,' Tommy says uncertainly.

I sit back and take a sip of wine, my heart thudding in my chest.

–

The next morning we set off back to London, via Bath. Tommy is virtually silent for once, but Rae and I chatter on, partly about our suspicions of Edgar, Harmony Moon and Mia, partly about what Tommy and I should do in Bath while she has her client meeting. In the end, her business lunch takes two and a half hours, which adds a further delay to our trip home, then to make matters worse, as we join the M4 rain begins pouring down, hammering on the car roof. I gaze through the streaked windows of the car, watching as the traffic ahead slows to a crawl.

By the time we get back to north London, it's almost seven p.m. Rae – who has been behind the wheel for the entire journey, refusing to let either Tommy or me drive her Audi – looks totally shattered.

I insist that she drops me at Mum's place with Tommy. I can find my own way home from there. I call Rob as we pull up, hoping he'll offer to pick me up, but it turns out he is just about to pop Iris in the bath so can't leave. I tell him I'll get a taxi home soon and go into the house. Tommy is chatting with Mum in the kitchen. I scurry into the living room and call Savannah, now at her mum's house in Leeds, to see how she's doing. I can just imagine how frustrated she's feeling at the doctor's instruction to "avoid stress" for the remainder of her pregnancy.

'I'm bored, bored, bored,' Sav says. 'Have you spoken to Edgar?'

'Yes, and Harmony Moon.' I explain about our trip to her commune, and our conversation about the "justified lie" email.

'Tommy's not sure, but Rae and I still think that the lie refers to Mia,' I say.

'So… so…' Sav's voice cracks. 'Do you think it's possible that Mia and Edgar and this… this Harmony Moon… that the three of them might really have killed Zane?'

'I don't know,' I sigh, not wanting either to upset her or raise her hopes that we've made any progress. 'To be honest, Sav, there's nothing to tie them directly to it. In fact, Uncle Edgar and Mia have alibis for that night.'

'They could easily have got someone else to carry out the hit-and-run for them.' Sav's voice rises, full of passion and fear. 'I'll come back to London tomorrow. Help look into it.'

'No,' I say firmly. 'Tommy, Rae and I are on the case. We *will* get to the bottom of it. I promise. You need to spend the next few weeks doing as little as possible.' I hesitate. 'Did Rae call you about the police saying it was okay to… that we should be able to have the funeral before too long?'

'Yes,' Sav says with a sniff. 'She was very nice about it, actually. We're going to organise things together. You know, where and… and how.'

'Good, well, I'll see you then, if not before.'

'Okay,' Sav reluctantly agrees, 'but you will keep me posted if you find out anything else? Promise?'

I make the promise but privately decide that I'm not going to contact her again unless I have definite news. Certainly not before I see her at Zane's funeral.

Wandering back to the kitchen after the call, I discover Mum has cooked a big bowl of pasta and insists I stay for the evening meal. Tommy clearly hasn't told her where we've been – or why – and I'm careful not to mention it either.

It's not just that any reference to Dad's second wife might upset her; I also need time to think about what we found out today – to try and make sense of it.

After we've eaten, Tommy mumbles that he's due to meet a friend and slips upstairs to change. We hear the front door shut behind him a few minutes later.

'Is he still clubbing most nights?' I ask, wondering where my brother finds the energy. It's not yet ten p.m.

but I'm already exhausted after our long drive back from Devon.

'I worry about him,' Mum says. 'Dad worried too. He always thought I babied him; we had endless conversations – arguments, really – about it.' Mum pauses. 'Personally, I think he was too hard on *all* the boys. All that nonsense about being happy to help you and Rae with your mortgage deposits, but not his sons.' She shakes her head sorrowfully.

'What d'you think was behind that?' I ask. 'I know it upset Tommy at the time.' My thoughts shoot back to a rare row with my younger brother about four years ago, during which he argued that Dad's gift to me and Rob was both unjust and unjustifiable.

Mum looks at me, thoughtfully. 'He was convinced that the boys needed goals… to have to strive in order to become men. *Especially* Tommy.' She turns away, clearly lost in the memory of some long-ago conversation. 'Dad used to say that Tommy was the child least like him. *No drive*, he'd say.' She smiles sadly. 'He had this idea that the rest of you… how did he put it? *They're all driven: Zane to make money, Rae to get her way and Cassie to look after people, but Tommy just drifts.*'

'What about Adam?' I ask. 'Did Dad think *he* was driven?'

'Oh, yes,' Mum says. 'Adam was very idealistic when he was a teenager. He often argued about politics with your dad. *Driven to save the bloody world* was Dad's take.'

'And yet Adam stole all that money?'

'*Tried* to,' Mum corrects. 'Dad was devastated, took it very personally. He'd been so proud to have both his older boys working at Carson and felt terribly let down. He really lost his rag that night, said things I'm sure he regretted. He was heartbroken when it was clear Adam had run off never to be seen again. After a while Dad hardened himself. He had to. But it nearly destroyed him.'

I sit back. 'When was this *exactly*?'

'Ooh, autumn 1999. October, I think. Everyone was very preoccupied with the "millennium bug", worrying every computer in the world was going to break down as soon as the new year started. That's how Adam's attempted theft came to light: Uncle Edgar was doing a security review of the finances.' She smiles. 'I shouldn't really say it, but Adam was far and away my favourite of Dad's older kids. Kind and gentle and great with you and Tommy. Not that it was much of a contest. Zane looked down his nose and barely said a word to any of us. As for Rae.' She shakes her head. 'I mean, she was still a teenager at the time, and she'd had a tough childhood, what with the break-up of her parents' marriage, then her dad's relationship with Harmony Moon being so volatile and short-lived.'

'Was that second split really hard on Rae?' I ask.

'Divorce is *always* hard on children,' Mum says. 'And after everything Rae had gone through with both marriages ending, it was always going to be difficult for her to trust *me*, the next wife.' Mum sighs. 'To be honest, we never really got past that to... to build the kind of bond I'd have liked.'

'What about...?' I frown. 'Did you really not know Dad was unfaithful with Mia's mum?'

'No, I didn't.' She pauses. 'Still, I'd be lying if I said I was totally shocked.'

'Oh, Mum.' I reach for her hand.

She waves me impatiently away. 'I'm just saying your father wasn't a saint. But he was always there for his children.'

I yawn and Mum asks if I'd like to stay the night. I check the time. It's now almost ten thirty. Mia won't be back from her modelling trip till tomorrow. Meanwhile, Rob will be heading to bed soon and Iris should have been asleep for ages.

I send Rob a text explaining that I might as well stay here and that Mum will like it. He replies saying it's no problem. He's going in late tomorrow and can easily drop Iris at nursery. I head to my old room at Mum's house, intending to be up early and home in time to take Iris to nursery with Rob. But, when morning comes, I sleep through my alarm, not waking until twenty past eight. It's a scramble to make it to Sound Heals by nine thirty, but I'm there and ready for the two clients whose sessions were postponed from yesterday. The first is Amara, a fifteen-year-old with cerebral palsy and a love of playing air guitar to loud rock music; the second is Bob, a middle-aged stroke victim who is flexing his motor skills playing the piano. As Bob and I work together creating little tunes on my keyboard, I find my mind drifting to the mystery of Mia.

I am going to have to face her tonight and, after all the events and discussions of the past twenty-four hours, I don't have any more concrete proof to go on than I did when she turned up on Mum's doorstep over a month ago.

NINETEEN

I leave Sound Heals at midday that Tuesday and go straight to the nursery to pick up Iris. Mia will be back from her modelling job today but I have no idea when she'll arrive home and the last thing I want is to have to make small talk with her.

Determined to delay my return home, I decide to take Iris to a city farm in the East End and we spend a fun couple of hours feeding the hens and petting the goats and donkeys. I even manage to put the whole Mia situation out of my head, delighting in my daughter's rosy cheeks and excited squeals as we trudge around the various hutches, pens and stables. The place probably seems enormous to Iris but to me, after the windswept fields of Devon and the Lissay Commune, the city farm and its precious acre of land seem small and confined.

As we reach the car, Iris starts telling me a jumbled story about a donkey called Blue. Clearly prompted by the animals at the city farm, it takes me a while to unravel that she's actually referring to a character in a book she heard at nursery yesterday.

'Ah, was it read at assembly?' I ask, as I lift her into her car seat. 'Or was it reading time with Miss Stacy at the end of day?'

'Reading time with Miss Stacy,' Iris declaims. 'Blue was about to make friends with a rabbit, but then we had to stop and all put our coats on and then Mia took me swimming.'

I freeze, staring at her. 'Mia met you after nursery yesterday?' My voice is faint, a whisper of sound on the strong wind blowing the smell of manure towards us.

'Yes, Mummy,' Iris says impatiently. 'I just said.'

'And… and she took you swimming?' I say, clicking the restraints of her car seat into place.

'Yes, I swam a whole width without arm bands.' Iris chatters on as I close the door next to her and numbly take my place behind the steering wheel.

What was Mia doing back at our house a day early?

An horrific thought grabs me. Did Mia actually leave in the first place? Or was her modelling job another lie, designed to reassure me that she would be out of the way and not wandering seductively around my home?

'I thought Mia went away,' I say, starting the engine, 'just after I left on Sunday.'

Iris considers this thoughtfully as I steer the car out of the city farm car park and onto the main road.

'Mia *did* go away,' she says at last. 'But she came back yesterday.'

I still can't wrap my head around what she's saying. If it's true, then why didn't Rob tell me Mia was there when we spoke last night?

Feeling sick, I drive on autopilot the whole way home. As I park the car outside our house, Iris asks if Mia will be inside.

'I don't know, sweetheart,' I say. I check the time. It's nearly half past five. Rob should be back from school by now. Are he and Mia in there together?

I switch off the car engine, then unclip Iris from her car seat. She skips ahead of me towards the house. My heart thuds, hard, as I unlock the front door, then shut it quietly behind me. If Mia's already home, she'll probably be in the kitchen preparing yet another delicious meal. But where is Rob? I glance into the living room as I pass. It's empty.

A sudden sense of foreboding overwhelms me. I hurry after Iris, who is already opening the kitchen door, one sleeve of her coat off already and dangling on the floor in her eagerness.

As I reach the door myself, I sense movement at the kitchen table, the quick drawing back of two people springing apart from each other. Rob and Mia look up as we walk in.

'Daddy!' Iris squeals, rushing over.

Rob's eyes are on our daughter, but Mia meets my gaze. She's wearing a satin blouse. My mouth gapes as I clock the colour and the small, pearlised buttons. It's another item of mine from that damn charity shop bag. Mia is fumbling with the top button, as if… as if doing it up.

Shit, shit, shit. Why the hell was it undone?

My stomach gives way.

'Hey, Cas.' Rob beams at me, Iris in his arms.

'What are you doing?' My words shoot at Rob like bullets.

He frowns. 'Helping Mia with an email to her lawyer.' He points to his open laptop on the kitchen table, then looks up at me. There's a wariness in his eyes. Is that genuine confusion at my manner? Or is it subterfuge and guilt?

I close my eyes, willing myself to calm down. I mustn't jump to conclusions. Rob may have a perfectly good explanation for avoiding mentioning Mia's early return.

After all, I've never doubted him before.

Iris is now clamouring to be put down. Rob eases her onto the floor, still staring at me.

'Cassie, are you all right?'

I want to tell him everything I'm feeling. To demand a reason for his lack of honesty last night. But not here. Now. Like this, with our daughter in the room. I glance at Mia and I swear for a second there's a look of triumph in her eyes. Then she blinks and claps her hands together, making big eyes at Iris.

'Hey, lovey, would you like a drink?'

Iris nods and Mia wanders to the fridge. As she pours a beaker of orange juice, I move over to Rob. He pulls me towards him.

'Cas?' His hand is warm on my shoulder.

I lean against him, my thoughts in turmoil. He sounds like he always does. But I can't help feeling I interrupted him and Mia just now. I pull away.

'I hear from Iris that you came back early from your work trip, Mia.' I can hear the edge to my voice. 'What happened?'

Mia glances over, her cheeks pinking slightly. 'Oh, they did my stuff first, so I wasn't needed for the final day and the café wanted me in for a shift this morning so…' She brings the juice over and sets it on the table next to Iris.

Beside me Rob tenses, as if feeling awkward. Is that just because he didn't mention Mia's early return last night? Or does he have more to hide?

My guts twist. Now I'm standing here with the two of them, the idea that they slept together last night simultaneously seems less likely – just the barefaced gall of it in my own house – and yet also somehow more likely – Mia is so pretty and Rob so… on edge.

And yet, surely Rob wouldn't do that to me? To our family?

'Can I see your DBS certificate, Mia?' The words shoot out of me.

Mia's jaw drops.

Rob frowns. 'Cassie—' he starts.

'I just... I just want to see it,' I say. Heat rises through my neck and into my face. 'You mentioned you were checked for working with children, so...' I raise my eyebrows, avoiding Rob's gaze.

'You don't have to show us,' Rob says. 'Only people like employers have a legal right to see—'

'It's fine.' Tears bubble in Mia's eyes. She turns and scurries out of the room. As her footsteps echo across the hall, Rob turns to me.

'What the hell, Cas?' he hisses.

I cross my arms, feeling defensive. 'I just want to see some proof.'

Rob shakes his head. Along the table, Iris is watching us furtively.

A moment later, Mia appears, suspiciously red around the eyes. She holds out the paper certificate to me. I take it and study it. Having one myself, I'm immediately certain it's genuine. Apart from anything else, it would be very hard to fake that crown seal watermark.

'You can look online on the DBS Update Service site,' Mia says shakily. 'It's still current.'

I can feel Rob's eyes on me.

'No need,' I say, handing back the certificate. 'Thank you for showing me.'

Mia nods meekly, then sits down beside Iris. Rob, still exuding disapproval, stalks around the table and takes the chair opposite them.

I back away with a shudder. I *hate* feeling like this. I need to know the truth about Mia, once and for all. But so far all I have are suspicions and riddles and mysteries.

If Mia is a fake, there will be proof of it.

There *must* be.

I just need to find it.

I make an excuse about needing the bathroom and head upstairs.

Instead of going to our en suite, I make straight for Mia's room. The bed is neatly made with the duvet pulled straight and all the clothes put away. I bend down and look under the bed. Empty, apart from some spiky black stilettos, two pairs of trainers and a cardboard box of make-up and toiletries, which I pull out and quickly rummage through. I'm not sure what I'm looking for, but if Mia is really in league with someone and aware she is conning us, then maybe there'll be some proof of it somewhere. All I find under the deodorant and tampons are some lipsticks which look at least a year past their sell-by date – nothing incriminating. Grimacing, I shove the box back under the bed and lift the mattress. Nothing hidden there, either.

I blow out my breath, feeling frustrated, then open the wardrobe. Some clothes are on hangers; several are in a heap on the wardrobe floor. I scrabble about but find nothing odd among the jumpers and jeans. I turn to the three drawers by the bed and speedily examine each one in turn. As I sift through Mia's knickers, I experience a sudden wave of revulsion. What am I doing? Poring over her underwear like some horrible pervert. I shut the drawer and stand up, looking around. There's literally nowhere else she could be concealing anything. Perhaps I'm being an idiot. If Mia is a fraud, any proof of the fact will probably only be online. She's surely too clever to keep any physical item that might betray her. And certainly not in a place that was easy to find.

I'm about to turn away when, on impulse, I drop to my knees and check under the bed again. I shine my torch right into the furthest corner. A boot I hadn't noticed before is on its side next to the wall. I lie flat on the floor. At full stretch, I can just reach the heel. I pull out the boot. It's a black with a square toe. Funny, I've never seen Mia wearing this.

I reach into the boot. My fingers light on something hard. Plastic.

My heart thuds as I pull out a small, black phone.

I gulp. This isn't Mia's normal mobile, which has a bright pink cover and a beaded phone charm dangling from the end.

This is a burner phone.

TWENTY

My fingers tremble as I switch on the phone. The screen comes to life, registering one message, number withheld. I open it.

All good, Alecto

I stare at the text. What does *that* mean? Who on earth is Alecto? I quickly scroll to old messages, calls and contacts.

All are empty.

Which is weird as hell, isn't it?

Footsteps sound on the stairs. My hands are sweaty as I shove the phone back into the boot and replace it under Mia's bed. I scramble to my feet and leave the little room, my heart racing.

Rob is on the landing opposite, about to go into the bathroom.

'What was all that earlier, with Mia's DBS?' He frowns at me. 'Do you really think she was lying about that?'

I shake my head, still fixated on the burner phone and its mysterious message.

'No, the certificate was genuine,' I murmur.

'Are you okay?' Rob's frown morphs to a gentle smile, his face softening with real warmth. He reaches for my hand. 'I missed you the past couple of days.'

In an instant, all my fears over him and Mia vanish. There's no way he would betray me. I can see his love in his eyes right now.

'Oh, Rob,' I whisper, grabbing his arm and dragging him into our bedroom. I shut the door behind me.

'What is it?' he asks, looking alarmed.

'I've just found a phone under her bed.'

'Eh?'

'*Mia*. A burner. Hidden in a boot. How suspicious is *that*?' I hiss. 'She has a second phone.'

Rob blinks, bewildered for a second. Then his expression hardens. 'Why were you snooping in her room?'

'I *had* to, Rob.' I grip his hand. 'Please, there are too many weird coincidences around her.' I take a deep breath. 'You remember that email I told you about? From Dad's second wife to Uncle Edgar, about a lie being justified? Well, Tommy, Rae and I went to see her — Harmony Moon — on Sunday. In her commune in Devon.'

'You did *what*?' Rob wrenches his hand out of mine and paces across the room. 'Why didn't you tell me?'

He turns and glares at me. And, in an instant, I'm flung back to the horror of my doubts and fears about him.

'Why didn't *you* tell *me* about Mia being here when I spoke to you last night?' I demand.

Silence for a moment, then Rob shakes his head. 'That's not the same thing. I didn't *lie* about Mia. You didn't mention her so there was no reason for me to.'

'*Bullshit*,' I snap. 'You *knew* I wouldn't like her being here.'

'Well, maybe *that's* why I didn't say anything,' he says furiously. 'Because I knew you'd get upset.'

'Well, maybe that's why I didn't tell you about going to see Harmony Moon.'

We stare at each other for a few moments, then Rob sighs and holds out his hand again. 'Let's not fight, Cas.'

I nod, squeezing his fingers. He draws me towards him and I tilt my face to his. His lips brush mine, then he pulls me into a hug. I lean against him again, my mind whirling.

'So tell me,' Rob whispers. 'What did Harmony Moon tell you yesterday that made you feel you had a right to invade Mia's privacy just now?'

I draw back and gaze into his dark, sorrowful eyes. 'It was more what she *didn't* say. And how she tried to focus us on Dad by saying he was an "evil parent".'

Rob frowns. 'What did she mean by that?'

'She was just saying it to divert our attention away from *her*,' I insist. 'She claimed she'd never heard of Mia and that the "justified lie" she mentioned in her email wasn't anything to do with Mia's claim. But when we asked, she wouldn't tell us what it *was* about.'

Rob folds his arms across his chest. 'I see,' he says icily.

'No, you don't.' I gulp. 'I think Harmony was lying. She clearly hates Dad... and has reasons of her own for wanting his money... I don't know, some sort of revenge. And of course she isn't going to confess to fraud and murder. She'd go to prison.'

Rob sighs. He sits down on our bed. 'Isn't it more likely that Harmony Moon is just really bitter at Nathaniel for ending their relationship and determined to paint him in the worst light possible to his children? Maybe slagging him off is her revenge.'

'Sure,' I say. 'But it's not an either/or. She can slag off Dad *and* still be prepared to lie and kill to get her hands on his money.'

'Okay.' Rob's tone is gentle now, almost conciliatory. I have the sudden feeling he's treating me like one of his more truculent teenage students. 'I get that she might want to do more than just mouth off about Nathaniel but surely the next step isn't an elaborate fraud and… and two murders? And why act in such an extreme way *now*, so many years after they broke up?' Rob shakes his head. 'You have to admit it sounds a bit far-fetched, Cas.'

'It's not just Harmony Moon and her stupid email,' I say, sitting down beside him on the bed. My heart thuds in my chest. I'm determined to try and make Rob see Mia the way I do. 'It's… there's all sorts of stuff that doesn't stack up. Like… well, to start with, there's the coincidence that Mia happens to find out she's Dad's daughter just in time to challenge the will.'

Rob frowns. 'Are you certain you're not just looking for evidence to fit your suspicions?'

I shake my head. 'Rae's got serious doubts about Mia too. She's looked and looked and she can't find her *anywhere* online. Surely you have to agree that having literally no social media presence *is* suspicious?' My voice rises. 'Not to mention hiding a second phone under your bed.'

Rob frowns. 'Have you considered that there might be a really straightforward explanation for both those things?'

'Like what?' I stare at him.

'While you've been on your wild goose chase,' he says quietly, 'looking for proof that Mia is a criminal con artist, Mia herself has been telling me more about her life before we met her. She really opened up last night.'

I wriggle uncomfortably on the bed. 'What did she say?'

'Do you remember me telling you how her mum had an abusive boyfriend? And Mia saw some of the violence when she was little?'

I nod.

'Well, it turns out Mia recently had an abusive boyfriend herself. Last night she told me that he turned nasty when she tried to end things, so she had to leave in the middle of the night – that's why she doesn't have many clothes and has been borrowing yours. She went into a shelter for a few weeks, before moving in with her friend Ellis. The people at the shelter advised her to cut all contact with the boyfriend, so she ditched her phone and archived her socials. Hence no social media.' He stares pointedly at me. 'That "burner" mobile you're so excited by must be the one she bought at the time, so she had some way of contacting people. She told me earlier that she's only recently gone back to her smartphone using a new number and that she's really wary about opening up a social media life again.'

'Oh.' I stare at him, taken aback. 'Why didn't Mia tell us any of that before?'

'Because those are difficult things to talk about,' Rob says, sounding more and more exasperated. 'You're a bloody therapist; you know how it goes. There's a lot of shame attached to coercive control.'

'I do *music* therapy,' I say. 'It's not the same thing.'

Rob shakes his head. 'The Cassie I knew until recently would be sympathetic to someone in Mia's position.'

'I *am*,' I protest. 'If it's the truth.'

'Jesus.' Rob gives a frustrated sigh. 'What Mia told me last night sounds a whole lot more plausible than some mad tale about faked DNA tests and burner phones. Don't you think?' He stands up. 'Look, I've got work to finish. I'll see you downstairs.'

I sit on the bed, my head spinning. As I listen to the pad of Rob's footsteps going down the stairs, my mind drifts the message Mia received on her burner phone a couple of hours ago.

All good, Alecto.

I do a search for the name.

> Alecto. One of the Erinyes or Furies in Greek and Roman myth, who had snakes for hair and blood dripping from their eyes. Representing a furious desire for revenge, Alecto's role is to punish the moral crimes of humans. Associated with battle and death.

I gasp, then reread, a cold, hard stone settling in my guts. It doesn't matter what Mia has told Rob; every instinct I have tells me that the use of this name by whoever sent the text to Mia isn't a coincidence. It's a clear sign that whoever they are is motivated by revenge – which definitely puts Uncle Edgar and Harmony Moon at the top of the list.

I might not be able to prove exactly who is behind Mia, but they're clearly prepared to go to any lengths to get their hands on Dad's inheritance – Zane and the DNA clinic nurse are already dead. I swallow hard, unable to quell the anxiety churning in my guts. Even though Rob and Iris don't directly inherit from Dad's will, they are surely in danger too, especially with Mia right here under our roof.

What I need now is proper evidence against her. All the small clues I've gathered so far, from the weird coincidences to the suspicious bits of behaviour, count for nothing when set against Mia's legally verified DNA test results. I'm almost certain now that the nurse in charge of that DNA test manipulated the findings, then was murdered to keep her quiet. Zane was killed too, for getting too close to the truth. But nobody other than me, Sav, Rae and Tommy believe either death was anything other than an accident.

It all comes down to Mia's DNA.

An idea sparks in my head. I need to get another test done. That will surely prove Mia isn't Dad's daughter, once and for all.

I just need a sample of her DNA and a place to test it.

TWENTY-ONE

I quickly realise there is no way I can legally submit Mia's DNA for testing without her permission. Well, there's an easy fix for that: I'll say it's *my* DNA. If it comes back confirming that Dad is my father, it will just look like I'm double-checking the paternity. But if it comes back saying the DNA is not a match, I'll be able to provide the results as an initial proof of Mia's treachery.

It turns out there are two types of DNA tests. Mia has already produced a legal DNA test. These have all sorts of restrictions and conditions attached and would be impossible for me to pull off, especially as I'm pretending the DNA is mine.

I decide to go for the less supervised "peace of mind" test, which can be done by post. They send out the kit; you supply the DNA. Thanks to the paternity test report from twenty years ago, I have access to Dad's DNA data and I quickly find a London-based service, where I can scan and upload those details. There's normally a turn-around of a week, so I pay extra to cut this down to forty-eight hours from receipt of DNA. If I return the kit the same day I receive it, the clinic should get it on Thursday and I'll be emailed the results on Saturday.

Those results won't hold any legal weight but should raise sufficient questions to force Mia to undertake a second test.

I hesitate before giving my address as the place to which the clinic should send the kit. Not only might Mia spot it landing on the doormat and be suspicious, but if Rob discovers what I'm planning he'll be furious.

I text Rae, explain what I'm doing and ask if I can use her address.

She responds immediately with a thumbs up and the message:

> Great idea, I should have thought of it straightaway.

So far, so good. Now all I need is a sample of Mia's DNA to pass off as my own.

I scroll quickly through the list of possible items that can be submitted: saliva and blood are top of the list, but I can't see a way to get hold of enough of either for a valid sample, without Mia being aware of it. It also turns out that though TV shows often suggest the opposite, lip marks around the rim of a drinking glass rarely leave enough DNA for a reliable test.

Hair is the next best option. But it must include the follicle. There was no hairbrush in Mia's room earlier, but she must have one somewhere.

Perhaps it's in her bag, which she usually has next to her.

I slip downstairs to the kitchen. Mia and Rob are now at opposite ends of the kitchen table; Iris sits in the middle. She's drawing a picture, her tongue peeking out from between her lips as she concentrates.

I glance across at Mia's faux leather tote bag on the chair beside her. It's zipped shut.

'Hey, tell me about your picture,' I ask, sitting down next to my daughter.

As Iris explains that the brown smudges on her paper are donkeys and that each one is going to have a different colour saddle, I look over at Rob. He is focused on his work, but I can tell the frustration he expressed earlier is still bubbling under the surface.

Mia, on the other hand, seems serene and entirely absorbed in her phone. She must sense me watching her, because she looks up and smiles. It's such an open, warm, gentle smile that, for a moment, I hesitate. Am I being paranoid to think this girl is capable of monumental fraud and involved in two cold-blooded murders?

I grit my teeth. These doubts are precisely why I need to take Mia's DNA and get another test done.

I keep my eyes on her bag. The only time she lets it out of her sight is when she goes to the loo after dinner. As soon as she's left the room, I glance around to check Rob isn't watching. His back is turned as he stacks the dishwasher. I scurry over. Holding my breath, I unzip the tote, then gently prise the opening apart.

Yes! The hairbrush is right there. And covered in Mia's blonde hair. Heart racing, I select several long strands. The clinic recommends seven as the ideal amount, but says five should be enough, so long as the follicles are attached. With trembling fingers, I carefully peel the chosen strands away from the brush and rezip the bag.

'What are you doing?' Rob's voice echoes across the kitchen.

'Nothing.' I spin around, shoving my hands behind my back. Rob is looking at me, curiously. 'I'm just going to check on Iris.'

I hurry out of the room, almost bumping into Mia in the hall. I swerve past her without speaking. Upstairs, I fetch a small envelope and place the hairs inside, then seal the envelope and shove it under a pair of socks in my underwear drawer.

Rob is still distant with me when we go to bed, giving me the briefest of goodnight kisses, before turning over and switching the light out immediately. He falls asleep within a couple of minutes, but I lie awake, my mind racing in the dark silence of the night.

–

At last morning arrives. No work today, thank goodness; I doubt I could focus on anything. Mia is still in her room when Rob leaves to drop Iris on his way to the office.

As soon as the front door closes, I grab the envelope containing her hair and head over to Rae's. I'm there when the DNA test kit arrives a couple of hours later. I open the envelope and tip the strands of hair into the pack – the instructions emphasise touching the sample as little as possible – then I seal it up and we take it to the post office. Now all we have to do is wait until Saturday for the results – it feels like an eternity away.

Rae is exultant, suggesting a celebratory lunch at the Wolseley, but I don't feel like celebrating. There is no good outcome from what we've just done. Either we're right and Mia is a sham, which will turn my family upside down and lead to a full investigation into Uncle Edgar and possibly Harmony Moon as well. Or we're wrong, in which case I'll have to bear the shame of my deceitfulness and find a way to repair things with Rob, while still worrying that there's a sexual attraction between him and Mia.

I take the noisy, rattling Northern line home. I'm braced to face Mia when I get in, but she isn't here. I stand in the doorway of her little bedroom and wrestle with myself. Has she had any more messages?

I crouch down and drag Mia's boot out from under the bed. I shove my hand inside. My fingers close on air. That second mobile is gone. Did Rob tell Mia I'd found it?

Feeling deeply troubled, I catch up with some paper-work, then collect Iris and lose myself in a game of "teacher", in which Iris conducts a class of simple maths and is alternately exacting and encouraging to me and the five dolls propped against the wall who make up the rest of the class.

Mia finally walks in at 5.30 p.m., followed just a minute later by Rob himself. I hover at one end of the hall as they chat by the door. Their conversation is innocuous enough, just pleasantries about their days... bad traffic... the weather, but I can't help but feel suspicious. Were they together? Just arriving separately for appearances' sake?

I catch sight of myself in the mirror on the wall opposite. Lank hair and a lined forehead frame panicky eyes. I touch my face, remembering how Uncle Edgar had commented on the similarity between my colouring and Mia's.

Well, we might both be fair-skinned and blonde, but that's where the similarities end. Mia is everything that I used to be, before age and the worry of work and parenting took over. Her face is still smooth, her hair still falls in soft waves and her body – I think with a jolt – is not that different from the body I had when Rob and I met.

It's not just the body, either. Right now, the extra pounds I've been carrying since having Iris are hidden under a shapeless jumper and wide-leg corduroy trousers. Mia, in contrast, is dressed in tight jeans and a cropped, celadon-coloured sweater that brings out the blue-green of her eyes.

She smiles shyly at me as she passes and goes into the kitchen. Rob follows her, his eyes fixed on his phone.

I put my hand on his arm as he reaches me. He looks up, distracted.

Rob has aged too, I think. There's a deep groove on his forehead and an ongoing weariness in his expression, neither of which were there when we met.

'Everything okay?' I ask.

He nods. 'Just school politics.' He indicates his phone. 'Bloody staff WhatsApp. I can't wait for half term.' He leans closer and kisses my cheek. 'How was your day?'

I almost tell him about the DNA test – but then I remember how cross and disappointed he sounded yesterday when I confided my suspicions about Mia.

'My day was okay,' I say, flatly. 'I'm glad you're home.'

Rob smiles and the years fall away in the light that shines from his eyes. I smile back, my spirits lifting instantly. After all, in all the time we've been together, Rob has never given me a single reason to suspect him of being unfaithful. He might not understand why I'm so wary of Mia, but surely I'm being ridiculously paranoid to imagine they are having an affair?

In the kitchen, Rob, Mia and Iris settle themselves at the table. Iris is drawing with her crayons, while Mia scrolls through her phone and Rob opens his laptop to make a start on tonight's marking. There's always more to do in the run-up to any holiday and, with half term coming next week, Rob is, I know, trying to get as much out of the way now as possible.

I scan the kitchen cupboards, trying to decide what to make for dinner. Over the past few weeks Mia has cooked a series of delicious vegan dishes and tonight I'm determined to produce something decent of my own.

'Can I help?' Mia asks softly, as I stand, gazing into the fridge and feeling distinctly uninspired.

'No, er, thanks,' I say.

Mia shrugs and returns to the kitchen table. I reach for a carton of tomato and basil sauce lurking behind the tin of baked beans. It's not very imaginative, but maybe I can tart up a basic pasta dish with a nice salad.

I focus on setting a pan of water to boil, then chopping some cucumber and spring onions.

Rob's laugh makes me look up.

My stomach hurtles into my mouth.

He has moved to the seat next to Mia, while Iris sits opposite. The crayons and laptop have made way for a pack of Go Fish cards. I frown. How on earth did I miss them deciding to play a game? And what on earth persuaded Rob to join in? He usually insists on getting his work finished before putting his laptop away.

The chopping knife rests in my hand as I watch my daughter clutching her cards, peering intently at the selection she's been dealt. Rob and Mia have their backs to me. I stare, transfixed, as Mia leans towards him, a lock of her wavy blonde hair brushing his shoulder. She's too close. There's something almost confidential in that tilt of her head, as if the two of them are sharing a secret. And then Mia sits back and gazes dreamily at his face. Jealousy sears through me as she leans towards him again, this time to pick a piece of fluff off his sleeve. Her fingers rest for a second on his arm, then trail delicately away.

It's simultaneously nothing, a momentary touch – and everything, a gesture both private and intimate.

My throat constricts. Only a lover would touch him like that.

I grab a saucepan off the rack and thump it down on the countertop.

Rob jumps in his seat and looks around, eyebrows raised.

'Sorry,' I say, through gritted teeth. 'It slipped.'

I catch Mia's eye. For a second I am sure I see the hard glint of amused contempt in her expression. Then it fades away into her more usual doe-eyed look of concern.

'Are you all right, Cassie?' she simpers.

'Fine, thanks.' I force a smile.

Rob clears his throat. 'I forgot to say earlier, but Jamie wants me to go for a drink after dinner.'

I nod, my mind still reeling. Jamie is Rob's younger brother and lives about ten minutes' drive north of here. I can't help but think that if Rob ever wanted anyone to cover or lie for him about *anything*, including an affair, he'd ask Jamie.

'I won't be late,' Rob goes on. 'If Jamie wants a big night he can do it with his mates at the weekend.'

I nod again and Rob turns back to the game.

I finish preparing our pasta and salad while Mia clears the table and Rob takes Iris to wash her hands. The three of them chatter as they eat, but the food tastes like dust in my mouth. I say I have a headache and sit there feeling sick. I snatch repeated glances at Mia and Rob. I'm not bloody imagining it. He is self-conscious around her tonight, while every move she makes is just one degree too intimate.

Something is happening between them.

After we've eaten – or, rather, after the others have eaten and I have pushed my pasta around my plate, Rob gets out his laptop and settles down at the end of the table to work again, while Mia gathers up the plates and gets Iris to help her carry everything over to the sink.

I sit watching Rob, half hoping that he will look up and see the anxiety on my face and somehow be able to say something that will, at a stroke, destroy my fears.

But Rob doesn't look up. For the next five minutes, his fingers fly over his keyboard as he finishes off his marking. At last, he heaves a tired sigh, packs the laptop away and announces he's leaving.

'Jamie's already in the pub,' he says, bending to kiss my cheek, then he picks up Iris and blows a raspberry on her neck.

As Iris giggles with delight, Rob sets her down, nods at Mia and disappears into the hall. I hurry after him, still hoping against hope that he will do or say something to set my mind at rest.

But he is distracted, trying to find his wallet, and hurries out of the house with just a cursory final glance. I lean against the front door, as Mia appears from the kitchen, a yawning Iris at her side. 'We're going to get ready for bed, then I've promised her three stories.'

'Lovely,' I say, trying to force a smile.

They head upstairs and I wander back into the kitchen, my head spinning. I've been such an idiot. It's clear to me from this evening that Mia is after Rob. She doesn't just want to take a portion of my inheritance; she wants to take over my life.

And in that moment, the realisation lands.

I'm certain that the DNA test I've sent off will prove she's a fake – and by inference, an accomplice to murder – but I can't wait until I get the results.

I can't have her in the house any longer.

An hour later she saunters downstairs and into the kitchen. I stand up, ready to go and say goodnight to Iris, but Mia airily informs me my daughter is already asleep.

'Oh,' I say. 'I see.'

'I'm actually going out now myself,' she says with a smile, flicking a wave of hair off her shoulder.

To meet my husband?

I can't help the thought that shoots painfully through my head. I clench my fists. 'Tell me, Mia, who's Alecto?'

Those sea-green eyes widen, clearly startled. 'What?'

We stare at each other for a moment. My guts twist and churn.

'I stumbled across your second phone,' I say. 'There was a message. *All good, Alecto.* I was just wondering what that was about.'

Annoyance flares in Mia's eyes. 'You *stumbled*?' she asks icily.

We stare at each other and I cross my arms, feeling defensive.

'I'm not going to apologise for being suspicious of someone who hides a burner phone under their bed,' I snap.

'Is that right?' Mia narrows her eyes. The usual sweet softness of her expression has hardened into something far more ferocious. 'Well, for your information, Alecto is just a nickname for my friend Alec.' She hesitates. 'He's another model. Someone I trust. That's why he has that number.'

I press my lips together. I'm still certain she's lying, but there's no point me challenging her any further. She's either going to deny the accusations or make up stories to explain them.

It doesn't matter what she says; I just don't trust her.

'I think it's time for you to move on, Mia,' I say evenly.

She blinks rapidly, her expression returning to wounded kitten mode. 'You... you mean *leave* here?'

I nod. Tears spring to her eyes. For a moment, I waver. Is this all really acting? Jesus, if it is then the woman deserves an Oscar. She's brilliant at it.

'I'm sorry to be brutal,' I say, guilt creeping through me in spite of my anger. 'But this was only ever meant to be a temporary arrangement.'

'Of course. And I've been looking and looking; there's just nothing available.' Mia puts her hand on her forehead. 'I... I don't understand what I've done wrong?'

I hesitate. There's no point getting into it with her. In a few days I'll have the test result on her hair that will, I'm sure, prove she is not Dad's daughter. Then she'll be forced to admit her lies. 'Do you have somewhere to go tonight?' I ask pointedly. 'I'm sorry that neither of the Carson company flats are available, but perhaps you could go back to stay with your friend... Ellis, is it? Just for a bit?'

'You want me to leave *right now*?' Mia looks shell-shocked. 'It's... this is so out of the blue. I thought you liked me being here? I get on so well with Iris. And Rob.'

'Oh, yes, I've noticed how well you get on with my husband.' The words are out of my mouth before I can stop them.

Mia recoils. 'Are you—?' She clasps her hand over her mouth. 'Cassie, I would *never*— You can't think—'

'Don't, please,' I interrupt, my throat tight with emotion. 'Just… please just pack up your things and go. I can pay for a hotel for tonight if you don't have—'

'This isn't fair, Cassie.' It's the angriest I've ever heard her. 'I haven't done anything wrong. I bet Rob doesn't even know you're doing this.'

I stare, stonily, back at her. She juts out her chin. 'I thought you were different,' she says, a savage bitterness now twisting through her anger. 'But whatever it is you've decided to believe to justify getting me out of your life, you should know that I got an email from Edgar earlier. I felt a bit awkward telling you; I know he wants to get everyone together at the weekend to announce it.'

'What are you talking about?'

'The verdict is through,' she says. 'The courts have legally accepted that I'm Nathaniel Carson's daughter. My claim to an equal share of his estate is upheld.'

And, with that, she slams her keys down on the kitchen counter and stalks out of the room. A few minutes later, she has gone.

TWENTY-TWO

I'm in bed and pretending to be asleep when Rob returns from his evening out with his brother. I've left Mia's door shut, so he can't yet know what I've done, unless of course Mia has already called and told him.

That thought keeps me awake long after Rob falls asleep, his breathing growing slow and shallow in the darkness of our room.

The next morning, everything's the usual rush. Rob makes no comment on Mia's non-appearance while we're having breakfast. I don't whether that means he assumes she's sleeping in – or whether he knows that I've kicked her out of the house. Either way, I don't mention her absence. Iris is around right now and I don't want to trigger a row in front of her. Plus, I'm scared, not just that Rob will be angry with me but that he really has fallen for Mia, and that his reaction to me sending her away will make that horribly, painfully clear.

Rob takes Iris to nursery, saying as he leaves that he's got a free afternoon so will do the pickup too. A few minutes after they've left, Uncle Edgar emails to invite us to a family lunch at his house on Saturday. This must be the meeting Mia mentioned. Rae is on the phone immediately, asking if I've seen the invite.

'Yes, and—' I start.

'There's a good chance the DNA test results on Mia will come through while everyone's at the lunch,' Rae says excitedly. 'Let's get together with Tommy and plan what we're going to say once we've exposed her.'

'What do you mean?'

'Come on, darling.' Rae tuts. 'It's not going to be enough for you to say, "Look, here's some DNA results that say they're mine, but which are actually Mia's that I passed off as mine."'

'No?'

'*No!* Think about it. Uncle Edgar's back will be against the wall. He'll probably make a big deal out of the fact that you did something actively illegal. And I can totally see him and Mia claiming you only *pretended* to use her DNA.'

I frown, feeling stupid that this hadn't occurred to me before. 'Okay,' I say. 'But even if we do get those reactions, surely all we have to do then is insist Mia does another DNA test – under supervised conditions, with us as witnesses – to clarify everything? Nobody could object to that. If Mia does, it'll look super suspicious.'

'Mmn,' Rae says with a doubtful sniff. 'It's not that simple.'

'What d'you mean?'

'I asked Uncle E. straight out and he admitted the courts have now accepted Mia is entitled to a share of Dad's estate.'

'I know,' I say. 'Mia told me.'

'Well, now *that's* been established, there'll be nothing preventing Mia from getting her hands on Dad's money as soon as probate comes through.'

'But surely if everyone accepts there's uncertainty over Mia's claim?'

'That gives us grounds, but we'll need to serve an injunction as soon as possible, to delay Mia acting on the court ruling until we've got more evidence against her.' She pauses. 'I'll draft an application this morning. Then I'll message Tommy and meet you both for lunch to go over it. Sound like a plan, darling?'

'Yes,' I say firmly.

A few hours later, I find myself in Soho Grind with Rae, waiting for Tommy to join us. Rae shows me the injunction application that she's composed. It's full of legalese and makes little sense to me, but Rae seems confident it will do the job.

'Of course, once the injunction is in place, we still have to wait for Mia to accept it and agree to another test.' She takes a swig of her skinny cappuccino, then sets it noisily down in its saucer.

'Surely she'll have to do that straightaway?'

Rae rolls her eyes. 'I wish, darling.'

'So… so what time frame are we talking about? Worst case?'

'A full legal challenge to Mia's court-ratified entitlement to an equal share of a multi-million-pound estate?' Rae shrugs. 'It could drag on for months.'

I sink back in my seat. I can't bear the thought of this nightmare hanging over us for such a long time. And what about Rob? Until now, I'd imagined that Saturday's DNA test results would allow our relationship to begin healing. But if Mia's identity isn't resolved, then maybe the tensions between us won't be resolved either.

Rae meanwhile is scanning her phone. 'Where the hell is Tommy?' she snaps. 'He was supposed to be here at one. It's so typical of him to be late.'

I gaze out of the window. It's 1.15 p.m., but the skies are darkening as if for a storm, a nearby streetlamp flickering on and off. Another quarter of an hour and I concede this really is late, even for Tommy. We message and voice note, then try calling him. His phone goes straight to voicemail.

'It's so rude,' Rae grumbles. 'He doesn't even bother to make up an excuse.'

I freeze, my thoughts flickering anxiously back to Zane and his sudden death. 'You don't think anything's happened to him, do you?'

'You mean from Mia or Edgar?' Rae stares at me, a look of alarm crossing her face. 'I guess it's possible they might already be targeting another sibling. It's in their interests to increase their share of the inheritance after all. But why go for Tommy before you and me? It's us who are actively investigating them.' She frowns. 'Did you say something to Mia about any of us being suspicious when you chucked her out?'

I wrinkle my nose. 'Not in so many words, but I did ask about "Alecto".' I frown. 'Anyway, Harmony Moon and Edgar already know we suspect Mia's a fake, so if they're all in league…' I trail off, gripped with worry over Tommy.

—

I'm still feeling anxious two hours later. Tommy didn't show up at Soho Grind. Nor has he messaged either me or Rae.

I arrive home to find the house strangely quiet. This does nothing to settle my nerves. I distinctly remember Rob saying he would pick up Iris earlier. Shouldn't they be back by now?

I take off my jacket and place it on the rack. I stare numbly at the empty peg beside it, where Mia's threadbare green coat spent much of the past few weeks. Feeling suddenly exhausted, I turn and trudge towards the kitchen.

To my surprise Rob is sitting at the table in the fading light. There's no sign of Iris. He stands up as I walk in, his eyes intense.

'What the hell have you done, Cassie?' he demands.

My insides seem to shrink. 'Where's Iris?' I ask.

'With your mum,' Rob says. 'I called her earlier. Asked her to pick Iris up and give her some tea. I'll go and collect her later.' He stares stonily at me.

'O-kay.' I walk over and stand in front of him. My heart thuds. 'Er, what's the matter?'

'You bloody well *know* what the matter is, Cas,' Rob snarls. 'I had Mia on the phone to me in tears earlier. She says you ordered her to move out *last night*. No warning. No reason.'

'I *do* have a reason, Rob, I—'

'Oh, what? That Mia and I are having an affair?' Rob asks, his voice dripping with sarcasm. 'How dare you think I would do that?'

'I'm not saying that you have. Not yet—' I stop, trying to work out how to explain my fears. 'But I've watched you together. I've seen it. The way she acts around you, touching your arm, leaning too close or springing away the second she senses me. It's… it's too intimate. And the way you get all self-conscious when she's around.'

'I *don't* get self-conscious!' Rob blurts out. 'I have no idea what you're talking about.'

'Please, Rob.' My voice breaks. 'Even if you haven't… acted on it just yet, you must see how she's behaving? She's flirting with you and—'

'That's just her manner,' Rob says. 'It doesn't mean anything.' He glares at me. 'I can't believe you didn't talk to me before you kicked her out. Jesus, you didn't even tell me this morning before I went to work.'

I look away.

Rob sighs. 'I have to say, Cas, that this is all reminding me of the time after Iris was born. You remember? How you got so... so dark and emotional about everything?'

I frown. 'That was the start of post-natal depression. Caused by hormones and lack of sleep. This is completely different.'

Rob shrugs as if there's no point arguing with me about it. 'Look, I promised Mia that I would speak to you. In fact, I suggested she might come round this evening so we can hash things out. But she said she was settled back with her friend Ellis and didn't want to upset you. I just don't get it, Cassie. How can you do this to her? She's your *sister*.'

'No.' I meet his gaze. 'She *isn't*. I'm certain of it. And in two days' time I'll be able to prove it.'

Rob frowns. 'What are you talking about?'

I take a deep breath and tell him about the DNA test on Mia's hair. 'It arrived at the clinic this morning and there's a forty-eight-hour turnaround.'

Rob stares at me in horror. 'You've passed Mia's DNA off as your own?' He clutches his forehead. 'Do you realise how wrong that is? It's not just unethical, it's *illegal*—'

'I *had* to, Rob.' I reach for his arm but he snatches it angrily away. 'Mia is dangerous. I think she's a fraud. And though she couldn't have killed Zane herself, I think she's working with the person who did.'

Rob gasps. 'This is *crazy*, Cassie. Mia's the sweetest kid and she's been through so much. She's got nobody else. And Iris adores her.'

'Don't bring Iris into this,' I snap.

I can see the disgust Rob's eyes, and it kills me. He thinks I'm being insecure, paranoid and unreasonable. And I don't know what to say to change his mind.

'Listen,' I say, my voice trembling. 'How about we agree to disagree until I get the result of the DNA test on Saturday. I'm *sure* that's going to prove Mia is a fraud, which will also mean she's almost certainly in league with a murderer. And that sweet personality of hers is a total fake.'

Rob shakes his head. 'And what will you do if the DNA test proves Mia is exactly who she says she is – your father's daughter and your own half-sister and nothing to do with fraud or murder?'

I take a deep breath. 'If the test result says Mia is genuine, then I'll be the first to invite her back to the house.' I hesitate, as the image of her picking that piece of fluff off Rob's sleeve leaps before my mind's eye. 'Though I think we should also try and help her find somewhere else to stay. For her own sake, as well as ours.'

'I guess that's something.' Rob sighs. 'Okay, Cas, I'll let her know.'

He turns back to his phone. For a moment I feel like I'm on the outside of his relationship with Mia. It hurts. I wander to the fridge and get out some cheese. I make us toasties, which we eat mostly in silence.

–

The next morning when I wake, I'm alone in our double bed. I wander downstairs to find that Rob has already left for work. He normally brings me a cup of tea when he leaves early. Feeling numb at the distance between us, I get Iris up and ready for nursery. As soon as I've dropped her, I message and call Tommy again.

There's no response, so I text Rae to see if he's been in touch with her. Rae answers twice, first in typically brisk fashion:

> No, heard nothing. Where the hell is he?

After a few more minutes, she sends another, more thoughtful, communication:

> Hard not to worry after Z. I'm stuck at work all day. Worth checking on T at home?

It's a good idea. Mum will know where he is.

I call her, but her phone goes straight to voicemail. I grimace. *Of course*. It's Friday, which means she'll be spending most of the day at Highbury Spa. I leave a message for her to call me when she picks up, then head off to Sound Heals for my regular back-to-back group music therapy sessions.

I'm distracted all morning, unable to focus properly on anything. Thankfully, Iris is on a playdate this afternoon so, as soon as my sessions are over, I catch the Tube to my childhood home in Highgate. Mum herself won't be there yet, but hopefully I'll find Tommy chilling in his room and my fears will be put to rest.

Leaving the warm stench of the Underground, I make my way through the crisp, cold streets. The temperature seems to have dropped since this morning and my fingers are frozen in my pockets. As I hurry along Mum's road, I have the sudden sense that someone is watching me. I spin around. Apart from a couple walking their dog on the opposite pavement the street is empty. A shiver slithers down my spine as I keep going to Mum's house, crunching quickly along the gravel drive and letting myself in with my key.

I call out for both Tommy and Mum but there's no response. Hoping my brother just has headphones on, I take off my coat and boots and hurry upstairs to investigate. There are four rooms on the first floor, including my parents' huge bedroom, and the two rooms which were mine and Tommy's growing up and which are now elegant spares. I keep going, up to the second floor. This is Tommy's domain now.

'Tommy?' I rap on his door. There's no reply, so I go inside.

A gigantic bed dominates the room: empty, unmade and scattered with clothes. A display tray of watches lies open on the carpet, next to the half-empty coffee mugs and yet more discarded clothes. I withdraw, glance quickly through the open door into the shower room, then move to the room opposite, which is effectively Tommy's gaming room.

It's also empty.

I gaze around. I haven't been in here for ages. Tommy has set up a long table against the far wall, set with two desktop computers and an array of cables, consoles and other gaming paraphernalia, as well as two plush high-backed leather chairs. I stare at the various keyboards and Xbox controllers and selection of headphones next to the PCs. Tommy's tablet and laptop are lying here too. No wonder Tommy has no desire to move out. He must love his life here, playing computer games and partying to his heart's content, though this entire set-up would surely be a massive "manchild" red flag for any girlfriend. Tommy's had a few over the years, but nobody has stuck and he's single right now. At least, there's certainly no one serious enough to tell me and Mum about.

I run my hand over the dusty surface of the long table, wondering vaguely if any of the clutter it contains might offer a clue as to Tommy's whereabouts. I sigh. Who am I kidding? If Tommy has noted down anything, it'll be online. I idly press the keyboard of one of the PCs. The password prompt flashes up. Of course it does. No way will Tommy have done an Uncle Edgar and written his passwords in a book.

I'm about to turn away and trudge back downstairs, when I notice the area to the right of the PC. Unlike everything else in Tommy's personal space, it is neat and ordered with no overflowing papers spilling out. Most strangely of all, it's topped with a book on gardening.

I frown. I remember this book. Mum gave it to Tommy for his birthday two years ago. Everyone laughed at the idea Tommy could ever be interested in pruning or planting anything, but Mum protested people can change and that, if Tommy tried working outside, he might actually enjoy it.

I know for a fact that this book was shoved straight onto Tommy's bookshelf and has been gathering dust there ever since. It seems strange that it's now out on his desk.

I lift the book. And gasp.

Underneath is a phone. Tommy's phone. I pick it up. It's on silent and almost out of battery. I can't open it, of course, but I can see my many missed calls and messages registered on the screen, as well as several from Rae and other names I don't recognise.

I set it down on the desk and stare at it.

Tommy never goes anywhere without his phone. I can't imagine he would have deliberately left it behind when going away for a few days. And there's something strange about the way it's been placed under the gardening book – not so obviously hidden as to suggest it's been put out of sight on purpose but sufficiently concealed to make it hard to spot.

My heart shrinks in my chest. Surely this discovery, more than anything, suggests that Tommy is in trouble.

TWENTY-THREE

The sound of the front door closing means Mum is home. Holding Tommy's phone in my hand, I fly down to the ground floor.

'Mum, do you know where Tommy is?' I ask.

She looks up, eyes wide with surprise. 'Cassie, hi,' she says, smoothing a strand of hair off her face. 'I wasn't expecting you.'

'But what about Tommy?' I urge. 'Have you seen him? He was supposed to meet me and Rae yesterday, but he didn't show up or answer when we messaged.'

I'm braced for her face to fill with anxiety. Instead, she smiles.

'Well, that certainly sounds like Tommy,' she says. 'Nothing's wrong. He's just away for a few days.'

'Did he *tell* you that himself?' I ask. 'In *person*?'

'Er, yes. We spoke yesterday morning, just before he left. He was off on a climbing trip.'

'How long for?'

'Three or four days, I think. He said he'd already mentioned it to you.'

I frown, trying to remember. Now I'm thinking about it, I do have a vague recollection of Tommy mentioning an upcoming climbing trip that afternoon we spent in the hospital with Savannah.

I take a deep breath. Perhaps I'm worrying over nothing. Though it's still seriously odd that he didn't take his phone. 'Did Tommy say where he was going?'

Mum shakes her head. 'And I didn't ask.' She gives a little shudder. 'The fewer details the better as far as I'm concerned.'

'What do you mean?'

'I'd rather not know if he's gone on one of those really steep, dangerous climbs.' Mum rolls her eyes. 'Anyway, you know what Tommy's like. Gets tetchy if you try and pin him down, just like Dad used to.' She hesitates. 'What's the matter? Why are you so upset?'

I hold up my brother's mobile. 'In what world would Tommy go away and leave his phone behind?'

Again, Mum's reaction is far more lowkey than I'm expecting. Instead of looking alarmed, she just shrugs. 'Oh, you know what he's like, especially when he's in a rush. I expect he just forgot the thing, and by the time he realised, it was too late to come back. You know they use sat phones when they're climbing half the time anyway.'

I sink down onto the bottom step of the stairs, struck by her lack of panic. Am I really making too much of this?

Mum pats my shoulder. 'Why are you so worried, love? It's not like Tommy's never gone away without giving us details before. He might be a bit... *directionless*, but he's not an idiot. I'm sure he'll be fine, with or without his phone.'

I nod, trying to find some relief in her calm logic.

Mum makes tea and I open up about my fears that Mia isn't who she claims to be. I focus on her behaviour, avoiding any mention of my suspicions that Uncle Edgar and Harmony Moon are involved or that Zane was deliberately killed. I also don't tell Mum about the DNA test on Mia's hair sample; there's no need to drag her into that.

Mum is as sceptical as Rob. 'But Mia seems such a sweet little thing,' she says. 'Kind eyes, too. And Iris adores her.'

I stare at the steam rising from my tea. 'Appearances can be deceptive,' I murmur. 'I'm fairly certain she's interested in Rob.'

'Oh, come on, Cassie.' Mum shuffles awkwardly in her chair. 'Even if that's true, Rob's not the type to cheat.' She pauses. 'I should know; I'm very familiar with the signs.'

I look up, struck by the sudden bitterness in her voice.

'Er, Mum, d'you remember what you said the other day? About not being "entirely shocked" to find out Dad had slept with Mia's mother?'

Mum raises her eyebrows. 'What are you asking?'

'Were there other women?' I lean forward in my chair, the horror of what I'm asking curling around me like a snake. 'A *lot* of women?'

Mum sighs. 'All I'll say is that there are certain signs when men are… are preoccupied. Drinks with "clients" on too many nights of the week… lots of vague "working late" stories. Getting flirty with other women when he thinks you're not looking.'

I stare at her, shocked. 'Rob doesn't do any of those things,' I say, 'but then he wouldn't have to; Mia is in the house with us.' I lay my hand on her arm and she looks up. 'I don't understand, Mum. You… you seemed so happy with Dad.'

'I *was*.' Mum rolls her eyes. 'Your generation sees things in such black-and-white terms. Dad was a wonderful man. He just had… poor impulse control.' She gives a wry

smile. 'So long as nothing he did threatened our family...
us...' She trails off.

'How could it not be a threat?' I demand, thinking
of how corrosive my suspicions about Mia and Rob have
already been.

Mum shrugs. 'I don't expect you to understand, Cassie;
my point is simply that if *I* can accept Mia is your father's
daughter, I think everyone else should be able to.'

I shake my head but say nothing. As we sit in silence,
a text from Rob pops up on my phone.

> Granny Annie is free this weekend, so am
> thinking of picking up Iris from her playdate
> and taking her off for a couple of
> dad-and-daughter days by the sea. Give
> you time to think, esp once those DNA
> results come in. Let's talk after that. Love
> you xx

I stare at the screen, feeling in my bones the rejection that
lies behind the message. Not to mention the assumption
that the DNA test on Mia's hair will prove me wrong
about her. I try to remind myself how close Rob is to
his mum, known to Iris as Granny Annie. An only son,
he tries to spend as much time as possible back in his
childhood home in Norfolk, and Gull Cottage is a magical
place for Iris to visit – set on the side of a cliff with
amazing views over the sea and what's effectively a private
beach in Gull Cove below. Of course, when the tide
comes in that beach can get cut off, so it's not without
its dangers, but Rob knows everything about the local
tides and would never let anything happen to Iris. In fact,

under the circumstances, perhaps Iris will be safer there, away from London… and Mia.

Unless – I think with a jolt – Rob's message is a cover and he's really taken Iris somewhere *with* Mia. No. I push the thought away. That would be too big a lie, involving both his mother and Iris – and far too easy for him to be caught out in.

As Mum's chatter drifts back to her earlier spa treatment and the perfect temperature of the hot stones her massage therapist used, I focus on the words at the heart of Rob's message.

Give you time to think.

What is he really saying there? That I should reflect on how crazy and paranoid I am being to see Mia as a threat to my family?

I grit my teeth. Tomorrow, Saturday, the test results will come through and, once I can prove Mia lied about her DNA, I'll be on my way to exposing her – and whoever she is working with – as a murderer.

I text Rob back to say if he wants to take Iris away over the weekend then I won't stand in his way, but I'd like her to be back for Monday and the start of half term.

I end up staying at Mum's until the light starts to fade from the day. I've half been hoping that Tommy will make a reappearance, but he doesn't. Despite Mum's dismissal of my worries, I still feel anxious about him leaving home without his phone. Though, I suppose it does explain why he didn't message Rae and me to explain he couldn't meet us yesterday – and why he isn't in touch now.

A sudden thought strikes me: if he doesn't have his phone or any of his other devices, will he even know about tomorrow's lunch at Uncle Edgar's?

As I set off home, Rae sends a text asking if I fancy a drink tonight. She ends:

> We can talk more about how we'll handle the big DNA reveal tomorrow! Martinis on me, darling xx

I hesitate, wondering how to respond. My half-sister might enjoy anticipating the confrontation to come, but the prospect of it makes me feel sick to my stomach. I text Rae to say I've been out all day and am going home for an early night, then shove my phone in my pocket and head for the Tube.

TWENTY-FOUR

The temperature has dropped several degrees by the time I arrive home. I fumble in my pocket for my keys, my fingers frozen. As I touch the cold metal, I have the same sensation as earlier outside Mum's house: someone is watching me.

I spin around, my heart racing. A tall, slim man is standing by the gate at the end of the path. His face is illuminated in the streetlamp. He's older than me, in his late forties I'd guess, with grey streaks in his hair and a lined, weatherbeaten face.

'Cassie?' His voice is warm. Low. As if he knows me.

I frown.

The man holds up his hands. He's dressed in a thick, padded coat with a beanie pulled low over his forehead. 'Don't you recognise me?' He smiles and a vague memory rises through the sea of the past.

I gasp. '*Adam?*'

He nods, his smile deepening. There it is, in that smile, the half-brother I knew all those years ago as a child. More than that, I see Dad in his colour of his eyes, Zane in the slope of his nose.

'I'm so sorry to barge in on you,' Adam says, walking up the path towards me. 'I wanted to speak to you after you finished work this morning, but—'

'Was that *you* following me earlier?'

He nods, looking awkward. 'I'm sorry if I scared you. I wanted to talk without your mum around.' He pauses. 'That's why Rae suggested going for a drink, a neutral space for us to meet.'

I let this fresh revelation settle. 'Rae knows you're here?'

'I'm staying with her,' Adam says. 'Truth is, I've been in touch with her a few times over the years. Nothing regular, but we've messaged and talked every now and then.'

My eyes widen as I remember the multiple times Rae has claimed no knowledge of our brother. 'Seriously? She never said a word.'

'Rae was still a teenager when I left and going through a rough time.' He sighs heavily. 'Leaving her was the hardest part of it. I couldn't cut all ties.' He hesitates. 'Maybe if I come inside I might explain? I think I can shed some light on the situation with Mia too.'

'You know about that?' I ask.

'Rae's filled me in,' he says grimly. 'I'm sure that DNA test you've done on Mia will prove she's a fraud.'

I hesitate. This Adam in front of me is a stranger and it would be crazy, under most circumstances, to invite a stranger into my home, especially when nobody else is there. But he is also my half-brother, who I remember as caring and kind from my childhood. Nothing about his manner or his words suggest he wants to do me harm. Plus, Rae clearly trusts him.

'Come on then.' I open the front door and Adam follows me inside. I turn on the light as Adam removes his coat and leather boots. I can't help but notice that his jeans and jumper are old and shabby and his boots covered in scuff marks.

He sees me noticing and grins. 'I guess I don't feature in the sartorially successful section of the family.'

I look away, my cheeks burning. 'Adam, I have so many questions...' I falter, unwinding my scarf. The craggy lines of his face and the calluses on his hands suggest a life lived outdoors involving very little self-care. And yet the kindness I remember still shines from his eyes. 'It's been... what? Twenty-three years?'

'Twenty-five,' Adam says. 'You were only eleven when I left. Man, I remember the last time I saw you like it was yesterday. We played catch. You, me and little Tommy, who I'm sure isn't so little anymore. Your mum made delicious hot chocolate. How is she, by the way, Donna?'

'Fine, she's fine.' Feeling dazed, I usher him into the kitchen and we sit at the table. Iris's latest drawings are scattered at one end.

Adam gazes at them. 'I hear you have a daughter?'

I nod. 'Iris. She's almost four. Do you have kids?'

He shakes his head. 'I imagine you're wondering why I'm back out of the blue?'

'Go on.'

'As soon as Rae told me she thought Zane had been murdered I started making plans to come back. I got here two days ago.' Those soft, kind eyes of his harden with anger. 'I had – I have – to help find out the truth.'

My head spins. 'You came home after all this time because of *Zane*?'

'He was my brother,' Adam says simply. 'An arrogant arsehole when we were younger, for sure. But still my brother.' His lip trembles. 'Apart from anything else, I want to be here for his funeral.'

'But…?' I stop, overwhelmed with the many questions rising in my brain. 'Where have you been living all this time?'

'Lots of places,' Adam says with a shrug. 'At first, I travelled, till the money ran out. I went through a bad phase. Lots of drugs. Fights. I ended up in Colombia, then Peru. I don't remember most of my late twenties, to be honest. It's a miracle I survived them.'

I swallow. 'How did you? Survive them, I mean?'

'A shelter run by a charity in Lima. They took me in. Cleaned me up. They had a clinic for local people. To help with vaccinations, infections… that kind of thing. Once I was on my feet they sponsored me to train as a doctor. I had the A levels for medical school already. They paid for my studies, on the proviso that once I was qualified I'd work there for ten years.' He pauses. 'I ended up staying for fifteen. In fact, I still go back there for a month every year. But I travel round too, a kind of mobile physician, getting help out to all the villages in the area.'

'Do you have a partner?' I ask.

'A few boyfriends but nothing permanent.' Adam sighs, suddenly looking older. 'It's hard to trust after what I went through.'

I frown. 'I… I get that Dad sending you away must have seemed extreme, but—'

'Uncle Edgar framed me,' Adam interrupts, sounding bitter.

I stare at him. '*What?*'

'I never stole a thing,' Adam goes on. 'I was working in the finance department for a few months. Dad liked us to get a feel for all the different areas of the business, so we'd spend a bit of time in each one.'

I nod, remembering Tommy's work at Carson Enterprises many years later running along similar lines.

'I came across an account containing money that had clearly just been siphoned off from other accounts. It looked suspicious, so I told Uncle Edgar. He acted really weird about it and told me he'd handle it.' Adam grimaces. 'Next thing I know, I'm being hauled into Dad's office and he's yelling at me for trying to steal from the company, pointing to the money that I told Edgar about, which is now in *my* account.' He shakes his head. 'Uncle Edgar must have moved the money once I realised he was trying to embezzle it.'

'Wait.' I frown. 'You're saying *Uncle Edgar* tried to steal from the company?'

'Absolutely.' Adam leans forward, intent on his tale. 'You must know the story of how their father left everything to Dad? And how resentful Edgar was because of it?'

I nod, slowly.

'So Edgar was already feeling out of sorts and let down and then, to rub salt in the wound, Dad puts him in charge of the unglamorous accounts department on a fixed salary, while Dad himself does the high-profile, high-status work of company chief, with annual bonuses on top.' Adam pauses. 'It makes sense Uncle Edgar would have wanted to take a chunk of the company's money. And it's easy to believe he thought he'd get away with it. He had the skills to shift the funds – it was all paper-based then – *and* to cover his tracks. He was just unlucky that I caught him before it got away with it. Then, realising the game was up, he turned the tables to made it look like *I'd* tried to steal hundreds of thousands of pounds.'

'No way,' I breathe, my heart thudding. All this time my one niggling doubt over Uncle Edgar was whether he'd really have the balls to plan a fraud and two murders.

I don't doubt that now.

Adam sinks back in his chair. 'To be honest, the worst thing was how easily Dad believed I was the thief.'

'Why d'you think that was?'

'I imagine because back then Dad and I rowed a lot. I was always having a go at Dad for being an evil capitalist, spouting the values of anarchy and socialism.' He sighs. 'I'm sure Dad saw it as a rebellion. That I wanted the money to fund some political cause. You know, a Robin Hood sort of thing.' He pauses. 'I think he probably thought me being gay was a rebellion too.'

I gaze at him. Was Dad really so out of touch?

Adam catches my eye. 'A lot of people thought like that then, that being gay was a lifestyle choice rather than part of your fundamental identity. Dad was never cruel about it, or unaccepting, but it was obvious he'd rather I was straight, like Zane.' He pauses. 'To be honest, out of the whole thing, what hurt the most was that Dad refused to believe my story. That he had totally bought into Uncle Edgar's loyal servant routine and trusted him over me.'

'Was that when he told you that he never wanted to see you again?'

Adam nods, his face wreathed in the pain of the memory. 'Looking back,' he says slowly, 'I don't think Dad meant it to be forever – after all, in the end no money was actually stolen – but he did use those words in his anger and I was too proud and too angry myself not to take them literally. I hated him for years for how he handled things. Probably more than I hated Edgar. That's why I wasn't even here for Dad's funeral.' Adam fixes me with sorrowful eyes.

I clear my throat. 'You said you were back here for Zane? And that you thought you could shed light on Mia…?'

Adam nods. 'I don't have any proof of course, but I'm certain you and Rae are right, that Uncle Edgar is behind the whole thing: the DNA fraud… Zane's murder…'

I shiver. 'Do you think *we're* safe?' I ask. 'I'm already a bit worried about Tommy. He went away yesterday and left his phone behind. I mean, it didn't *sound* suspicious. He told Mum he was going on a climbing break with a few friends, and it's like him to be a bit vague and unreliable, but even so…'

'You're concerned,' Adam finishes. 'I don't blame you. Look, there's nothing we can do for Tommy right now. And I admit, coming back my priority was Rae. But I don't want anything to happen to you either. Where's your husband? Rob, is it?'

'He's visiting his mum with our little girl for the weekend,' I explain, not wanting to go into detail about the way my marriage feels like it's hanging by a thread.

'Mia was staying with you, wasn't she?' I nod. Adam narrows his eyes. 'Has that caused any, er, problems?'

I look up, struck by his intuition. He meets my gaze and I can see from the sympathy in his expression that he fully appreciates the misery in mine. I nod, slowly.

'Rae says Mia's very attractive,' he says thoughtfully. 'Do you think she may be trying to drive a wedge between you and Rob? To make you think there's… something going on between them?'

'Rob says I'm crazy to even think it.' Tears bubble into my eyes. 'And to be honest, sometimes I wonder if he's right. I feel like I am going a bit mad, unsure what's real anymore.'

Adam nods. 'Classic divide and conquer. Edgar wants you preoccupied with your marriage, not investigating him.'

I look up. 'Do you know about the lunch he's organised at his house tomorrow?' I grimace. 'He says he wants to welcome Mia into the family now the court have approved her inheritance claim?'

'Yeah, Rae told me.'

'Well, we're expecting the results of Mia's DNA test while we're there.'

'I know.' Adam pauses. 'Rae wants me to turn up as a surprise guest, but I think I'm better off keeping my powder dry. For now, I'd rather no one apart from you and Rae know I'm back. Is that okay? Not to tell anyone about me just yet?'

I nod. Adam leans forward and reaches for my hand. There's a small, curved scar just above his right eye. 'That from a fight?' I ask, gesturing to it.

'Yes,' he says then adds, wryly, 'and it's not the only scar I carry.' He squeezes my hand. 'Hey, why don't you come and stay with me and Rae tonight? Safety in numbers.'

'I'll be okay here,' I say. 'But thanks.'

'Things are likely to get really heated once the DNA results come back and show Mia's a fraud,' Adam says thoughtfully. 'I don't think Edgar will go down without a fight.' He gets up to leave and I show him to the door. As he puts on his coat, he turns to me and asks, 'By the way, you did make sure the hair you sent off still had a follicle attached? You can only do a mitochondrial DNA test with cut hair. It's not enough for proper proof.'

I stare at him. 'How do you know that?'

'I'm a doctor, remember?' He moves closer and we hug. Adam smells of herbs and leather. It's a comforting scent. He draws back. 'Take care, Cas,' he says. 'Call Rae if you're worried about anything. Promise?'

I nod, suddenly overwhelmed with emotion. I want to tell Adam that I'm glad he's back and safe. But before I can find the words, he has stepped outside and shut the door behind him, leaving only a swirl of freezing cold air.

TWENTY-FIVE

It's a sunny Saturday morning, but the front of Uncle Edgar's red-brick home is overshadowed by the cluster of tall pine trees that line his drive. They sway in the breeze, casting a gloom over the north London house that matches my own mood. There are so many things on my mind. The upcoming DNA test results… my relationship with Rob… his with Mia… Adam's revelations about Uncle Edgar last night – not to mention Tommy's whereabouts.

I haven't talked to Mum about any of these except the last. Right now she is strolling up Uncle Edgar's drive beside me, attempting to reassure me that I'm being silly to worry about Tommy. As she keeps pointing out, it's typical of my brother not only to swan off at a moment's notice but also to be sufficiently disorganised to have left something important behind. Maybe I am overreacting, but after losing Zane so recently, I can't bear the thought of anything happening to Tommy.

Meanwhile, Rob is at his mother's house in Norfolk, clearly angry with me. And even though I'm certain that the DNA test results I'm expecting in the next hour or so will prove that I was right to suspect Mia of fraud, I'm also aware of the massive upset the revelation will cause.

As Mum raps the ornate brass knocker on the front door, these dark thoughts circle my head like a kettle of hawks.

Uncle Edgar welcomes us inside and I follow him and Mum through the hall in silence. I've never really thought about it before, but Edgar's house is considerably smaller than the one I grew up in, as well as further out from the centre of London, in Southgate. Did these differences in what each brother could afford rankle with my uncle more than I've realised? He's certainly made up for the relative modesty of the house by filling it with a load of costly furnishings. The living room is decorated like a gentleman's club from the nineteenth century, with dark-wood panel walls and a gilt-framed mirror over an ornate, Victorian fireplace in which a real fire crackles and burns.

Mia is curled up in one of the wing-backed leather armchairs staring into the flames. She turns her head as we walk in and looks warily up at us.

'No Tommy?' Uncle Edgar strides over to his drinks table, which is laden with bottles of wine and gin, as well as a decanter of whiskey, a jug of orange juice and several rows of sparkling crystal glasses.

'Tommy's away,' I say, watching him carefully for signs that he knows full well where my younger brother is – and what has happened to him.

'Ah, I see, I didn't get a reply from him about today,' Uncle Edgar says, sounding a little irritated.

'He left his phone behind.' I glance at Mia as I say this, but she is gazing into the fire again, her expression hidden.

The grandfather clock in the corner ticks into the silence, as Uncle Edgar pours Mum and I each a glass of Sancerre and refreshes Mia's orange juice.

Dauphin, Edgar's King Charles spaniel, is asleep on the armchair opposite Mia's, close to the warmth of the fire, so Mum and I sit at either end of the large chintz sofa opposite.

'This is very nice, Edgar,' Mum says politely, indicating the polished wood table where dishes of cold chicken, poached salmon and rice salad have been laid out. A stack of porcelain plates stands at one end. I count six as well as the same number of ornate silver cutlery sets.

Uncle Edgar gives a self-congratulatory nod. 'Thank you, Donna.'

I stare at him, remembering everything Adam revealed last night. I've always seen my uncle as a small personality, pompous and pinched – a weasel lurking in the leonine shadow of my father.

But today he seems more like a snake: secretive, poisonous and deadly.

The doorbell buzzes insistently and Uncle Edgar disappears into the hall. A second later Rae strolls into the living room. She scowls at Mia, air kisses Mum, then seats herself beside me on the sofa.

'I hear you had a visitor last night?' she whispers.

I nod, wondering how to ask her why she never said anything to me about being in touch with Adam over all these years.

Before I can speak, Rae is leaning close again. 'Any news, darling?' she hisses, prodding at my phone.

She means the DNA results.

'Not yet,' I whisper back.

Another buzz at the front door.

'Who else is coming for lunch?' Mum's enquiry brings me back to the present moment.

'I'm not expecting anyone else unless...' Uncle Edgar frowns, glancing at the Rolex he inherited from Dad. 'Perhaps that's Tommy after all.'

'Actually—' Mia starts.

But Uncle Edgar has already trotted out of the room. The sound of low voices drifts towards us from the front door, then Edgar reappears. 'Looks like we'll be six after all,' he announces.

My jaw drops, as Rob materialises in the doorway.

'What are you doing here?' The words fly out of my mouth like an accusation. Rob glances at Mia, who beams back at him. My stomach flips over.

'I'm here because Mia asked,' Rob says, turning back to me.

The atmosphere in the room tenses.

I can feel both Rae and Mum staring at me and feel sure my shock is written all over my face.

'And you're most welcome, Rob,' says Uncle Edgar hastily. 'I'm intending this to be an informal buffet, a chance to welcome Mia to the family.'

'Great,' says Rob, sounding awkward.

Mia gives a quick, self-conscious smile. It strikes me that there's an unusually jittery quality about her today, as if she's nervous about something. Is that because of the lies she's telling? Or is it because she's aware that inviting Rob here as *her* plus one is such a slap in the face for me?

I stare at her. She's gazing into the fire again, ignoring all of us. She's dressed differently than normal too, I think, in a loose-fitting mini dress and thick black tights. No skin on display for once.

As Edgar pours Rae a gin and tonic, I hurry over to Rob.

'Why didn't you tell me you'd be here?' I mutter.

'Because after how you've acted over Mia, I knew you'd be angry if I showed up here to support her.' He gazes sorrowfully at me. 'Mia doesn't have anyone else in her corner so when she asked me, I felt I couldn't say no.'

I think back to Adam's question last night. *Do you think she may be trying to drive a wedge between you and Rob?*

'Right,' I say. 'Where's Iris?'

'Still with my mum in Gull Cottage,' Rob says. 'I drove back this morning.' He looks at me hopefully, lowering his voice. 'I know these results of yours will be through soon. I didn't mention them to Mia when she called and asked me to be here.'

I look into his eyes. There's real care and concern in his expression. For the first time in days, I doubt all my fears over him and Mia. Surely he couldn't be carrying on with her and still look at me with such tenderness?

'Oh, Rob.' My voice breaks.

'I'm actually thinking that it would be nice for Iris to stay at Granny Annie's for the whole of half term,' he says hesitantly. 'Perhaps once you've got the reassurance you need, you might come back there with me?'

I press my lips together, not trusting myself to speak.

Uncle Edgar appears with a tray of canapes. He offers them round, then shoos Dauphin off the second armchair and sits down. Meanwhile, Rob fetches one of the chairs from around the table and plants himself beside Mum at the far end of the sofa. He declines a drink, but refills my glass, which, in all the stress, I appear to have drunk in about five minutes flat.

I take a sip and check the time. It's almost one p.m. Soon, I should be able to expose Mia and, hopefully, start the process that will lead to unmasking Zane's killer. I look at Uncle Edgar again. He is gazing awkwardly at his guests, offering clumsy and overformal titbits of small talk and generally appearing tense and on edge.

Is that because he knows about the test results I'm about to receive? Or is it just his social anxiety? This dry-as-dust party is typical of the social gatherings he occasionally hosts. Unlike Dad, he is no master of ceremonies. Even when he's surrounded by family like this, the more people he has to deal with the less relaxed he becomes.

The canapes do another round, then Uncle Edgar urges us to fill our plates from the buffet in the corner. He takes my seat next to Rae on the sofa, leaving me forced to perch on the armchair opposite Mia. She has barely said a word to any of us and is careful not to catch my eye now, her legs folded under her as she picks listlessly at some rice salad.

I fix my gaze on the glass-fronted cabinet behind her, where Uncle Edgar's antique coin collection is on display.

Across the room, Mum and Rob are talking about Iris – with Mum avoiding any enquiry into why I didn't know my husband would be here this morning. Meanwhile Uncle Edgar and Rae are also chatting, though their voices are so low I can't hear what they're saying.

I check my phone again. Still no sign of the DNA results. Surely they are overdue now?

My heart lodges in my throat as Uncle Edgar clears our lunch plates, then brings us slices of almond cake and coffee. Mum, as usual, oohs and aahs over Edgar's antique Wedgwood coffee cups. And Uncle Edgar, as usual, tells the rather boring story of how he found the set by chance, during a driving holiday in the Lake District about ten million years ago.

Once the story is told and most of the cake is eaten, Uncle Edgar clears his throat and we all look at him expectantly.

'The first thing I feel I must do is acknowledge the absence of dear Zane, who should of course have been here with us today.' He looks over at Rae.

I feel a stab of guilt. I've been so fixated on other things I hadn't thought much about Zane – or whether being at a family gathering like this without him might be hard for his sister.

Rae presses her lips together, her eyes glistening.

'I spoke to Savannah this morning,' Uncle Edgar continues. I look up. 'No sign of baby yet, but she's doing well.'

'Oh, that's good to hear,' Mum murmurs.

Uncle Edgar gives a self-conscious cough. 'Now, as I have already informed everyone,' he says, 'I had hoped that today would offer a chance to welcome Mia to the family.' He pauses, presumably for us all to offer some sort of verbal welcome.

Silence fills the room.

'Anyhoo,' Uncle Edgar goes on, 'those who perhaps aren't already aware should know that Mia's legal application to be included as one of Nathaniel's heirs has been upheld.'

Across the room, Rae stiffens, the soft sad quality vanishing from her eyes. She raises her eyebrows at me, clearly asking if the results of our DNA test have come through yet.

I glance quickly at my phone again, then shake my head.

'I am certain,' Uncle Edgar goes on, 'that welcoming Mia into the family is what my brother would have wanted. His will states that he wished his estate to be divided between each and every one of his children, except where specified by name. And the only name excluded was Adam's.'

'Such bullshit,' mutters Rae beside me.

Uncle Edgar frowns in her direction. 'What was that, Rae?'

She sits forward and I suddenly realise what she's about to do.

'No, Rae!' I gasp. She mustn't say what we've done *before* the results come through.

But it's too late.

Rae launches into our tale of suspicion and anxiety. Rob knows most of it already, of course, and keeps his gaze on the carpet, but I watch Uncle Edgar's and Mum's jaws drop as Rae explains how I took strands of Mia's hair and passed them off as my own.

Mia herself doesn't seem surprised by the news, just stares sullenly at me. Perhaps Rob did tell her about that, despite what he said earlier.

'So you see,' Rae finishes defiantly, 'any second now we'll have proof that Mia isn't who she says she is.'

An awkward silence descends on the room.

'I… I have to say I'm shocked that you two would do this,' Mum murmurs quietly.

'I'm more than shocked,' adds Edgar, drawing himself up. 'I'm *appalled*.' He glares at Rae. 'Especially at *you*, Rae. As a lawyer, you must know that the taking and testing of DNA without consent is illegal? And that a peace of mind test carries no legal weight whatsoever?'

'We just want the results to prompt a fresh test,' Rae says smoothly. 'I'm sure Mia won't mind agreeing to that?'

All eyes turn to Mia, who scowls back. Rob shakes his head in disgust. My heart sinks. This is so *not* how I wanted to expose Mia. Rae is making it too much of a public humiliation.

'As I said, the results should be through any second.' Rae turns to me, a fresh urgency in her gaze. 'Any news, Cassie, darling?'

I check my phone again. A new email has arrived. It's from the clinic. My throat tightens and I sit bolt upright. 'Yes,' I say. 'It's here.'

I can feel everyone's eyes on me as I look at the email. The report is an attachment. My fingers are trembling as I open it. At first all I see is a blur of numbers.

I scan to the bottom. That's where the result of the DNA test into Dad being Mia's father will be.

probability of paternity = 99.9998%

No, that can't be right. I blink, trying to take in what I'm looking at.

'What is it?' Rae snatches the phone off me. She reads the results, her mouth gaping.

'What's happening?' Mum asks.

Mia unfurls herself from the armchair like a cat. Her blonde hair glints in the firelight. Suddenly, all her confidence is back.

'The results confirm that I am Nathaniel Carson's biological child, don't they?' she demands.

I nod. Then look at Rob. He is shaking his head.

I close my eyes. How can this have happened?

Have I been wrong about everything?

TWENTY-SIX

Time seems to slow down. Beside me, Mum's hand is over her mouth, eyes wide with disbelief, while Rae is still transfixed by the email that confirms Mia's hair sample has matched with Dad's DNA.

I gaze around the room. Emotions are huge on every face: Rob is watching me with a mix of shock and concern, while Uncle Edgar looks scandalised, his mouth gaping. I glance at Mia. For a second, I'm sure I see triumph flaring in her eyes, but almost instantly this subsides into stony and resentful anger.

I shrink back, wishing the sofa would swallow me up. 'I… I'm sorry,' I stammer. 'I really thought…'

'Don't apologise, for goodness' sake.' Rae shoves my phone back at me and rises to her feet, hands on her hips. 'It's obvious what has happened. The sample must have been tampered with.'

'The sample that Cassie stole and put in a sealed envelope until you both took it to the post office?' Rob's voice is withering. 'I don't see who could have tampered with it.'

Rae turns on me with an accusing look. 'You *told* him?'

'Only afterwards,' I explain. 'I wanted him to understand.'

215

'Oh, I understand.' Rob's voice rises. 'You're consumed with nonsensical suspicions and poor Mia has to—'

'No,' I protest. 'It isn't like that.'

'Please don't be cross with Cassie.' Mia jumps up, wringing her hands. Every trace of both anger and triumph have vanished from her face. 'She's lost her dad and her brother; it's been a really difficult time and it's no wonder she wasn't sure about me. I wouldn't have been either.'

Every face turns towards her. My heart sinks. This is the Mia that Rob sees: soft and kind and loyal and brave. I'm sure there is more to her than that, but perhaps – oh, God, how can I have been wrong about this? – perhaps it doesn't actually amount to fraud.

'Oh, very good, darling.' Rae begins a slow hand clap. 'Fantastic performance. Where did you train? RADA?'

Mia's lip wobbles.

'For God's sake, Rae,' Rob begins angrily.

'I do wish everyone would calm down,' Uncle Edgar says, helplessly. He gestures with his hands for those standing to sit again.

'No way will I calm down!' Rae gesticulates wildly. 'I don't care how many DNA tests you find a way out of, Mia, I think your whole story is a massive con and I'm going to prove it.' She turns to me. 'Forward me those results, Cassie. Now!'

I frown. 'Rae—'

'*Now!*'

I do as she says, as Rae storms across the room. She stops in the doorway, her Strathberry dangling from her hand, and gives a theatrical toss of the head. 'Goodbye, all!' She glances contemptuously in Uncle Edgar's direction.

'And thanks so much for a lovely lunch, *dear* uncle.' She stalks out.

Silence falls. A hand on my arm. I glance over. Mum is gazing at me with a worried expression on her face. 'Are you all right, Cas? This is just... I, er... I had no idea you felt so strongly about Mia that you'd go to such lengths...' She trails off.

I can see in her eyes that she thinks, as Rob does, that my behaviour is dangerously paranoid and obsessive. I'm taken straight back to the terrible first few weeks after Iris's birth, when I couldn't seem to claw my way out of the deepest darkness I've ever felt and my calm, caring mother joined forces with my practical, loving husband to insist I talked to a doctor.

Of course, they were right to do so. But that was then and this is different.

Though it's obvious I'm not going to be able to convince either of them that I'm not spiralling down into anxiety and depression again.

'I'm fine, Mum,' I murmur.

She frowns, clearly unconvinced.

I look away. If Mia *isn't* a con conjured up by Uncle Edgar and Harmony Moon, how do I make sense of the burner phone and the "Alecto" text and the way she's got my husband on her side? Are they all simply coincidences? And, if Mia is genuine, then does that mean that Zane's death was an accident after all? And the fact that the nurse from the first DNA clinic also died in an unexplained hit-and-run just an unhappy quirk of fate?

Every instinct I have tells me that I've been right to suspect Mia. And yet how do I square that with not one but, now, two DNA results that claim the opposite?

'Cassie?'

I turn. Rob is standing in front of me, that expression of deep concern still on his face. Across the room, Mum and Uncle Edgar are talking in low voices. Mia is nowhere to be seen.

My world shrinks to the two of us. 'Oh, Rob.' My voice cracks.

'Come here.' He pulls me towards him in a hug, rubbing my back. 'I know this is tough but, honestly, what did you think would happen?'

I sink into him. 'I was certain the DNA would prove—' I break off. 'I'm sorry... this is all such a mess.'

'Hey.' Rob pulls back, holding me by my shoulders. 'Mia's right, it's been a really difficult time.' He hesitates. 'Look, I don't think she's going to move straight back in, but if the two of you make up, I'm sure she'll come round soon enough.'

Make up? Move back in?

'Do you really want her to live with us again?' I stare at him.

Rob frowns. 'Not permanently, *obviously*. You were right that we need to help her move on. But we should let her stay until she gets back on her feet. We promised her that weeks ago, remember? When her flatshare fell through.'

I bite my lip.

'Helping Mia is the right thing to do,' Rob insists. 'Once she gets her share of your dad's money, she'll be able to afford whatever she wants and—'

'No.' I step back. I glance across the room. Mum and Edgar are still talking, taking no notice of us. Mia is still absent from the room.

'What do you mean "no"?' Rob asks.

'I don't want Mia back in our house,' I say. 'I… I just don't trust her.'

'But you have the proof now that she's exactly who she says she is!' Rob glares at me, his expression a mix of confusion and exasperation. 'Is this about her and me? Because I've already told you there's *nothing* going on.' He pauses. 'Come *on*, Cassie, this isn't like you.'

'Isn't it?' I look miserably at him. 'Why don't you believe me when I say there's something off about her?'

Rob's eyes widen in bewilderment. 'Are you serious?'

I look down. The rug at my feet has an old-fashioned border, woven with strands of red and gold. Several of the red strands have come loose, creating a break in the pattern.

'Where is Mia, anyway?' I mumble.

'She's just gone to the bathroom,' Rob says, flatly. 'Jesus, Cassie. If you really don't want her with us, then…' He trails off.

I stare at him, sullenly.

'Okay, then,' Rob says quietly, his tone suddenly more distant. 'I'm going to give Mia a lift to Ellis's flat. That's where she's staying.'

'What about after that?' I can hear the need in my voice.

'Er, well, like I said, I think it'll be great for Iris to spend the week at Gull Cottage. There's the wood for her to play in and… and the beach.' Rob hesitates. 'Cassie, why don't you come back there with me? Sound Heals is closed for half term, so you don't have clients. Maybe the break will… you know, help.'

He means help me stop being obsessive and paranoid about Mia.

I pull away. 'I… I need a bit of time by myself first,' I say numbly.

No way can I spend the next few days with Rob and his mum hovering over me like I'm a fragile piece of porcelain. I need to get my head sorted. Decide once and for all whether to accept Mia as she is or try and work out how on earth she managed to manipulate that DNA test on her hair.

Rob frowns. 'Are you sure?'

I peer up at him, soaking up the love that radiates through the frustration in his eyes. Perhaps he really hasn't been romantically seduced by Mia, but he still trusts everything she tells him. And as long as he does that, there is going to be a chasm between us.

'Do you really not see anything odd about Mia? The way she behaves around you?' I persist.

Rob sighs. 'Honestly, Cas, the only one who is behaving oddly is *you*.'

I take a step away from him, my heart hardening.

'Like I say, I need some time alone.'

Rob opens his mouth to speak again, but just then Mia appears beside us, now wearing her threadbare green coat. She glances at Rob, ignoring me.

'Are you still okay to give me a lift back to Ellis's?' she asks.

Rob nods. I take another step back, a dull weight settling in my guts.

Pointedly ignoring me, Mia thanks Uncle Edgar for including her in the lunch, then turns and leaves the room. Rob kisses my cheek and whispers he loves me, then follows. I stare after them. It feels like my entire world is collapsing.

'What a debacle!' Uncle Edgar's haughty voice cuts through my thoughts. 'You and Rae have certainly made a mess of things, Cassie.'

I hang my head.

'Cassie, why don't you come home with me?' Mum sounds worried.

I shake my head. If I don't want Rob fussing over me, I certainly don't need Mum doing so.

'What were you thinking, faking a DNA test?' Uncle Edgar is brimming with outrage and holding it in with some difficulty.

'Edgar.' Mum's voice is soft, but it sounds a warning note. As if I'm too delicate to be challenged.

Suddenly I can't bear to be around them.

'I'm going to leave,' I say, not making eye contact. 'I'll make my own way home. I'm… I'm sorry for all the fuss, Uncle Edgar.'

He starts replying, but I am already hurrying out of the room.

TWENTY-SEVEN

I push my worries about my relationship with Rob to the back of my mind and spend the rest of Saturday trying make sense of the DNA test results on Mia's hair sample. How is it possible that they appear to prove she is exactly who she says?

I call Rae, who remains completely convinced that the results are wrong – and part of a far larger conspiracy. She insists that Edgar must have found a way to get to the DNA clinic we used and tamper with the sample we sent. I point out, again, how unlikely it is that our uncle could have even known what we were doing, let alone manipulated the DNA sample in the time available, but Rae doesn't want to hear it.

'Adam thinks something is off too,' she says.

Not wanting to argue, I move on to the other thing that's on my mind.

'Talking of Adam, why didn't you tell me you've been in touch with him this whole time?' I demand. 'I asked you lots of times if you'd heard from him. Why did you lie?'

Silence on the other end of the line. Then Rae clears her throat. 'I promised Adam I'd keep him a secret. I felt bad not telling you… everyone… we were in touch, but it was what he wanted. It wasn't like we were talking on a regular basis and I didn't actually see him in the flesh until he turned up earlier this week.' She pauses. 'I'm really sorry, Cassie, you're the last person I wanted to lie to.'

A few hours after our call, Rae sends a text:

> Adam has gone to Cambridge to stay with a scientist friend and get him to check out ALL the DNA results. There must be something in them that doesn't add up.

Clearly neither of them is going to stop insisting that Mia is a fraud.

Part of me wishes I had their conviction, instead of the doubts and fears that gnaw endlessly away at me.

I sit alone in the kitchen, wishing Tommy was here. Mum reassures me again that he's simply off with his mates for a few days, so I'm trying not to worry. But it's unsettling for so much family drama to be unfolding in his absence.

As night falls outside, I video call Iris, who appears to be having a great time with Granny Annie. Rob comes on and is so sweet and concerned for me, I almost wish I was there with them. But, in my heart, I know I need to be on my own like I told him, trying to make sense of everything.

'We're going to find a way through this,' Rob says confidently. 'But – and please don't take this the wrong way – maybe you should talk to someone? It really helped when… after Iris, didn't it?'

Yes, I think. *But that was when I was grappling with post-natal depression. Can't you see this isn't the same?*

'I don't see how talking to someone would help,' I say.

'I get that, but...' He sighs. 'But maybe it would be good to try and work out why you've been so... why you see so much bad in Mia, when the rest of us just see good.'

Not all of the rest of us, I think, reflecting grimly on Rae and Adam's continuing insistence that Mia is a fraud.

We ring off with mutual 'I love you's, but everything left unresolved.

I eat a slice of toast at the kitchen table, my mind running over and over everything that has happened since Mia walked into our lives. So many secrets unearthed and lies revealed. Members of my own family accusing each other of the worst possible crimes. I don't feel I can truly be sure of anyone anymore.

Night falls while I'm sitting here. The weather is milder than it has been, but the temperature still drops when it's dark. I realise I'm freezing and put the heating on. It doesn't help ease the chill deep in my bones.

I drag myself upstairs just after eleven p.m. As I'm about to undress, my phone rings – a withheld number. It seems really late for a call, so I ignore it. If something was wrong with Iris, it would be Rob or his mum on the line. And if it's important, whoever is calling me will leave a message.

But they don't. Instead, the phone rings again imme-diately.

I pick it up. 'Hello?' I say cautiously.

'Cassie?'

It's Tommy. My heart swells with relief at the sound of his voice. 'Are you all right?' I ask. 'Why didn't you tell me where you were—?'

'I told Mum,' Tommy interrupts. 'And I was going to call you, but I forgot my mobile and didn't realise till it was too late to come back. I bought a basic phone from a service station earlier so that…' He pauses. 'Listen, Cas, I've been on a climbing trip.'

'I know. Mum said. Why—?'

'We've been all over but today we went to this spot in Devon and I kept thinking about our talk with Harmony Moon the other day, so after dinner I went to see her again.' He pauses. 'I had this hunch… and I knew that if I just explained why it mattered so much, I'd get her to talk to me.'

'Why didn't you call before and say any of this to me?' I demand. 'You could have borrowed a phone, couldn't you?'

'I didn't have your number – not until I got it off Harmony Moon. You gave it to her, remember? Anyway, like I say, it was just a hunch,' Tommy replies. 'I didn't want to talk about it until I was certain. Now I am.'

I frown. *Certain about what?* 'Listen, Tommy, I got the results of the new DNA test and—'

'Mia is really Dad's daughter,' he says. 'Yeah, I know.'

'You do?'

Tommy blows out his breath. 'Yeah,' he says. 'At least I figured she must be. It took *hours*, but I finally got the truth out of Harmony Moon just now.'

'The truth?'

'About that email she sent Edgar. It's nothing to do with Mia. It's about *Adam*. And what's more he's back in the country, which—'

'I know, Tommy,' I interrupt. 'I've seen him, but—?'

'*Seen* him? *Shit*, Cas, are you okay?'

'Yes.' I frown. 'Why wouldn't I be?'

'Because Harmony Moon says that all that stuff about Adam stealing from the company and betraying Dad was *bollocks*.'

'I know, Adam told me the same thing,' I say. 'He says that Uncle Edgar set him up.'

'Yeah, that's right.' Tommy pauses. 'But it's not the *whole* truth.'

'What are you talking about?'

'Why don't I let Harmony Moon tell you herself.' Tommy lets out a shaky breath.

'She's there with you?'

'No, but I recorded what she said. I'm sending it to you now.'

A moment later I open the recording. The sound of Harmony Moon's slightly resentful voice fills my ears.

'*Edgar did frame Adam,*' she says. '*But only because Zane made him.*'

Zane? I sink onto my bed.

'*What did Zane do?*' Tommy asks her.

'*He found something out… about me and Edgar.*' Harmony Moon's recorded voice swells with defiant embarrassment. '*We had an affair – a long affair – while I was married to Nathaniel and afterwards too.*'

I gasp.

'*Zane said nothing when he found out, but years later…*' She trails off.

'*What happened?*' Tommy's voice is full of urgency. I can just imagine him leaning forward, intent on Harmony Moon's face.

'*Adam spotted a bit of dodgy accounting in the company books and took it to Edgar,*' Harmony Moon says at last. '*Edgar quickly realised the culprit was Zane. He confronted him, insisting he was going to tell Nathaniel.*' She heaves a sigh. '*But Zane turned the tables. He blackmailed Edgar into making Adam look responsible for the attempted theft. He threatened to tell Nathaniel about our affair if Edgar didn't do as he said.*'

The recording ends abruptly and I resume my call to Tommy.

'I can't believe it,' I say before he can speak.

'I know, right?' Tommy says. 'But Harmony Moon wasn't lying, I'm certain. And if you think about it, what she says makes sense. Zane always had a mean streak. Look how horrible Mum says he was to her when they first met. And as for Uncle Edgar, he'd have done anything to avoid Dad finding out about him and Harmony Moon. Plus he was in charge of the company accounts. It would have been easy for him to frame Adam.'

'Why hasn't Harmony Moon told anyone before?' I ask.

'To protect Uncle Edgar. He fiddled the books to make an innocent man look guilty of a crime that lost him his entire family. That's sackable. Probably jailable.' Tommy hesitates. 'She only told Adam because he threatened to kill Edgar.'

'*What?*' I frown. That doesn't sound like the Adam I met last night.

'Yeah, apparently he turned up at her door, ranting and raving that Uncle Edgar ruined his relationship with Dad and now Dad was dead and they'd never be reconciled. He was totally blaming Edgar, of course, but Harmony Moon made it clear that Zane is the person he should really be furious at.'

I shake my head. 'Adam didn't sound anywhere near that angry when I spoke to him. How long ago did he talk to Harmony Moon?'

'Months. It was just after Dad died,' Tommy says.

'But Adam told me that until this week he hasn't been back to England for twenty-five years.'

'He was lying,' Tommy insists.

'But *why*? And why didn't he tell me about Zane?' I demand.

'Isn't that obvious?' Tommy sighs. 'Adam hasn't told anyone that Zane framed him because he doesn't want anyone to know he had a motive for murder.'

I grip the edge of the bedside table. 'You really think *Adam* killed Zane?' My voice is faint with shock.

'I do,' Tommy says solemnly.

'I can't believe Adam would...' My heart races. 'I'm going to call Rae, see what she makes of—'

'I already tried her; she didn't pick up,' Tommy says. 'I left a message warning her about Adam, but...'

'You... you don't think she'll have confronted him, do you?' I stammer. 'You know how forceful, how impulsive she can be.'

'I hope not,' Tommy says. 'Because however nice Adam seems, he's gone to a lot of effort to conceal his real motives. If he really killed Zane, he's more violent than you think.'

'But he wouldn't hurt Rae, would he? He adores her.' I frown, remembering Rae's text. 'Anyway, Adam's not there right now. Rae messaged earlier. He's in Cambridge.'

Tommy sucks in his breath. 'Man, you don't think... Suppose Rae called him and... and got really mad? I mean, Zane was her brother too. They were close. She might have threatened to go to the police. Adam might be on his way back to have it out with her... or worse.'

I shudder. 'Okay, I'm going to call her myself right now. If I can't get hold of her, I'm going over there.'

'No, Cassie, please don't do that,' Tommy says. 'Wait for me so we can go together.'

'But... but aren't you in Devon right now?' I ask.

'If I set off now, I can be with you in about four hours.'

I check the time. 11.13 p.m. 'No, Tommy, that's crazy.' I take a deep breath. 'It's gone eleven and you've been climbing all day. Stay put, get some sleep and come in the morning.'

'Okay, but— *shit*! Cassie, this stupid phone's about to die, the battery's down to—' The line goes silent.

A chill wriggles down my spine as I scroll to Rae's number. The call goes straight to voicemail. 'Listen, Rae, it's Cassie. We need to talk. It's urgent. Call me. Doesn't matter how late.'

I put down my mobile and wait, my heart thudding in the silence of the night. I check the time again: 11.20 p.m.

Rae must be okay, right? It's hardly strange that her phone is set to voicemail at this time of night. She's probably asleep.

The question is, what did she do before going to bed? Did she blow up at Adam and threaten to expose him over Zane?

Might he really be on his way home and intent on stopping her, whatever it takes?

I pace around the kitchen. No way will I be able to sleep until I know she's all right.

I hurry into the hall, pull on a pair of boots and grab my keys.

My Uber arrives a few minutes later. I hurry into the stale, warm air of the back seat and check the time again. I should get to Rae's house in ten minutes.

TWENTY-EIGHT

The air bites at my cheeks as I race up the path to Rae's front door. I step into the porch and reach out to ring the bell.

My heart jolts. The front door is ajar. I hesitate. There's no sign of a break-in; the door is on the latch. Did Rae somehow accidentally leave it like that? Goosebumps prick the back of my neck as I push the door fully open. A stretch of tiled flooring gleams dimly in the streetlight. Everything around it is in shadow.

'Rae?' I call out. 'It's me, Cassie. I rang just now.'

I step inside and fumble for the light switch. Instantly the hall illuminates in front of me. Rae's house is, in design terms, the opposite of Uncle Edgar's. Everything here is bright and minimal. The paint on the walls is sunshine yellow and the floor a mass of orange and yellow squares, making walking into the hall feel like entering a giant egg yolk.

'Rae?' My voice quavers as I call again, this time more loudly.

My boots echo in the silence as I creep across the hall to the bottom of the stairs and peer up to the shadows of the first floor. 'Are you up there, Rae?'

Still no reply.

The intense quiet of the house presses in on me. I peer into the unlit downstairs rooms. Nothing seems out of the ordinary.

Then I see it: a dark viscous line trickling towards me out of the kitchen. My heart in my mouth, I step towards it and look more closely.

A slick of red shines starkly against the yellow tile.

Blood.

Avoiding its trail, my throat tight with fear, I step into the kitchen and turn on the light.

Rae is lying on the floor by the central island, her body unnaturally still. Blood pools around her left side, seeping away towards the hallway.

I'm too late.

I fly towards her. Drop to my knees.

'Rae! *Rae!*' I put my hand to her cheeks. They are cool to the touch. I reach to her side, where the blood seems to be coming from. My hand comes away warm and sticky. A sharp, steel kitchen knife lies on the floor next to the wound. I stare, transfixed for a second.

Did Adam do this?

Fingers trembling, I feel for a pulse in Rae's neck. *There*. Thank goodness. It's faint. Very. But it's regular.

'You'll be okay,' I murmur, praying that it's true. 'Just hold on.'

I snatch a tea towel from the counter and press it against the wound, trying to staunch the flow. As I fumble, one-handed, for my phone, my eyes light on a small marking in the blood next to Rae's hand. Keeping pressure against the wound, I peer more closely.

It's the letter "A". Rae must have drawn it before she passed out.

A for Adam.

My stomach lurches into my mouth. I grab my phone. But before I can dial 999, the crunch of breaking wood echoes from the hall, followed by an almighty crash. I start. Is that the front door being smashed in? I'm certain I left it open. I drop my phone, grab the knife and turn towards the kitchen door, still keeping one hand pressed against Rae's side. It's like a nightmare, as time slows down and before I can speak or move, a uniformed police officer storms into the kitchen.

'In here!' he yells, catching sight of me.

'Help—' I start.

But another much younger officer is already in here and talking over me into his radio. The first officer points at my hand. 'Drop it!'

I follow his gaze and realise I'm still holding the knife.

I let it go; it clatters onto the tiles.

'Get her!' orders the older officer.

And before I can think, hands are on me, pulling me away. I'm bundled into the hall, my arms twisted behind my back. Paramedics rush past me, into the kitchen.

I stare helplessly after them. My brain feels like it has slowed to a crawl. Gradually, I register that I'm in handcuffs and the older officer is talking to me.

'What is your name?' He's speaking slowly, as if repeating a question to a sleepy child.

I meet his gaze. The man must be in his fifties: grey-haired, his forehead scored with deep lines. He raises his eyebrows. '*Name?*'

'Cassie,' I say, my voice hoarse. 'Cassie Carson. That's my sister, Rae.' I nod towards the kitchen. 'How is she? There was so much blood. Is she all right?'

The officer frowns. 'I have to ask. Are *you* injured?'

I shake my head, as the officer ushers me out of the house and into the squad car outside. I sit in the back, next to a female officer who glances at me but says nothing.

I can't process what is happening. All I can think about is Rae. The shock of the blood. My fear for her life.

The paramedics haven't reappeared. I ask again how Rae is, but the female officer remains resolutely silent. Time seems to pass slowly, yet also very fast. More people rush into the house.

After what seems like hours, a gurney emerges from the house. Rae is lying on it, her eyes still closed. A paramedic is holding a drip bag over her.

'I want to go with her in the ambulance!' I protest.

The female officer beside me shakes her head and I slump back. As the gurney passes the squad car I lean closer to the window.

'Is she going to be okay?' I shout through the glass.

'Touch and go,' the paramedic says back, earning a glare from the female officer beside me.

I stare helplessly as the gurney trundles towards the ambulance parked just in front. The sound of a squeaking wheel echoes through the night air. Otherwise, everything is silent.

I hurl myself against the door of the car. 'I have to go with her!' I insist.

'No.' The female officer speaks for the first time. 'Now are you coming with me peacefully, or do I have to put you in restraints and arrest you?'

'Arrest me?' And in that instant my mind speeds into the light, as all the realisations slam into me at once.

I've been caught with a knife in my hand, standing over a stab victim. Tommy was right: Rae was in danger. I got here too late to stop Adam attacking her.

233

And now it looks like I just committed attempted murder.

The wail of sirens echoes through the night air, as the ambulance carrying Rae speeds away, out of sight. I close my eyes, praying Rae is all right. I need to call Mum. Get her to go to the hospital. But I don't have my phone. I dropped it on the kitchen floor when the police stormed in. They must have it.

'I need my mobile,' I say, my voice breaking.

'That's not possible right now,' says the female officer crisply, as the police car pulls away. House lights are on up and down the street, despite the late hour.

—

At the station, people stare at my coat. I look down. It's covered in blood. I give my name, age and address to the sergeant at the desk, then I'm ushered into a small, bleak room with bright lights, where the female PC tells me to take off all my clothes.

'Why?' I ask stupidly.

'They're evidence,' she says, holding open a large brown bag.

I strip to my underwear, then numbly put on the grey sweats that the woman offers me. They swamp me and I have to roll up the legs and arms. My bare feet are cold on the grubby vinyl floor and I ask for socks. These, also, are too big, but I put them on anyway and sit, huddled on a chair.

I'm left on my own for about an hour. The female PC brings me a plastic cup of water. She says the detectives will be in shortly.

Five minutes later, two men stride into the room. They are not much older than I am, I'd guess, and both dressed in grey suits, though one suit is crumpled and poorly fitting, while the other is sharply cut and neat as a pin.

Neat Suit asks me to sit down at the table, while Crumpled Suit adjusts the recording machine by the wall. They introduce themselves, but I'm too overwhelmed and jittery with anxiety and don't properly focus on either their ranks or their names. I ask how Rae is and they say that she's being operated on at the hospital, refusing to give any kind of prognosis.

They go through my name and address details with me again. I'm not being charged, but they say I can have a lawyer if I want one. I refuse. Why should I need a lawyer? I've done nothing wrong. They also tell me that Mum and Uncle Edgar have been contacted and are, presumably, on their way to the hospital now. I sit back. That's something at least. The detectives offer me the phone call I asked for earlier, but the only person I want to call is Rob and the clock on the wall says it's two a.m. If I call him now, I'll wake him up. Plus I'll have to explain everything while my head is spinning.

I look up. 'You haven't arrested me,' I say. 'Does that mean I can leave?'

The two officers look at each other.

Crumpled Suit nods. 'You can indeed leave, Cassie. But if you're as upset about the attack on your sister as you seem, I'm sure you'll want to tell us everything you know about what happened.'

I nod.

Neat Suit takes this as a cue to lean forward and narrow his eyes. 'Let's start at the beginning,' he says firmly. 'What were you doing in Rachael Carson's house at 11.30 p.m.? Was it a social call?'

'No.' And then it all pours out of me. I tell them everything, from Mia's claim to be Dad's daughter, right through to Adam's reappearance and how Tommy rang in a state earlier, convinced Adam killed Zane. I'm trying to keep to the key facts and follow a timeline, but I can hear my account is jumbled and see the looks of confusion on both detectives' faces.

'So you see I went to the house to warn my sister not to confront Adam on her own,' I finish, feeling desperate. 'But I... I guess I was too late. I found her passed out and bleeding on the floor.' As I say this, an image of the pool of blood on the ground beside Rae flashes before my mind's eye. I gasp. 'There was a letter, did you see it? The "A" that Rae wrote in her blood before she passed out?'

The detectives exchange a look.

'It's been noted,' Crumpled Suit says briskly. 'Now perhaps you could tell us how the knife you were holding got into your hand?'

I frown. 'I picked it up when... when I heard the front door being smashed in.'

Neat Suit raises his eyebrows. 'How did you get in the house, if your sister was already unconscious?'

'It was open. The Yale was on the latch.'

'Not when our officers made entry,' says Crumpled Suit.

I shake my head. 'I can't explain that; I didn't close it—' I suck in my breath. 'Unless the person who killed her – Adam – was still there when I arrived and let himself out after I'd come inside.'

The Suits look at each other again. I can't tell if they believe a word I've said.

They leave me, saying it will just be for a few minutes. My heart is thudding in my chest as time ticks away. A few minutes become ten, then twenty. Suddenly half an hour has passed.

Crumpled Suit reappears. 'We're just having your statement typed up, Cassie. Once you've signed it, we'll take you home.' He smiles.

I stare back, thrown by his change of manner.

'Do you have any news on Rae?' I ask, hoping the change signals that he'll be more forthcoming than earlier. 'Did the operation go okay? Is she all right?'

Crumpled Suit nods. 'Rae has come through the operation and is stable for now. They've put her in an induced coma.'

Thank goodness. I heave a sigh of relief, as Neat Suit walks in and sits down next to his partner.

'It seems your story checks out, Cassie,' Neat Suit says sympathetically. 'In fact, according to the doctors and paramedics, you probably saved your sister's life by trying to stop the bleeding when you did.'

'So... so... was it Adam?'

Crumpled Suit presses his thin lips tightly together. 'We can't confirm that, but preliminary forensics suggest the knife attack would have taken considerable force and from the angle was probably carried out by someone several inches taller than the victim.'

'Most likely a man,' Neat Suit adds.

The clock on the wall ticks silently round.

'We have an alert on Adam Carson,' Crumpled Suit says.

'And a police guard outside your sister's hospital room,' Neat Suit adds.

I nod. *Thank goodness*.

A few minutes later I've signed my statement and the detectives stand up.

'Cassie, please understand that you're a key witness to an attempted murder and we may need to call you in for further questioning as the case progresses,' Crumpled Suit says.

I look down at the grey sweats I was given last night. 'Can I get my clothes back?'

'I'm afraid we need to keep all items of your clothing as evidence,' says Neat Suit. 'We're also going to hold onto your phone while we copy any relevant data, though we should be able to return that to you tomorrow, or today rather,' he corrects himself. 'We'll have a car ready for you soon.'

TWENTY-NINE

I ask the police car to drop me at Mum's house rather than my own. After everything that's happened, I can't face going straight home alone. I'm not expecting Mum to be in, but she has just got back from the hospital, having left Rae out of immediate danger, but still in an induced coma.

'Poor Rae,' Mum gabbles. 'The police called and I was still reeling over her being attacked when they said *you'd* been arrested.'

'I wasn't *arrested*, Mum,' I say. 'I was just held for questioning.'

'What were you doing at Rae's house?'

I outline everything as quickly as I can. Mum hangs on every word, her eyes widening when I explain that I'm certain Adam attacked Rae. I check the time again. It's almost five a.m. I am desperate to call Rob, but Iris will be awake in an hour or so and I don't want to deprive him of that last bit of sleep. Plus, now I'm no longer at crisis point and able to think properly, I'm apprehensive that if I tell him about Adam, he'll start insisting this *proves* I should make up with Mia. And I still don't want her back in our house.

'How did Rob sound when you spoke to him?'

Mum glances sideways at me. 'Worried. I'm not prying, but it's obvious there's... that the two of you are having issues at the moment.'

I look away.

'Rob wanted to drive straight back to London,' Mum goes on, 'but it was after one a.m. at this point and I told him to wait until I'd got more information rather than get in the car and fall asleep at the wheel. I had this terrible image of him dead and you in prison.' She shudders. 'I know it was silly, but what would happen to Iris?'

'She'd come here and live with you and Tommy,' I say. 'Mum, the police have kept my phone. Can I borrow yours?'

I send Rob a text for the morning saying that I've talked to the police and that I'm at Mum's house now and totally fine, though very tired. I don't mention Adam or go into too much detail about Rae. I add that I'm going to catch up on sleep for a few hours and will call him when I wake up.

I give Mum her phone back. 'How come the police turned up at Rae's house when they did?' I ask.

'Anonymous tip-off,' Mum says. 'Apparently one of the neighbours saw you entering the house.'

'Right.' I sit back. It strikes me again that Adam could easily have still been inside when I arrived, hiding as I crept through to the kitchen. The thought makes me shiver.

'I wish I could get hold of Tommy,' Mum mutters.

'He called me last night,' I say. 'He said he should be home at some point today.' I hesitate. 'He went to see Harmony Moon.'

Mum shoots me a sharp look and I tell her everything Tommy told me, and how that prompted my visit to Rae's house.

'You're very lucky Adam didn't attack *you*,' Mum says with a shudder. 'I hope the police find him soon.'

A few minutes later, I'm yawning, barely able to keep myself awake. I change into a pair of Mum's leggings and one of her jumpers, then fall quickly asleep in my old bedroom. I wake only when Mum brings me some coffee and am shocked to discover that it's already the afternoon. Mum tells me Rae is still holding her own in hospital and that Rob called twice while I was sleeping.

'He wanted to make sure you were okay,' Mum explains with a smile. 'The police also rang me. They've examined your phone and released it.'

I nod. 'I'll go over and pick it up,' I say.

'No need.' Mum smiles again. 'I already sent a taxi for it. Here.' She hands it to me.

I give her a grateful hug and she holds me for a moment, like she used to when I was little.

'I suspect you'll want to call your husband,' she says, pulling away, and slips out of the room, back downstairs.

I prop myself up against my pillows and call Rob. It's good to hear his voice. He is full of concern, even though I keep stressing that I'm fine.

'I don't think you should go home until I'm back in London,' he says, sounding anxious.

'That's fine, I'll stay with Mum another night,' I say.

'I can put Iris in the car; we can be with you before it's dark.'

'Actually...' I hesitate.

'What?'

I take a deep breath. The truth is that, after the horror of last night, I'd love nothing more than to have my husband and daughter beside me, to cuddle Iris then dissolve into the safety of Rob's arms. But I'm also aware that his concern for me in this moment of crisis only serves to paper over the deep cracks in our relationship.

He is still convinced I have treated Mia badly.

And I'm still unsure about her.

Perhaps she really is Dad's daughter and had nothing to do with Zane's death. With Adam now the prime suspect for Zane as well as Rae, it certainly looks that way. But I don't – can't – trust her. And Rob doesn't get that at all.

'Let's talk tomorrow, Rob,' I say, 'see how we feel then. You and Iris can always drive back in the afternoon. Meanwhile, I'm fine here with Mum.'

'Okay.' He sounds reluctant. 'I miss you.'

'Me too.'

Feeling troubled, I ring off and pad downstairs. Much to my delight, Tommy has arrived. He got home from Devon while I was asleep. We hold each other tightly, aware of what a close shave I must have had last night.

'I'm certain Adam was still in Rae's house when I arrived,' I say quietly.

'I'm so sorry, Cas, I should never have mentioned that I couldn't get hold of her,' Tommy says, looking stricken. 'The last thing I wanted was to put you in danger.'

'I wasn't in danger,' I protest. But I don't say the words with any certainty. Tommy and Mum don't look convinced either. After all, hard though it is to accept, if Adam attacked Rae, he could easily have assaulted me too.

Tommy pats my arm. 'Don't worry, Cas. The police will find Adam soon.'

'Yes, and once Rae comes round,' Mum adds, 'she'll be able to identify Adam as her attacker and the police will have even more reason to go after him.'

–

I sleep surprisingly well on Sunday night, considering the maelstrom of emotions I'm feeling. I'm shattered from being up for most of the past twenty-four hours and it's easy to let Mum look after me a bit, to regress to childhood.

Mum makes me and Tommy scrambled eggs on toast on Monday morning, then they both leave. Tommy is intent on going to the police to give a statement on everything he's found out from Harmony Moon about Adam.

'He's already killed Zane and attacked Rae. Who knows who'll be next.'

Mum, meanwhile, has a meeting for a charity gala she's helping to organise. She offers to stay with me, but I insist she keeps the appointment. The gala is coming up next week and I know there's a lot still to plan.

It's actually lovely to have the house to myself for a little while. After several grey days, the morning is crisp and clear, the sun shining brightly in a strikingly blue sky. I make myself a coffee and take it onto Mum's patio.

A click of the back gate. I spin around. Gasp.

Adam is walking towards me.

THIRTY

I drop the coffee cup. It smashes onto the stone flags of the patio.

'Cassie.' Adam's voice is full of concern. 'Are you okay? How is Rae?'

I back away, bumping into the small, wrought-iron table Mum leaves outside during the winter months. 'Get away from me!' My fingers grip the sides of the table, icy cold to the touch.

Adam stops walking. He raises his hands, a gesture of surrender. He is holding a brown envelope. 'It wasn't me,' he says. 'I didn't attack Rae. I've been set up. Just like I was twenty-five years ago.'

I shake my head. 'You're lying.'

'No... let me explain,' Adam urges, 'but first, *please* tell me how Rae is. I've made a couple of anonymous calls to the hospital, but they won't give out any information. And I can't say who I am. There's a warrant out for my arrest.'

'Rae's stable for now; they've put her in an induced coma.' My breath mists in the air in front of me. The "A" that Rae drew in her own blood flashes before my mind's eye again. A tendril of fear creeps around my heart and squeezes. 'You killed Zane, didn't you? Are you here to kill me?'

'How can you think that?' He looks horrified. 'Please, just listen to me, Cassie. I haven't... *couldn't* hurt *anyone*. I swear that's the truth.'

'I already *know* the truth.' My voice rises. 'All about what you did to Zane and what he did to you years ago. Harmony Moon told Tommy the *real* story. About Zane. How he blackmailed Uncle Edgar into framing you.'

Adam looks away.

'Why didn't you tell me?' My voice cracks. 'How could you come back here after all those years away with a bunch of lies and—'

'I didn't lie,' Adam protests. 'Everything I told you was true. Edgar did frame me. I just... I left out Zane's involvement because he's dead now and Rae loved him and... and I didn't want to ruin his memory for her. Or you.'

The two of us stand in silence as the cold wind whirls around us. When Adam speaks again, his voice is smaller and sadder than before.

'Please listen to me, Cassie. I only found out that Zane was part of it just over a week ago. He sent me a letter after Dad died, admitting it all and apologising, but he only had the vaguest idea where I was, so it didn't reach me for months. As soon as I read it, I decided to come home and talk to him, but I was too late. He was dead before I arrived.'

'But you were here months ago. You threatened Harmony Moon,' I insist.

'No, I told you! I didn't get back here till last week. Anyway I haven't talked to Harmony Moon in years. If she's saying I did, she must be working with them.'

'With whom?'

'With the people who are trying to frame me. With Mia.' He runs his hand through his hair. 'Mia's behind everything and she's had help from inside the family. I originally thought that was Edgar, but now...' He hesitates.

'According to the DNA test on her hair sample, Mia's exactly who she says she is,' I snap. 'Surely Rae must have told you?'

'Rae didn't believe that test result.' Adam narrows his eyes, gazing intently at me. 'And I can see it written all over your face: you don't trust Mia either.' He takes a step towards me.

I shrink back. 'You really need to leave, before I call the police.'

'Just *listen*.' There's genuine agony in Adam's expression. 'You've got all of this upside down,' he pleads. 'So has Tommy. Harmony Moon's fed him a pack of lies. Don't you see that framing me takes the spotlight off the real killers? Who knows what they'll do next. I'm terrified they'll hurt you and Tommy, like they did Rae.' His voice cracks. 'That's why I'm here. Look, please can we go inside? I have some things I want to show you.'

I hesitate. Despite the look of unhappy sincerity on Adam's face, there's no way I can truly be sure he's not going to hurt me. Perhaps he wants to lure me inside, where the sound of my screams would be muffled. A shiver shoots down my spine.

'If you've got something to show me, you can do it right here,' I say, folding my arms.

For a moment we stand in silence on opposite sides of the iron table. The icy wind whirls around us.

'Fine,' Adam says. He removes a piece of paper and a passport from the envelope in his hand and passes them to me. The paper is a printout of a boarding pass; the passport is his. My fingers are numb with cold as I open it.

'Flick through and you'll see the stamp showing when I left Colombia,' he says. 'The dates match the ticket. That passport proves I hadn't set foot in this country for years, until I flew in *after* Zane died.'

I turn the pages of his passport. He's right. According to this he wasn't in the UK when Zane died. My stomach ties into knots. I look up. 'People can have more than one passport. This doesn't actually *prove* anything.'

'Okay.' Adam turns to the envelope again. 'But this does.' He hesitates, then draws out another sheet of paper. 'This shows beyond a shadow of doubt that Mia has been lying. But before I show it to you, I want to explain what I've done.'

'Done?'

'When Rae said that the DNA test you did with Mia's hair sample showed she was Nathaniel's daughter, it was obvious that one of two things must have happened.' He takes a deep breath. 'Either somebody at your DNA clinic fabricated the results, like I'm certain happened at the first clinic. Or the hair sample in the envelope wasn't Mia's.'

I frown. 'But—'

'Hear me out,' Adam says. 'It can't be the DNA clinic. Rae explained that the two of you picked it at random and never told anyone the name. Anyway, there wouldn't have been time for anyone to interfere.' He grimaces. 'Somebody must have switched the hairs in the envelope before you sent them to the lab.'

'That's impossible,' I counter. 'The envelope was sealed from the moment I put Mia's hairs inside.'

'It was a plain white envelope, right?' Adam asks. 'I'm guessing you have more than one of those at home?'

'Yes, but I—'

'Whoever switched the hairs used a fresh but identical envelope. There would have been no way of telling.'

'Wait.' I shake my head. 'Back up. You keep saying someone switched the hairs that were tested, but the results showed Mia is Dad's daughter. That means the hairs used must have been from—' I stop, the realisation of what he's saying hitting home. 'You think they were *my* hairs?'

Adam places the sheet of paper on the wrought-iron table, then looks up at me. 'The DNA test carried out was simply to determine whether the sample in the hairs you provided matched for paternity with the old test of Nathaniel's from years back. They could definitely have been yours. I have never met Mia in person, but Rae showed me a picture and your hair and Mia's is similar in both colour and length. They could easily be mistaken for each other.' He pauses. My heart thuds. It's true that several people have commented on our colouring being similar; I even noticed it myself.

'Here's the key point,' Adam goes on. 'I've shown the report to a scientist friend of mine and there *is* a discrepancy.' He taps the paper, his calloused finger landing about halfway down. 'There's data here that apparently suggests the DNA submitted belonged to someone more likely to be in their late thirties than their late twenties.'

My stomach falls away.

'It's a process called the Horvath age clock. It uses DNA methylation data to determine the age of a person within about three years. And this is too old to be Mia.' He pushes the piece of paper towards me. I glance down. It's a printout of the same test results I've already got on my phone.

My head spins as I try to piece it all together. 'So... so you're saying somebody took *my* hair and put it in an identical envelope and put that in my underwear drawer? All without my noticing?'

Adam nods, his face very serious.

'But... but how could anyone have managed all that? Nobody apart from Rae knew what I was doing,' I protest.

'Didn't they?'

I stare at him. 'No. I didn't tell anyone until *afterwards*. I took the hairs and hid them in the evening, then left home with them the following morning. Nobody came to the house all that time.'

'Who was *in* the house already?' Adam asks. 'Who was there all along, with access to your personal items, including your phone to sneak a look at your plans and... and your clothes or a hairbrush to take hair from?'

'Just Mia and Rob. And Iris, of course, but...' I look up. 'You think Mia did all that?'

'Not on her own,' Adam says flatly. 'But then she wasn't the one sleeping next to you, familiar with the place in the house you kept envelopes or where you were most likely to hide a DNA sample.'

Our eyes meet and I realise what he is saying. 'No!'

My hand flies to my mouth and all the weeks of suspicion coalesce around this one new and horrific fear.

Has Rob been working with Mia all along?

THIRTY-ONE

I shiver.

'Can we go inside, now?' Adam asks.

My head reeling, I take him into Mum's dining room. The air in here is warm, almost stuffy, after the crisp chill of the back garden. Adam takes off his thick padded jacket and lays it carefully over a chair. He's wearing a faded black jumper underneath; his chin is covered in stubble.

I sink into a chair. Surely it can't be true? The idea that *Rob* has been in league with Mia from the start is unthinkable. I'd imagined an attraction – possibly even an affair. But not endless lies going back months.

Not the organising and executing of a terrible con trick.

Not murder.

But what if Rob has been in thrall to Mia all this time? Totally manipulated by her? I feel sick to my stomach, my brain ricocheting from thought to thought. The *planning* this would have taken. The cold, cynical calculation of it.

I look up. Adam is gazing at me, eyes full of sympathy. His pity somehow makes it worse.

'I… I don't believe Rob could… there's no way…' I stammer.

Adam says nothing, just places another piece of paper beside the one already on the table. 'There's something else I need you to look at.'

I try to focus on the new paperwork. It's another set of DNA results. I catch the initials "N. C." and "M. I." and look up.

'What is this?'

'It's a copy of Mia's original DNA test. The one that Edgar organised. The one that led to the death of the nurse who dealt with Mia. These results reveal the whole thing was a fraud.' He pauses. 'And how much planning went into it.'

I nod, staring numbly down at the columns of DNA data and the probability statement at the end, which shows that N. C. is the father of M. I. 'What do you mean?'

'See there?' Adam points to one of the middle columns. 'That was the first alarm bell. It says Mia's DNA came from her hair, rather than a mouth swab, which would be more normal for an in-person DNA test.'

'Okay,' I say, 'but that doesn't actually prove anything.'

'No,' Adam says. 'But there's more. Far more.' He takes a deep breath. 'These original test results are identical to the results of the test *you* organised last week, where your hair was substituted in place of Mia's.'

My jaw drops. 'You mean they used my DNA for the original test too?'

Adam nods. 'The DNA report says the sample was taken in situ, but the nurse could have lied about that. My guess is Rob got hold of some of your hair for this test, then Mia took it to the clinic and somehow persuaded the nurse to use it instead of her own – a bribe, most likely. She and Rob must have worried the nurse would say something, so...' He makes a face. 'She had to go.'

'You're seriously suggesting that Rob... *my* Rob... ran her over?' My voice cracks. 'Adam, I swear there's no *way* Rob is capable. He's the gentlest, kindest person. He wouldn't hurt a fly.' Tears bubble in my eyes, blurring the words on the report.

'I know this must be incredibly hard,' Adam says gently, 'but you have to see Rob has questions to answer here, like… like where he was when the DNA nurse died.'

I wipe my face and look up at him. 'That was nearly two months ago.'

'Okay, what about the night Zane was killed? Where was Rob then?'

My mind zooms back to the evening of that terrible phone call from Savannah. Rob *did* pop out that night, just briefly, for a drink with his brother Jamie. I press my lips together as I remember thinking that Jamie would cover for Rob over anything.

Adam reaches across the table and squeezes my hand. 'I'm so sorry.' He pauses. 'But if there's a chance Rob murdered Zane it's also possible he tried to kill Rae. Did the police say anything about her attacker?'

'Just… just that from the angle of the wound, they thought whoever attacked her was taller than her. And stronger.' My voice shrinks to a whisper. 'Probably a man, they said.' An image of the pool of blood surrounding my unconscious sister lying on the kitchen floor flashes in front of my mind's eye again. My heart thuds as I see the letter she scrawled in the red. 'Wait!' I frown. 'What about the "A" beside Rae? She drew it in her own blood.'

'The "A"? Show me.' Adam indicates the paper in front of me. 'Draw what you saw.'

I snatch up a pen and replicate the letter as I remember it. Adam turns the paper and peers at what I've drawn, then he turns it back to me and tilts it slightly to one side.

'This could just as easily be an "R",' he says quietly.

I stare at my drawing. Shit, he's right. *"R" for Rob.*

I sink back in my chair, my head in my hands. It *can't* be true.

It just *can't*.

Adam clears his throat. 'Cassie, I think you—'

'It doesn't make sense!' I look up, feeling sick to my stomach. 'Even if Rob was somehow brainwashed into helping Mia, why kill Zane?'

'Zane was investigating the DNA results, wasn't he?' Adam asks. I nod. 'Sooner or later he was bound to stumble across the discrepancy I found.'

I gasp, remembering the last message he sent me. 'Zane texted me the day he died, saying he had "important news". There were no specifics, but Savannah – his partner – she said he'd found something that he thought might lead to proof about Mia.' I look at Adam. 'Maybe he'd got wind that there was something off with the DNA sample?'

Adam nods. 'If he had evidence of that, Rob and Mia couldn't risk it coming out. They must have felt they had to kill him, just like they killed the clinic nurse.'

'Okay, maybe that's *why* he was killed, but no way did Rob do it. And what about Rae? Why attack her?'

Adam shrugs. 'Maybe she was getting too close to the truth too.'

I shake my head. 'At least Rae is safe in hospital,' I say. 'They put a police guard outside her room.' I look up. 'To protect her from you.'

A look of pain passes across Adam's face. He gives himself a shake. 'Look, there's one more thing I need to say,' he says slowly. 'It's the hardest thing of all.'

'What?'

'I'm worried Rob and Mia might hurt *you*.'

'No!' I insist. 'No way! Even if you're right about the rest of it, Rob would *never* hurt me or allow anyone else to.' I glare at Adam. 'Apart from anything else, if Rob wanted to… to harm me, he could have done it a million times by now. So could Mia.'

Adam sighs. 'I understand why you're saying that, Cassie, I really do. But if Rob and Mia are in a relationship, then I'm guessing Rob might have designs on your inheritance, not just the share Mia is going after.'

'What do you mean?'

'That Rob needs to stay married to you long enough for you to inherit Dad's money.' He grimaces. 'But after that point, once the money is yours, he'd inherit it himself if… if you died.'

I stare at him, utterly horrified. 'No way! However it looks, there's just no way Rob is involved. Not in *murder.* And definitely not killing the mother of his child. I'm going to talk to him.' I reach for my phone then stop, my fingertips resting on the screen. A phone call is not the way to handle this. I need to be with Rob as we speak. 'I *know* him,' I say. 'And I *know* I'll see the truth about this if I'm with him, face to face.' I turn to Adam. 'I'm going to drive to Rob now. He's at his mum's place in Norfolk. I'll show him all this DNA stuff. If he has the slightest bit of knowledge about any of it, I'll see it in his eyes. Then we can go to the police together.'

'I don't think that's a good idea.' Adam looks alarmed. 'I mean, about confronting Rob.'

'Well, you don't have to come with me,' I say, jumping to my feet and grabbing Mum's car keys off the table. I'll have to borrow her car; Rob has taken ours.

Adam follows me to the front door. 'Wait, Cassie. Do you know where Mia is?'

'No. That is, Rob said she was staying at her friend Ellis's flat, but for all I know she could be anywhere.' I open the front door. 'You're wrong about Rob. I swear.'

Adam nods. 'Okay, maybe I am. But it's still too risky for you to confront him on your own.'

'Rob won't hurt me.' I give a dry, bitter laugh. 'You said it yourself. If you're right, he needs me to stay alive long enough to inherit Dad's money.'

I stride down the path, holding the key fob in front of me.

'I'm coming with you.' Adam runs after me, pulling his coat on. 'I'm not letting you go alone.'

It's clear Adam isn't going to take no for an answer, so I let him into Mum's car and we set off.

I call Tommy on the way. It goes to voicemail, which isn't surprising if he's still talking to the police. I leave a brief message, telling him to be on his guard and explaining that new information about the DNA tests has come to light, then adding that I'm driving to Rob's mum's house now. I don't mention that Adam is with me.

I can't rely on Tommy not to panic and tell the police – and the last thing we need is to be stopped before we get to Gull Cottage.

THIRTY-TWO

The coastal road that leads to Rob's family home dips and weaves along a cliff edge that – at various points – lurches vertiginously over the roaring sea below. I keep my eyes on the road ahead, rehearsing what I will say to Rob when I get to Gull Cottage.

It's almost three p.m. by the time we arrive. As Adam and I get out of the car, the sky looms dense and low overhead. The darkness of the steel-grey clouds matches my mood.

Gull Cottage itself is an ordinary-looking fifties bungalow, but it's impossible not to be awestruck by its clifftop location.

'Wow,' says Adam, following my gaze around the side of the house to the garden, which leads directly onto the cliff path. Even from where we're standing, the view out to sea is breathtaking. 'This place is amazing.'

'I wonder where our car is. Mine and Rob's.' I stare at the empty drive. There's no sign of Rob's mother's battered old Volkswagen either. I turn to Adam. 'I hope after all this that he's here.'

'Assuming he is,' Adam says, 'how do you want to do this?'

'I think we should talk to Rob together,' I say. 'But I want Iris out of the way first.'

'Agreed.'

As we walk up to the front door, a salt wind blows hard in our faces. Exposed to the sea like this, the cottage is plagued by strong gusts and sudden squalls. Adam tugs his padded jacket around his chest. 'I'd forgotten how cold the UK can be for a supposedly mild country.'

I press the doorbell and a soft peal of chimes echoes inside. My stomach is in knots. I have no idea what I'm going to say to Rob, assuming he's even here. I have a sudden flashback to the last time I saw him – and the frustration and disappointment in his eyes.

And then the door opens and Rob is standing in front of me. The sight of his face brings up all my emotions and for a second I think I might burst into tears.

'*Cassie*, what are you doing here?' Rob frowns. 'What's happened? Is it Rae?'

'No, she's the same… she's okay.' I hesitate, wondering how to begin.

'Hi,' says Adam, beside me.

'Who's this?' Rob asks. There's just the hint of jealousy in his voice. If the circumstances were different, I would smile.

'Adam, my half-brother.'

Rob's eyes widen. 'Isn't…' He turns to Adam. 'Aren't the police looking for you?'

'They are,' Adam says grimly.

'Cassie?' Rob turns to me, aghast. 'What the hell?'

'Adam didn't attack Rae,' I say. 'He was set up. Er, can we come in? Where's Iris?'

Rob's cheeks flush a soft red. 'She's not with me.'

'What do you mean?' I frown. 'Is she with your mum?'

'No, er, Mum's out visiting a friend all day.' He looks guiltily at me. 'Her car is in the garage, so she borrowed ours.'

'So where's Iris?' Fear tightens my throat.

Rob takes a deep breath. 'Iris is… She's, er, she's with Mia.'

My stomach lurches. 'Mia is *here*? You've left our daughter with her?'

'Please don't start that again, Cassie.' Rob makes a face. 'I knew Mum would be out all day and I've got masses of exam prep to do, so I asked Mia to come last night. I thought she might appreciate the break, and that she'd mind Iris for a bit today while I—'

I barge past Rob and hurry into the hall.

'Iris!' I shout. '*Iris!*'

No reply. I turn to Rob. 'Where *exactly* are they?'

'I don't know. Outside somewhere.' He frowns. 'Cassie, what on earth is the problem? Whatever you think Mia has done, surely you don't believe she's capable of hurting Iris?'

I hesitate. Rob is right about that, isn't he? I glance at Adam. He clears his throat.

'Maybe it's better Iris isn't here for this,' he says, giving me a meaningful look.

I nod, slowly. The last thing I want is for our daughter to witness the confrontation that's about to ensue.

Rob frowns. 'Here for *what*?' he demands.

I say nothing, just lead the three of us into the open-plan kitchen-diner at the back of the house.

I peer through the window. There's no sign of Mia or Iris. All I can see is a sliver of lawn, then the cliff edge and the dramatic expanse of sea beyond. Sparkles of silver light dance across the waves. Even under the glowering sky, the water is beautiful. I pull the DNA paperwork out of my bag and set it out on the table.

'We wanted to show you these,' I say.

'Mia's DNA test results?' Rob frowns, looking up at me.

'Yes,' I say. 'The results from *both* the tests that were done – the original one that Edgar set up *and* the more recent one on what I thought was her hair,' I explain. 'In both cases, we're certain that the DNA sample wasn't Mia's.'

Rob stares blankly at me. 'What are you talking about?' he demands. He prods at the bottom of the two reports. 'It says clearly on these that the DNA tested belongs to Nathaniel Carson's daughter.'

'Yes,' I say. 'That's because it's *my* DNA.'

'What?' Rob's jaw drops.

'The age of the DNA is too old to be Mia's,' Adam says.

'And too young to be Rae's. It's *mine*,' I say. 'My DNA was used both times.'

Rob stares at me, eyes wide with shock. 'Are you sure?'

I nod, keeping my gaze on his face. I can see no panic in his expression. No deceit.

'We think that the person behind this was working with Mia from the start,' Adam says. 'They've been prepared to lie and cheat their way to the inheritance money – and to kill anyone getting in their way.' He hesitates. 'You can see why... how you look suspicious. Nobody would have had easier access to Cassie's DNA than yourself.'

Rob stares at him. I watch as the shock on his face morphs to disbelief. He turns to me. 'Seriously, Cassie? You think I might be capable of fraud? Of murder?'

'No. Course not.' My heart beats faster. 'We just need answers.' I look out the window again. Still no sign of Iris.

'Please call Mia and ask her to come back to the house. I really want to know Iris is safe.'

'Of *course* she's safe.' Rob's voice rises.

'*Please*, Rob.' Tears prick at my eyes. 'Call Mia and get Iris back here.'

Rob nods, then takes out his phone. He puts it on speaker and makes the call.

It goes straight to voicemail.

'No signal.' He glares at Adam. 'Which, for your information, is normal round here.'

Adam is already striding to the door. 'I'll go and find them then.'

'Wait,' I say. 'Let's all go.' I turn to Rob. 'Okay?'

Rob grimaces at me. 'Fine. I just need to put on my boots.' He disappears through to the little utility room.

I grab Adam's arm. 'I don't believe Rob did *any* of this,' I hiss. 'You saw his face. He couldn't lie that well.'

Adam gazes at me, a look somewhere between pity and fear. 'Cas, if Rob *is* behind fraud and murder, he's been lying to you for months. I don't know why you'd think you could spot it now, if you've missed it this far.'

It feels like he's slapped me. I lean against a chair, my head spinning.

Adam buttons up his jacket, then frowns. 'How long does it take to put a pair of boots on?'

My stomach leaps into my throat. I dart into the utility room. The stand where Rob keeps his boots is empty. I open the door that leads onto the garden and peer out.

'*Shit!*' Adam roars.

Rob has gone.

THIRTY-THREE

Adam and I stare across the grass. The wind blasts our faces. The garden stretches out on either side, with the wood opposite and the low wall that separates the garden from the cliff edge to the left. There's no sign of Rob.

'He must be trying to warn Mia,' Adam says. 'Which way will she have gone?'

'Probably the wood,' I say. 'The cliff path to the beach is really steep. And even more windy than up here.'

As we set off towards the trees, my phone beeps.

I glance down. It's a message from Mia:

> On the beach. I have Iris. Come now if you want to see her again. ALONE.

I stare at the text, my heart racing. The wind whips at my face.

'What is it?'

I start. Adam has doubled back and is standing in front of me, his expression full of impatience.

Silently, I turn the phone so he can read the screen.

'Oh, Christ!' He looks at me, stricken. 'How do we get to the beach?'

I put my hand on his arm. 'Mia says to come alone.'

Adam shakes his head. 'No way. The woman is responsible for a major fraud, two murders and the attempt on Rae's life. I'm not letting you deal with her solo.'

'But… but what about Iris?' I plead. 'I can't risk Mia hurting her.'

'Then you go on ahead. I'll follow but stay out of sight.'

I shake my head. Adam isn't going to find many opportunities to keep his distance, especially once the path broadens out towards the beach.

'I'm not discussing it,' he says firmly. 'I'm coming.'

My heart races. 'Fine,' I say, feeling desperate, 'but you *have* to stay back.' I shove my mobile in my pocket and sprint along the garden. The path down the cliffside is right on the edge of the property, around an "L" bend. As I start down the steps, the wind gusts more fiercely than ever. I bend my head to keep it out of my eyes, concentrating on my footing. The path is super steep, with nothing to hold onto for balance. How dare Mia bring Iris down here when it's this blustery? She could easily get blown off. I peer down to the deserted strip of the beach below that's visible and shiver.

As the path winds further down the cliffside, I grow colder and colder. I fix my eyes on the sea, trying to focus on the sound of the waves, but they're too turbulent, the wind whipping them up, then crashing them onto the rocks. About halfway down, I look back up the cliff. There's no sign of Adam. Good. If he stays that far back, maybe Mia won't spot him until I can distract her.

I reach the beach. There's no one here, but there's another bay and another beach just around the high rock to my right. Adam is still nowhere to be seen up on the cliffside. I raise my hand anyway, hoping he can see me, and point to the right. Then I shove my numb, cold fingers in my pockets, and crunch over the stones and into the next bay.

The pebble beach here is also deserted. I look around. No sign of anyone. The bay is horseshoe shaped and surrounded by sheer rockface. On a sunny day, it's a pleasant spot to bring a picnic, though at high tide it gets cut off. Right now, with the wind buffeting and the sea roiling and the skies the colour of lead, it feels ominous. Sinister.

My heart in my mouth, I put my hands to my lips and shout out.

'Iris! Mia! *Iris!*'

My cry is whisked away on the wind. I trudge across the beach, yelling louder. Where the hell are they? For a second, I have the terrifying thought that Mia has taken Iris into the water. I turn and scan the waves. They are fiercer than ever, eating up the pebbles in great gulps as they surge further and further up the beach. The tide is rising. My heart beats faster.

'Mummy!' Iris's shout is faint over the noise of the wind. I spin around. She's racing across the pebbles towards me. I hurry towards her and scoop her up, my heart pounding with relief. I clutch her to me, forgetting everything else for a moment. She is warmly dressed in gloves and a puffer jacket. A pink scarf I don't recognise is wound around her throat and her woolly hat with the blue pompom is pulled right down around her ears.

'You don't need to look so relieved; I'd never actually let anything happen to her.' Mia materialises in front of us.

I stagger back. Mia's dressed in a puffer jacket too, with jeans and a black beanie. Her long hair flies out from underneath it. She points to her bare throat.

'I gave Iris my scarf,' she says.

I clutch Iris more tightly. 'And giving her a scarf makes up for threatening to kill her?' I hiss. 'Not to mention everything else you've done.'

Mia stares sullenly back at me. 'I don't know what you're—'

'Oh, give it up!' My voice rises as I shout into the wind. 'You're a fraud and a murderer.'

I suddenly wonder if Rob is here too and look around again. I spot a small gap in the rockface at the back of the beach. It's too dark inside to see properly, but I'm guessing that's where Mia and Iris were just now.

Mia follows my gaze. 'We were sheltering from the wind.'

'Is my husband in there?' I demand.

Mia frowns. 'What? No.'

'Mummy, why are you so cross?' Iris demands, wriggling hard in my arms. She's too big to hold like that, so I let her down to the ground, keeping tight hold of her hand. She jumps up and down, tugging at my arm. 'We found a dragon's cave, Mummy. There's a nest and an egg and everything. Come and see!'

I hold tight to Iris, resisting her attempt to pull me towards the gap in the rockface.

I glare at Mia. 'Why did you get me down here?'

'Don't you want to see the dragon's cave?' Mia asks, lightly.

I frown. What the hell is she playing at?

'Please, Mummy.'

'Come on, Iris,' I say. 'I think we're going to go back up the cliff to Granny Annie's house. The tide is coming in and—'

'Cassie!' Mia's voice is like I've never heard before: dark and threatening. She unzips her puffer jacket and indicates the slim silver knife concealed inside.

I gulp.

Mia rezips her jacket. 'Just take a quick look inside the cave, okay?' she asks, resuming her light, cheerful normal tone. 'Then we'll all go back up together.'

I hesitate a moment. 'Okay.'

Iris drags me towards the opening in the rockface. I keep my gaze firmly on Mia. What is she doing? Why bring me down here if we're just going to return to the house in a moment?

I glance over my shoulder, hoping to see Adam charging towards us. But there's no sign of him. Iris pulls away from me as we reach the gap in the rock. It's wider than I'd thought from across the beach; there's plenty of room for someone to walk through.

I peer inside. The ceiling of the cold, damp cave is low, only half a metre or so above my head. Six grey rocks embedded in the ground form a rough ring in the centre of the gloomy space. A smaller seventh stone, oval and speckled, sits in the middle of the ring.

'Look, Mummy!' squeals Iris. 'See the dragon's nest and the egg?'

I nod, then step inside. There's no wind in here, but I'm shivering. What is Mia planning? She's by the entrance of the little cave, leaning against the rocky wall as if waiting for something.

I glance out towards the beach again. The tide is still rising. *Where is Adam?*

'*Mummy!*' Iris grabs me by the hand and pulls me over to examine the dragon's egg properly.

I stare down at speckled stone, too preoccupied to focus.

From outside, the sound of footsteps echoes towards us. I spin around. Oh, thank goodness. It's Adam. But something is wrong. He's staggering. The side of his head is dark and matted. Is that blood? As he reaches the cave I rush over, keeping hold of Iris's hand.

He clutches the wound. His eyes are glazed.

'Who's that?' Iris lisps, wide-eyed with apprehension. She wrenches herself away from me, scuttling back to the rear of the cave.

'It's okay—' I start saying, but just then Adam stumbles forward, half-collapsing onto me. I help ease him to the ground beside the ring of stones, one eye still on Mia by the entrance. She hasn't moved.

'What happened, Adam?' I ask. 'Who did this?'

'I didn't see,' Adam gasps, still holding his head. 'They hit me from behind. Grabbed my phone. It… it must have been Rob.'

'No.' I say the word, but in my heart, I don't really believe it anymore. After all, who else could have attacked Adam?

Iris creeps back over and huddles next to me. Her eyes are huge, her face pale.

'We… we have to get out of here,' Adam gasps, struggling to get to his feet. '*Now!*'

'I know!' I glance up, expecting Mia still to be standing by the entrance, with her back to the cave wall, watching us.

But Mia has vanished.

'Mummy, what's happening?' I can hear from Iris's voice and from the stiff way she holds herself that she's terrified.

'Everything's fine,' I say, trying to reassure her. But my own voice is shaky.

I look down at Adam. His eyes are closed. Has he passed out? I quickly take off my coat and cover him with it. How on earth am I going to get him out of here now?

'Look, Mummy!' I glance up. Iris has edged over to the cave entrance and is pointing out across the beach.

A terrible sense of foreboding washes over me as I hurry over to her and peer outside. To my horror, the sea is far higher up the beach than I'm expecting, the water already lapping at the rock that divides this bay from the one next door.

How has the tide risen so fast?

'Come on, Iris, we have to go.' I turn back to Adam and shake his shoulder. 'I'll get help, I promise.'

He murmurs something under his breath, but I can't make it out.

There's no time to waste.

I grab Iris, hoist her onto my hip and run as fast as I can over the pebbles to the stretch of rock that separates this bay from the one with the steps up to safety. I wade into the water. The sea is cold, already over my ankles. Water splashes up at Iris and she squeals.

'Keep still!' I order.

She shrinks against me. I wade further, my heart in my mouth. A bigger wave launches itself at my body, almost knocking me off balance. Iris is crying now. I hold her tight and take another step. My frozen foot knocks against a large stone underwater and I stumble, just as another wave – even larger than before – crashes over me.

Time slows as I fall, still clinging to Iris. And suddenly we're both in the shock of the cold water and time is speeding up as the current tugs and claws at my body.

All I can think is that I mustn't let go of Iris. But the tide is ripping her away. I lift my head, suck in a huge gulp of air, then I'm under again. I can't see. Salt water churns in my mouth. I'm choking, scrabbling to right myself.

Iris is gone.

THIRTY-FOUR

With a roar I force my way to my feet, bursting through the surface and back into the cold air. I scan the waves in front of me. 'Iris!' The water is only up to my thighs, but that's higher than her head. My heart threatens to burst out of my chest. 'Iris!' I yell again, desperate with panic. '*Iris!*'

I stare out to sea. I know how fierce the tide is here, how deadly the rocks that lurk under the water just a little way out can be. I'm about to dive under, to see if I can spot her. Then I hear a faint cry behind me.

'Mummy!'

I spin around. *Thank goodness.* The current has dragged her back to the pebble beach. She's standing there, drenched and shivering, but safe from the tide. Flooding with relief, I wade back to her and haul her into my arms.

She sobs against my chest and I stroke her wet hair. I'm making soothing noises as I stare at the sea, now properly crashing against the rock that divides our beach from the only way out of Gull Cove.

But inside just one thought screams in my head.

We are trapped and the tide is still rising.

I feel in my pocket for my phone, the wind slicing at my face. But it's not there. It must have fallen out when I went under.

I stare helplessly at the water. The waves suck and pull at the stones. The tide is now halfway up the beach and still rising. I examine the rockface that rises high all around us. Every inch of it is smooth and sheer. Maybe a really experienced climber might navigate it using tiny ridges for fingertip holds, but not me. Certainly not with Iris.

'Mummy, I'm scared.' Iris clutches my leg, like she did when she was a toddler.

'It's okay, sweetheart,' I say, trying to keep my voice steady. I unwind her hand and squeeze it tight. 'Everything's going to be all right.'

My heart pounding, I lead her back into the cave and check on Adam. He moans softly as I touch his shoulder but doesn't open his eyes.

'I'm here,' I say, trying to sound stronger than I feel. 'I'll work out a way out.'

'Tide... rising,' Adam gasps.

'I know,' I say, dully.

'What's wrong with him?' Iris whispers.

'He hurt his head,' I say. I squat down beside her. 'Why don't you go and bring that dragon's egg over here so I can see it properly. Okay?'

Iris nods and trots away, towards the circle of rocks in the centre of the cave. I look around. The cave isn't deep, maybe two or three metres across. I know that, at high tide, this beach disappears entirely, but what about in here? I look around for water marks, but I can't see any. That's a bad sign, isn't it? It means the cave must get full too. I wish I could ask Rob.

Except Rob is the reason I'm in here.

A memory flashes into my head from the early days of our relationship. It was summer and the first time I'd visited Rob's family and the two of us spent a magical afternoon down on the beach, making out and watching the waves crash against the shore. A rush of misery sears through my terror.

Is Rob really with Mia? Did he tell her to abandon us? To leave us to drown?

I push the thought away. Right now, I need to focus on getting us out of here.

Adam is still lying on the ground, clutching his head, his eyes shut.

'Can you move?' I ask.

He tries to sit up, then shakes his head very slightly. 'Dizzy,' he complains, then slumps back down.

Iris creeps back to me. She places the speckled oval stone from the centre of the circle in my hand. 'Here's the dragon's egg, Mummy,' she says quietly, one wary eye on Adam.

'Thank you.' I take the stone and kiss her head. She huddles next to my leg as waves lick at the beach just outside the cave. 'Sweetheart,' I say, 'in a minute I'm going to need you to be very brave.'

'Here you are!' A familiar voice rings out across the cave.

'Tommy!' I jump to my feet. My brother is striding into the cave, dressed in his climbing gear, a full body harness strapped across his legs and chest. 'How—?'

'Is that my favourite niece or a cave troll!' Tommy opens his arms wide and Iris races over to him, giggling wildly. He picks her up and swings her onto his hip. 'Ready to get out of here?'

I hurry towards him, filling with relief. It's a miracle that he's found us. Tommy scoops me into the hug with Iris. I cling to him for a moment, leaning my head against his shoulder.

'How did you know we were here?' I ask.

'I heard your voice note and decided to drive straight after you,' he says gruffly. 'I saw the car in the drive so I knew you must be here, but no one answered at the front, so I went round to the garden. I found the back door of the house wide open and footprints on the path down to the cove, so I figured you—' Tommy spots Adam slumped on the ground, his eyes closed. 'Who's that?' he asks. 'What's happened to him?'

I give Iris back the "dragon's egg", then rapidly explain everything to Tommy. His eyes widen as he takes in not just my story, but the presence of a brother he last saw as a little boy. 'You really think Rob attacked him? And that he's in league with Mia?' he whispers, looking horrified.

'What other explanation is there?' My voice rises with anxiety. 'I tried to get Iris out of the bay, but the current was too strong and now we're cut off and—'

'Easy,' says Tommy, hugging me to him again. 'When I realised you were probably here, I grabbed some equipment from my car and climbed down. Now we just have to get you back up.'

'But...' My panic rises. 'What about him?' I point to Adam, still lying on the ground with his eyes shut. 'He can't climb.'

'Okay, but I'm going to get you and Iris out. I'll jumar us up the cliff with—'

'You'll *what*?'

'Abseil upwards. *Climb*. I'll take Iris with me.'

My eyes widen.

'Don't worry, she'll be in the harness.' Tommy pats my arm and looks over at Iris, who is squatting in the centre of the ring of rocks. 'It'll be fun, won't it, cave troll?'

Iris nods, beaming broadly.

'Once I've got Iris up to the top, I'll call 999 from the house phone; there's no signal on my mobile.' He lowers his voice again. 'I can let down the climbing rope for you, help guide you up. But there's nothing I can do for Adam, not without better equipment. There must be a coastguard nearby, though. Or the RNLI. They can send a boat for him.'

I nod, glancing around at Adam. How long will all that take?

Tommy is already striding outside, Iris still in his arms. 'I can't believe Mia left you here,' he mutters.

'Did you see her up at the house?' I hurry after him. 'Or... or Rob?'

Tommy shakes his head.

'Watch out they don't— *Oh!*' I join him on the little beach; my guts give a sickening lurch. The waves are already two-thirds of the way up the beach and still coming, clawing at the stones. A rope dangles to the ground, whipping slightly in the wind. I peer up to where it's fastened at the very top of the sheer cliff, the equivalent of four storeys or so above us. I shiver. Tommy shifts Iris to his front and fastens her to his harness.

'You need to keep still while we climb, okay, Iris?' Tommy instructs.

She nods, her eyes wide as saucers, and stretches one arm out towards me.

I take her hand. 'It's all right, sweetheart, Uncle Tommy will keep you safe. Just do everything he says.'

Tommy clips his harness to the rope and glances up the cliff.

'Okay, Cas, once I'm up there I'll throw a harness down for you and—'

I hesitate. 'Actually, no. Tommy, there's no way I can leave Adam down here alone even if help is coming. He's only semi-conscious. I can hold him out of the water if I stay. Just make sure the coastguard understands how urgent it is. And don't let Iris out of your sight. Mia and… and Rob might still be up there somewhere.'

Tommy stares at me. The wind howls around us. 'Are you sure I shouldn't come back for you?'

I nod. Tommy tugs on the rope, then looks down at Iris. 'Okay, say goodbye to Mummy.'

There's something in the sound of his voice that sends another shiver shooting through me. It's as if he's telling Iris to say goodbye to me forever. I give myself a shake. I'm getting morbid. And I mustn't. I have to stay strong for Iris. And Adam.

I whisper into my daughter's ear that I love her, then I stand back.

Tommy meets my eyes. 'I'll get help to you and Adam as soon as I can. Wait inside the cave; don't risk the current. And don't worry.' He balances his feet against the cliff, pulling the rope taut. His gaze lingers for a moment. A look of apprehension passes across his face, as if he knows somehow that help is not going to reach me and Adam in time.

I frown, feeling uneasy again. 'Tommy?'

His expression hardens. 'It's going to be fine. Love you.'

I open my mouth to say it back, but Tommy is already climbing at speed, one foot against the other up the cliff-side. I watch his back, unable to see anything of Iris other than her little legs sticking out on either side of his waist. All other thoughts vanish as I clench my fists in sheer terror, watching as Tommy makes his way to the top.

It takes him just a couple of minutes to reach the grassy edge of the cliff. I watch him clamber over, then disappear. I wait a second, desperate to see Iris again, to make sure she's okay.

To my relief, Tommy reappears, the harness removed. He is holding Iris's hand. They stand on the clifftop looking down at me. Iris waves and Tommy salutes me, then they're gone.

A new fear grips me. Suppose Rob and Mia are up there, waiting? They've already tried to kill us once. I should have warned Tommy more forcefully to be on his guard. I should have insisted that as soon as he called the coastguard, he was to put Iris in his car and drive the two of them out of here as fast as possible.

'Cassie!' Adam's urgent cry drifts towards me from the cave.

I turn. *Oh, no.* While I've been watching Tommy and Iris climb, the tide has been rising. The sea has almost covered the beach. I look over to the cave. Waves are already lapping at the entrance.

I race over and go inside. Adam is staggering to his feet, looking dazed. 'Must… get out,' he stammers.

I take his arm. 'It's okay,' I say. 'Tommy just climbed up the cliffside with Iris. He'll… he's going to call for help for us.'

Adam looks at me, frowning. 'Is… is there time?'

'I think so,' I say. 'We're trapped in the bay but this cave goes a few metres back, so even if the sea comes further inside, I'm sure we'll be okay until the rescue boat gets here.' My lips tremble. I can see on Adam's face that I haven't convinced him. 'The important thing is that we stay out of the current. It's really strong round here.'

'Okay.' Adam blinks, then stumbles to the back of the cave. Another wave surges towards us. Water licks at the rocks that form the circle of Iris's dragon's nest. The ceiling at the back of the cave is only just above our heads. Adam leans against the wall, his eyes glinting miserably in the dim light as the water swills around our ankles.

Tommy must have made that call by now. Surely help is on its way.

I take a deep breath. 'We'll be okay,' I mutter, trying to convince myself as much as Adam.

'Cold.' Adam's teeth are chattering. 'Too cold.'

I nod. 'The lifeboat will be here soon.'

But even as I say this, fear creeps like poison through my veins. I can't help but feel that Adam and I are on our own.

THIRTY-FIVE

Several minutes pass. The water in the cave floor is up to our knees and so cold it burns. My feet and hands are numb.

'Surely the tide can't rise much further,' Adam mutters.

I wade to the cave entrance and peer outside. Not an inch of pebble beach remains in view and the waves are still washing towards us. My heart sinks.

I scan the horizon. The sun is out, the water gleaming in its light. There's no sign of a rescue boat.

'Tommy *definitely* told us to stay in here? In the cave?' Adam asks.

I nod.

'How long has it been?' He means since Tommy got to the top of the cliff with Iris.

'Fifteen minutes or so,' I say, then, trying to convince myself as much as him, I add: 'I'm sure the lifeboat is on its way.'

Another, bigger, wave rolls through the cave, splashing seawater against my thighs. My heart thuds. The cave is so quiet, the only sound the slap of water against the cold rock wall.

Five more minutes go by. I'm now certain that something has gone wrong. Suppose Tommy's message that we were in the cave didn't get through? Suppose Mia – or

Rob – stopped him before he could call the emergency services? Suppose no lifeboat is coming?

I grit my teeth. No way am I dying here, drowning inside this dank, gloomy cave. And outside, at least we might spot a passing boat.

'Change of plan!' I grab Adam's arm. 'We need to get outside, onto the beach.'

'What? But…' He frowns, still looking dazed. 'Okay.'

I help support him and we wade out of the cave. The water here is almost at my waist. The sun beats down but I'm shivering uncontrollably. I squint out to sea. Still no sign of any boats.

'Are they coming?' Adam's voice sounds very weak.

He is hunched over, clutching his head again.

'Is it worse?' I ask.

He nods. His face is horribly pale. 'It's… it comes and goes.' He winces with pain.

A huge wave surges against us, far more powerful than the smaller ones in the cave. I brace as my entire body is soaked. Another massive whoosh of water lifts me off my feet. And another. Suddenly I'm under the cold wet of the sea. Grit in my mouth, salt stinging my eyes. I scrabble with my hands, desperate to find the right way up.

My head bursts through the surface. I take huge gulps of the damp air. The waves calm a little. I look around for Adam. He is slumped over and floating face down a metre or so away.

Panic twists and swells inside me as I swim over and haul his face out of the water. 'Adam!' I shriek.

He opens his eyes. 'Cassie,' he splutters. Then his eyes roll back in his head and he slumps again.

I catch him under his armpit, keeping his face out of the wet with one hand, while the other pulls at the water.

I'm so cold I can't feel my legs. Adrenalin pumps through me, but I know I can't keep both of us afloat for much longer. I look around. We're drifting across the bay, propelled by the current. Another few metres and we'll be out of the bay and in open sea.

Cold, hard despair lodges in my guts. Maybe we should have stayed in the cave after all. Drowning in there would surely be gentler than out here, being thrown about by the waves.

'Adam,' I gasp. 'Kick your legs! *Kick!*'

He doesn't respond.

I find the strength from somewhere to drag him after me as I try to swim through the surging water and back towards the cave. I concentrate on keeping hold of Adam as each wave hits. Every time the sea splashes over us, he splutters and moans but doesn't open his eyes.

Without warning, the sun disappears behind a dark cloud and the wind casts needles at my face. This is hell, the waves battering my body, flinging me about. I'm shivering uncontrollably. The true horror of our situation hits me.

We're going to die.

Adam's body is limp in the water. I keep my hand under his chin, trying to keep his face out of the waves as best I can.

I think of Iris, praying Tommy can keep her safe.

'*I love you,*' I whisper under my breath. '*I love you.*'

Seawater lashes at my face. I'm getting lower and lower in the water. My strength almost gone. And then, rising above the crash and suck of the waves, I hear another noise. Faint at first, but then stronger, a chugging sound.

A small motorboat appears from around the rock. I blink the water out of my eyes.

A single figure is at the stern, hand on the tiller. Whoever it is, is dressed in yellow oilskins, their hood pulled low.

I raise my arm and the boat turns. As it pulls alongside us, I stare at the oilskinned figure. Who on earth is it? The engine cuts out and he leans out of the boat and reaches into the water for Adam. I peer closer, as a gust of wind blows back his hood.

'Rob!' I stare at the familiar face, confusion and fear racing inside me.

Why would he leave us to die, then come and rescue us?

There's no time to think. I have no energy to think. Or move. All I know is that Rob is pulling at Adam, trying to heave him into the boat.

'Push him up!' he yells.

I have no idea if it's some kind of bizarre trap, but Adam and I will die if we stay in this water, so I push as hard as I can. The boat bucks and sways, as Rob hauls Adam on board. He lands with a thud, the boat almost tipping on its side.

Immediately, a wave catches it and drives it away from me. I choke on seawater, flailing helplessly. I can see the terror in Rob's eyes as he grabs the tiller and steers the boat back to me.

I am struggling now to move my legs. The cold has seeped into every cell, paralysing me. I keep my gaze fixed on Rob's face. He's shouting something, but the words are muffled in my ears.

I try to raise my arm. To reach his outstretched hands. His fingertips brush mine, just as another wave crashes over me.

THIRTY-SIX

A searing pain shoots through my head. I jolt back to consciousness in the cold air, coughing and spluttering. I open my eyes, wild with agony. Rob's face is right in front of mine. He is holding me up by my hair – that's what the pain is – and yelling at the top of his voice.

'Grab the boat, Cassie! Now!'

Somehow my body obeys. I claw my fingers over the hull. The boat tips and rocks in the waves. And then Rob releases my hair, grasps me under my armpits and hauls me out of the water. The air is freezing. My clothes sodden against my skin. The floor of the boat rushes up to meet me as my legs bang against the sides.

'Cassie, where's Iris?' Rob's voice is urgent. Desperate.

I open my eyes. I'm lying in a heap inside the boat, coughing and shivering. Rob is right in front of my face.

'Iris?' He shakes me, his eyes full of terror. 'Is Iris still in the water?'

I blink, trying to focus. 'No,' I gasp. 'Safe.'

Rob nods, then scrambles back to the stern. His hand rests on the tiller as he steers the boat through the water. I push myself up. This is Rob's mum's boat. Normally moored at the boathouse half a mile along the coast.

Rob shouts something, but his voice is lost in the wind. I shuffle closer, wiping my face, trying to hear what he's saying.

'There's an emergency kit in the box under my seat. Get the foil blankets!'

I somehow manage to scrabble underneath his seat and pull out the metal box. The foil blankets are on the top, folded into neat squares. I take out two of them, but my fingers fumble with the Velcro fastening. Rob leaves the tiller and crouches beside me. In a second, the foil blankets are free. He wraps one around me, places the other over Adam, then quickly returns to his seat in the stern.

I look up, as the deep chill recedes a little. Our boat has reached the open water, leaving Gull Cove behind. Rob steadies the boat and, keeping well away from the coastline, which I know is full of submerged and dangerous rocks, steers us towards the boathouse. The sun emerges from behind a cloud, warming my face. I tilt my head back, feeling my body come back from the abyss. I feel bruised all over, but I'm alive.

What about Adam? I lean over him. He is breathing, but unconscious.

'We need to get him to a doctor,' Rob says grimly.

I nod, feeling dazed. I don't understand why or how Rob is here, but if he wanted us dead, he would surely have left us to drown.

'Rob?' I ask, desperate to understand. 'What—?'

'There should be a set of spare waterproofs in the emergency box,' Rob interrupts, his gaze set on coastline ahead. 'I'd put them on. Get out of your wet clothes.'

I glance down at Adam. 'What about him?'

'No way are we getting him into different clothes,' Rob says. 'It nearly killed me getting him into the boat.' He watches me as I open the box again. I rummage inside for the waterproofs. They're in a vacuum-sealed bag. As I rip it open, I spot a first aid kit, a stack of energy bars and a row of water bottles.

I swig some water and take huge bites out of the bar, then peel off my soaking wet clothes and pull on a waterproof jacket and trousers. Immediately I feel better, my body no longer shivering.

I take the water and crawl over to Adam. I hold the bottle over his lips and let a gentle trickle run into his mouth. I tuck his foil blanket more tightly around him and add the one I was just using on top of it. I touch his cheek. It's cold, but not deathly so. I examine his head. I can feel a huge bump, but there's no blood.

'How is he?' Rob calls over the wind.

'Still unconscious,' I say.

Rob nods grimly. The boat chugs steadily through the waves, thankfully now calmer than they were a few minutes ago. As he steers around the next rock, the boathouse comes into view. It stands at the end of a small, empty jetty.

'I'm so sorry I didn't believe you,' Rob says. 'About Mia.' His eyes fix on mine, his expression intense and deeply sorrowful.

I nod, the confusions building and swirling in my mind.

Is he truly innocent?

'Why did you run off and leave me and Adam earlier?' I demand.

Rob looks at me, his face filling with shame. 'I was so convinced you must be wrong about Mia... I went into the wood to find her and warn her. I couldn't believe she had deceived us... *me.*' He pauses. 'I really thought she was this vulnerable innocent who needed our help.'

We stare at each other.

'You were right,' he says huskily. 'And I should have listened from the start.'

I nod, slowly. 'What happened in the wood?'

Rob looks miserably at me. 'I called out for Mia but she wasn't there. I walked around for – I don't know – a minute or two I guess, looking for her and Iris.' He pauses.

'They were already down on the beach.' I frown. 'I don't understand, Rob. *What happened?*'

'Somebody else was there,' he says. 'Somebody I didn't expect to see.' He pauses. 'They took me by surprise. Threatened me. Took my phone. Tied me up and ran off.'

I stare at him. Who is he talking about? The same person who attacked Adam? My head spins. Is Uncle Edgar here? Or Harmony Moon? Why doesn't he name them?

'By the time I'd got myself free, the bay was already cut off. You had to be down here, so I ran to the boathouse and… here I am.'

The jetty comes into view and Rob slows the boat as we approach. He leans across and touches my face. 'I'm so glad you're okay. I should never have doubted you.'

'Me too.' I close my eyes for a second, letting him draw me close, allowing myself to feel the full relief of his being here. 'But who—?'

My eyes snap open.

The truth that's been in plain sight all along forces its way to the front of my brain. No way would my elderly uncle or Harmony Moon be able to overpower either Rob or Adam. But I know who *would* be able to. And I handed my daughter over to him just a few minutes ago.

THIRTY-SEVEN

'Tommy!' It's half a statement, half a horrified gasp. '*Tommy* attacked you.'

'I'm so sorry, Cassie.' Rob looks at me, agonised, as he eases the boat alongside the jetty. 'I… I know how much you love him. I—?'

'He's got Iris!' I jump up, my exhaustion forgotten. The boat rocks as I grab the jetty and haul myself onto dry land.

'*What?* Where?' Rob follows me, quickly fastening the boat's mooring line around the nearest cleat. He glances down at Adam, still unconscious in the base of the boat.

I grab his arm. 'There's nothing we can do for Adam right now,' I say. 'We need to get back to the house. Call for help. And we *have* to find Iris. Tommy took her earlier. God knows where they are now.'

'Look!' Rob's voice sounds hollow. I follow his pointing finger past the steps that lead from the boathouse, right up to the cliff top high above our heads.

Tommy and Mia are standing on the edge of the cliff, peering down at us.

There's no sign of Iris. I lunge across the jetty, my heart in my mouth. I climb the steps as fast as I can, but my limbs are exhausted. Rob passes me, taking my hand and pulling me on. I feel his determination in the press of his fingers.

It gives me the strength I need.

I'm panting for breath as I reach the top of the steps. The sun is bright and the sky now clear and blue, all the earlier clouds having burned away. The salt air has a fresh crispness as it buffets our faces. It's a beautiful afternoon, but as I stare at Tommy and Mia, all I can feel is despair. I have adored Tommy ever since he was born, and he left me to die.

'What have you done with Iris?' I shout.

'She's fine,' Tommy insists.

'I changed her into dry clothes,' Mia adds. 'I wouldn't have left her on the beach with you earlier, but the tide was rising and I had to get back to Tommy.' She glances proudly at him. 'I knew he'd save her.'

'Where is she now?' I demand.

'Just inside, doing a drawing. Totally safe.' Tommy pauses. 'We saw you in the boat and thought we should come down to talk.'

'What do you think you're doing, Tommy?' Rob takes a step towards him. He turns on Mia. 'And *you*! All those lies?'

Mia glares at him, contempt oozing from her eyes. 'I *told* you, Tommy!' she says fiercely. 'You should have dealt with that one properly in the wood.'

'*Dealt* with me?' Rob snaps. 'What the hell does that—'

'Stop talking!' Tommy explodes. He lurches forward, fists clenched. There is a righteous fury in his eyes, a ferocity that I've never seen before.

Shocked, Rob falls back, silent. He draws me closer to his side, his arm protectively around my shoulders.

'Tommy?' My voice cracks on his name. He turns and meets my gaze and I can see no trace of the easy-going

286

little brother I thought I knew. 'What is going on?' I glance from him to Mia. 'Are you two…? Was it the two of you from the start?'

Tommy sighs. 'You don't understand, Cassie.'

My throat tightens. 'I understand that less than an hour ago you left me and Adam to die.'

Tommy looks away, and that failure to meet my gaze sends an arrow through my heart.

'Did you do the rest of it too?' I ask, my voice shaking. 'Steal my DNA and pretend it was Mia's? Commit fraud? Murder? How the hell am I supposed to understand that? We're *family*, Tommy.'

Tommy looks up, bitter anger flaring in his eyes. 'Family?' he snaps. 'Is that what you call it? It's so easy for you, Cassie. You fit right into *your* family, don't you?'

'What are you talking about? My family *is* your family.'

'That's what *you* think. Dad treated you like a princess and me like a bit of rubbish stuck to the sole of his shoes.'

'What are you talking about?' Rob demands.

I frown, wracking my brain to try and understand. 'Jesus, Tommy. Is all this because Dad gave us the deposit for our house?'

'No.' Tommy sighs. 'It's *so* much more than that. It's that "evil parenting" Harmony Moon mentioned. *She* understood what Dad was like. She saw how he behaved towards Zane and Adam, always playing them off against each other. I reckon Dad pushed them to "be the best", in that narrow way of his – like he tried to do later with me – and *that's* what led Zane to frame Adam all those years ago.'

'You can't blame Dad for that!' I protest.

'Can't I?' Tommy folds his arms. 'Do you know what Dad said to me the last time I saw him? On his actual *death bed*?'

I shake my head.

'He told me to man up, that I needed to change to be the kind of son he'd be proud of.' Tommy's expression is one of hurt and disgust. 'He said that all the things I did, like gaming and… and climbing, were too childish for a proper adult. He said that I had no purpose, no ambition. That… that he was ashamed of the man I'd become. Can you imagine how that made me feel? That those were the last words he said to me?'

I stare at him.

'I don't see how anything Nathaniel said could justify you committing murder,' Rob says coldly.

'I just wanted to prove Dad was wrong about me,' spits Tommy. He turns to me. 'Look what I achieved, Cas! Look at the attention to detail! I came up with the fake birthday card that Dad supposedly sent Mia's mum. Then I took your hair and Mia bribed that nurse, Blossom, to fake the DNA test with it. Though the stupid cow immediately got cold feet, threatened to blab. But I worked out where there wouldn't be any CCTV on her route to the Tube *and* bought some fake plates for my car. I went the extra mile to make sure the hit-and-run couldn't be traced back to me.'

A cold shiver snakes down my spine. 'So you really did that… you really killed her?' I say flatly. 'And… and Zane? Your own brother?'

'Half-brother.' Tommy looks away. 'We didn't have a choice. Zane was on the verge of getting hold of the same proof Adam brought you. We couldn't risk him telling

anyone so… so I used the same MO as with the nurse.'
He makes a face. 'Zane never cared about me.'

'Are you kidding me?' I demand. 'What about Rae?
She cared. And you attacked her anyway, didn't you? Then
drew that "A" in her blood to frame Adam?'

'Rae brought that on herself,' Mia snaps. She hitches up
the sleeves of her puffer jacket, revealing the barbed wire
tattoo on her lower arm. 'I tried to talk to her, convince
her I was Nathaniel's daughter, but she wouldn't listen,
so—'

'So I snuck into her house,' Tommy says. 'She didn't
see me, she won't be able to ID me, but I made sure she
wouldn't be able to do *anything* for a while – at least until
Mia and I get our money.'

'You almost killed her,' I gasp. 'It was sheer luck that I
got there in time.'

Tommy rolls his eyes. 'You still don't get it, do you,
Cas? Luck had nothing to do with it. I deliberately left
my phone at home the whole weekend so I couldn't be
tracked. I was *there* in Rae's house when I called you and
when you arrived. I sent the police round too.'

My jaw drops.

'For God's sake,' Rob snarls. 'They thought *Cassie*
attacked her.'

'Only for a bit. I set the whole thing up to make
Adam look guilty, to get him out of the way.' A hint
of arrogance creeps into Tommy's voice. 'Don't you see?
Once I realised you and Rae weren't letting things go, I
organised *everything*. I merged truth with lies, so it would
be impossible to tell the difference. All that stuff about
Edgar and Zane framing Adam… all that was true. I even
recorded Harmony Moon saying it. But I made up that

Adam went to see her, and I talked to her myself a whole day before I told you.'

'Oh, Tommo.' I stare at the pride in his eyes and it feels like my heart is breaking. 'All that effort? Just for a bit more money than you would have got anyway?'

'*No!* Haven't you listened to a word I've said?' Tommy snaps. 'I did it to prove that I'm twice as smart and focused and high achieving as all the members of this family who've been looking down on me ever since I can remember.'

There's a long pause. The sun blazes down and the wind swirls around us. I tuck my damp hair behind my ears, my insides churning.

'Of course, the money is good too,' Mia says wryly. 'My share should set me up as a photographer. Plus it means I'll never have to do another stupid modelling job or fend off some sleazy man who thinks he can buy me with a cheap cocktail. Right, babe?' She slides her hand into Tommy's. As she does so, her jacket flaps open in the wind and I catch sight of the knife she threatened us with earlier.

She's planning to use that on us.

The thought sears through me. That's why she and Tommy are waiting here for us. To finish us off, once and for all.

My head spins with fear. I have to keep them talking, try and work out how we get that knife, get away and get to Iris. I glance at Rob, hoping he'll understand.

'So when did it start?' I ask. 'How did you two meet?'

'West End bar about a month after Nathaniel died.' Mia glances at Tommy. 'This one was full of how badly he'd been treated. But all I could think was how lucky he was. How unfair it was that he'd been born into a life with so many opportunities and all I'd had was a drug-addict mum and no money *ever.*' She pauses. 'The irony is that the story we came up with *could* have been true. Nathaniel *did* meet my mother. She told my gran he tried it on with her but she said "no", then got pregnant by someone else a few weeks later. According to Gran, Nathaniel punished her for turning him down. Made sure she struggled to find work. She really spiralled because of that.'

I stare at her, remembering Harmony Moon saying something similar about Dad putting paid to her own career. Was Dad really so vengeful? So petty? So abusive?

Mia turns and her jacket lifts a little, exposing that knife again. I glance at Rob. He is intent on the weapon. I am sure he's weighing up the risk of tackling her, trying to get the knife off her.

'So is that when you and Tommy started planning the fraud?' I ask.

Mia nods. 'Tommy came up with the original idea, that I should say I was Nathaniel's secret daughter. Then I helped with some of the details.' She smirks. 'Tommy said you'd be a soft touch, Cassie, and you were. It was ridiculously easy to get you to take me in. Even easier to make you think Rob and I were having an affair. A lingering glance here, a button hastily done up there. I even made up an abusive relationship to make Rob feel sorry for me, which turned out to be handy when you found my phone. You actually saw me on it that first night, outside on the patio? I said I was talking to my gran, but it was really Tommy.'

I nod, remembering.

'After that I was really careful to watch you,' Mia goes on. 'That's why I noticed you through the kitchen door last week, taking hairs from the brush in my bag.'

'Which you switched out with mine later that evening?' I ask.

Mia nods.

I glance at Rob. If we both go for her together, maybe we can get that knife off her.

'And… and the message on that phone from "Alecto", that was you, Tommy?' My legs feel like they're about to give way.

Tommy nods. 'Benefits of a classical education, eh? Though I've lost count of the times Dad said it was wasted on me. Guess he was wrong about that.'

'We've talked enough,' Mia says. She looks at Tommy. 'Let's get on with it.'

I gasp, feeling sick. 'We just want Iris!' I plead. 'Let us take her and leave.'

Rob nods, letting go of me and striding forward.

'That's far enough.' Tommy squares up to him.

'I'm afraid we can't let you go,' Mia says softly. The tone is more like the way I'm used to her speaking, but there's venom running through it now. She steps forward so that she's standing next to Tommy. The knife from her jacket is now in her hand.

Its long, silver blade glints in the low afternoon light.

THIRTY-EIGHT

All Mia has to do is make one move and that knife is inside Rob.

'Wait!' Tommy puts out his hand and places it firmly on Mia's arm.

'For what?' Mia snaps. 'We don't have time.'

'I need to say this to Cassie.' Tommy turns to me. 'You have to know that I love you and I love Iris. Please don't worry about her. Mia and I will look after her, I promise.'

My stomach falls away.

'Like hell you will,' growls Rob, his eyes darting between Tommy and the knife in Mia's hand.

I suck in my breath. 'You're seriously saying that you're going to kill us but it's okay because you'll take care of our orphaned daughter afterwards?'

'Come *on*, Tommy,' Mia urges.

Tommy glances at the edge of the cliff, just a metre or so behind us.

I follow his gaze. 'Is that the plan?' I demand. 'Push us off the cliff and make it look like we slipped?'

Tommy's expression fills with pain. 'I never wanted it to come to this, Cas. I told Mia from the start that Zane and Rae were expendable. But *not* you. *Never* you. But then you got all up in our faces with your suspicions and you kept digging and digging and now...' He pauses.

I stare at him, feeling sick.

'For God's sake, Tommy.' Mia raises her hand, the knife glinting in the light. 'Grab Rob. *I'll* deal with Cassie.' She takes a step towards me.

'No!' Rob lunges at her. Mia swipes sideways, the knife perilously close to Rob's face. He darts away, but Tommy grabs him and twists his arm behind his back, wrenching it up.

Rob yells out in pain.

I leap towards Tommy, intent on pulling him away from Rob. But a hand seizes me from behind, yanking me back, off balance. Cold steel presses against my neck as Mia pins my arm against my side.

'Keep still or I'll use this,' she hisses.

I freeze.

'You too, Rob!' Mia shouts over the wind. 'Stop struggling or she's dead.'

Rob slumps against Tommy, his eyes fixed on the knife at my throat.

'No, Mia, please.' My words rise up as a sob. I look over at my brother, but he won't meet my gaze.

'Rob first,' Mia orders. 'Now!'

Tommy nods. He tries to turn Rob around to face the cliff. Rob resists, his eyes still on me. This can't be happening.

Tommy pushes Rob so that he's right on the edge of the cliff. Earth crumbles under his boots as he scrabbles backwards. I stare, my heart racing, as the knife presses deeper against my skin. Rob twists around, looking at me. 'Don't hurt her!' he yells.

Tommy hesitates.

And then a terrified cry fills the air. Iris is running towards us, her little legs going as fast as they can, tears streaming from her eyes.

'Mummy!' she cries. 'Daddy!'

Everything happens at once. Tommy lets go of Rob, who hurls himself towards me, arms outstretched, grasping for the knife. I ram my elbow, hard, into Mia's side, just as Rob forces the hand with the knife away from me.

Mia howls, lashing out. Blood surges, a thin red line rising on Rob's hand. He yelps in pain, as Mia raises the knife to strike him again. Suddenly Iris is here, right in the middle of the fight. I scream, reaching for her, swooping her off her feet and into my arms, as Rob pushes Mia away. She stumbles back into Tommy and, with a roar of defiance, she raises her knife once more.

Her expression is pure rage. This time, I think, she will make the blow count.

I meet Tommy's gaze. And in a moment that lasts a lifetime I see horror and shame in his eyes. He looks briefly at Iris, who is clinging to me and sobbing, her face buried in my chest. And then he grabs Mia's arm and twists the knife out of her hand. It falls to the ground with a thud.

Tommy yanks Mia back, towards the edge of the cliff.

'I'm sorry, Cas,' he says.

As Mia tries to lunge forward, Tommy tugs her back again and they both lose their balance, teetering on the edge of the cliff and then falling down, down onto the rocks below.

Rob and I stand, open-mouthed as the wind surges around us. I'm still holding Iris, stroking her hair as she cries.

In the distance, a bird lets out a long, mournful wail.

THIRTY-NINE

TWO WEEKS LATER

It's been raining for days, but the sun is shining as we gather for Zane's funeral. The crematorium is packed with his friends and colleagues; almost the entire senior management team from Carson Enterprises has shown up. Our family occupies the first two rows. Savannah, her baby due any day now, is at the front between her mum and her auntie. She stares miserably at the floor.

I'm sitting between Rob and Mum on the row behind. Poor Mum has been weeping since we arrived, though I'm pretty sure it's more at the thought of Tommy's funeral next week than for Zane.

His body was found washed up on the rocks the day after he fell; Mia's hasn't yet been recovered. Unlike Mum, I haven't cried for Tommy – not yet. I feel numb at the thought of how the brother I adored was manipulating us with endless lies, as he plotted fraud and murder. Yet I know that, at the end, he also saved my life and Rob's too.

How do I make sense of that?

Rae and Adam are on Rob's other side, staring stoic-ally ahead as the celebrant delivers Zane's eulogy. Rae could have spoken at the service herself; she's been out of hospital for a week now and physically is on track to make a complete recovery. But since the attack she has been a far quieter, softer version of herself. She has even taken a six-month sabbatical from her job, ostensibly to look after Adam, who is recovering from his head injury at her house, but also, I think, to give herself time to heal and process everything that has happened.

Uncle Edgar and Harmony Moon are sitting together at the end of the front row. My uncle's fingertips are pressed together as he listens attentively to the eulogy. He and I went to see Adam last week and Uncle Edgar admitted, at last, how Zane blackmailed him into framing Adam all those years ago. I watched, open-mouthed, as my uptight, often pompous uncle clutched his nephew's hand and wept for forgiveness.

And then I watched in awe, as Adam somehow found the grace to offer kindness and mercy, laying his hand on Uncle Edgar's and whispering absolution.

–

The service ends and we troop outside into the bright sunshine. There is something I must say to Rae, something that I need to do before I can properly mourn all that I have lost. I find her around the back of the crematorium, in front of Dad's memorial plaque.

I stand beside her, not wanting to interrupt her moment. But she turns to me immediately.

'It's just us, now,' she says. 'You know, in terms of what Dad wanted.'

She means the inheritance. I nod. 'That's actually what I want to talk to you about,' I say. 'I know you plan to take over Carson Enterprises, but—'

'Actually, that isn't my plan anymore.' She sighs. 'Dad knew I wasn't interested in the business and he never pushed me, not like he did with the boys.'

She gazes sadly at me and I nod, to show I understand.

'So what *would* you like to do with the company?' I ask.

'Sell it.' Rae turns to face me, her eyes intent. 'I've been talking with Adam. He doesn't care about the inheritance per se, but we could do so much good with the money and I want to split my half of it with him. I want to sell Carson, as a going concern, making sure everyone's jobs are protected, then work with Adam to spend our share on something that really helps people. What do you think?'

I smile, remembering Rae's very different outlook just a few weeks ago.

'I think that sounds like a good plan.' I pause. 'I have some ideas myself.'

Rae raises her eyebrows. 'Go on.'

'I'd actually like to split our inheritance five ways,' I say. 'Adam should have a share, of course. But also Uncle Edgar. And Zane's baby, of course, though we'd put his money in a trust that Sav could manage until he's older.'

Rae blinks. I hold my breath.

'Okay,' she says. 'We'll talk to them all later, make it happen.'

I glance at Dad's plaque. 'You know, we wouldn't be here if Dad had made Tommy feel more valued.'

'Tommy was a grown man, darling,' says Rae, sounding more like her old self. 'He made his own choices.' She pauses. 'How's Iris, by the way?'

'Good, she's doing well,' I say. 'She keeps asking about Tommy and Mia, but we're trying to do what the psychiatrist recommended and keep what we say simple. That is, we're being honest to an extent, but avoiding the darkness until she's old enough for it.'

'I wish *I* could wait until I was old enough,' Rae says with feeling.

I squeeze her arm, then link it through mine.

We turn and walk back to the bustling square outside the crematorium. Rae drifts away to talk to Uncle Edgar and Adam, who are standing in the sunshine with Savannah and her mother. A moment later, Harmony Moon, resplendent in a long, lilac coat, glides over to the group and then, to my surprise, Mum joins them too. I hang back for a moment, enjoying the feel of the sun on my face and watching as they chat, at first awkwardly, then with real warmth.

How delicate life is, I think. How tiny but vital the difference between the small decisions that end up destroying us and the everyday choices which bind us together.

Across the square, Rob catches my eye as he heads towards the family group. Despite all the secrets and tensions of the past few weeks, after that terrible day on the cliff we are closer than ever.

I smile and walk towards him.

Acknowledgements

Huge thanks to the whole team at Canelo, especially Louise Cullen, Alicia Pountney, Kate Shepherd, Hannah Cowie, Rebecca McInerney, Deirbhile Brennan, Kim Yudelowitz and Micaela Cavaletto. Also to the brilliant Lou Kuenzler for her feedback and to my friends and family for their support and encouragement.